New Woman, New Fiction

New Woman magazine was launched with tremendous success
in 1988. Under the skilful editorship of Frankie McGowan, it
has made a name for itself for topical articles – on relationships,
people and current affairs – that entertain, inspire, inform. . .
while keeping humour intact. Original and readable fiction,
selected by the Magazine's Associate and Literary Editor Suzanne
Askham, is an essential part of *New Woman*'s appeal.

New Woman, New Fiction

edited by Suzanne Askham

Pan Original
London, Sydney and Auckland

This collection first published 1990 by
Pan Books Ltd, Cavaye Place, London SW10 9PG

9 8 7 6 5 4 3 2 1

This collection © Murdoch Magazines (UK) Ltd 1990

Introduction © Frankie McGowan 1990

For copyright in individual stories see page 282

ISBN 0 330 31756 3

Typeset by Selectmove Ltd, London
Printed in England by Clays Ltd, St Ives plc

Contents

Introduction Frankie McGowan 1

The Glimpses Penny Vincenzi 3

Olive Oil Alice Walker 29

Subject to Diary Fay Weldon 37

The Leap Louise Erdrich 51

Crumbs of Wisdom Penelope Lively 61

The Room Tim Parks 73

Princess Harafa's Revelation Georgina Tisdall 87

En Route to Algiers Douglas Kennedy 101

Teenage Wasteland Anne Tyler 117

The Bolshybally Lisa St Aubin de Terán 131

Baby Love Julie Burchill 139

Loosing the Shoe Mavis Cheek 151

116th Street Jenny Judith Rossner 161

Mike's Sarah Harrison 199

The Moses Basket Felicity Wood 213

Dislocation Patrick Gale 225

The Butterfly Rachel Billington 237

Glasnost Shirley Lowe and Angela Ince 251

Over the Road Bel Mooney 265

Acknowledgements 282

Introduction

One of the more pleasant tasks of editing *New Woman* is being given batches of short stories to read. For someone like me with a lot to pack into each day, the luxury of a full-length novel is reserved for holidays. A short story by a brilliant writer at the end of a hectic day is my treat.

When I was asked to edit the magazine a priority for me was fiction. Good, strong short stories reflecting the preoccupations of the nineties. Families, careers, relationships, love, life and bags of humour.

I wanted and – in the capable hands of literary editor Suzanne Askham – I got the kind of authors, the style, the wit, the nerve that has made *New Woman* fiction compulsive reading. The kind of treat that busy people appreciate.

In the two years since it first appeared *New Woman* has made a name for itself for excellent, readable fiction and it was, it seemed to me, high time it was given a launch pad of its own. *New Woman, New Fiction* is the result. The first collection of short stories especially commissioned by a women's magazine with the authors, the plots and style that have become the trademark of the magazine.

Suzanne Askham, who is also an Associate Editor of *New Woman*, has in her debut as an editor skilfully brought together a collection of stories and authors whose combined talents cover the delicate balance of family life: a welcome move away from the explicit sex scenes of the eighties (goldfish and diamonds have their place but it isn't here!) towards infinitely more erotic, complex, intriguing relationships in which the mind figures as much as the body, and that most prized ability so necessary to all of us – to be able to laugh at ourselves and each other.

Read on for the whole variety.

Frankie McGowan

Frankie McGowan
Editor, *New Woman*

Penny Vincenzi

The Glimpses

Penny Vincenzi made her fiction debut in 1989 with Old Sins, *a clever blockbuster about a will, manipulation and a bit of sex. Her previous career as a writer and editor on women's magazines gives her fiction a healthy regard for cliffhangers to keep the reader hooked. Married, with four daughters, Penny wrote* The Glimpses *from her own observations of what happens when people have babies: 'The wife takes on the role of being a wonderful mother, which is undeniably an ego trip for her but not a lot of fun for the husband.'*

James was a very lucky man. He told himself so quite often, and he listened to his mother and his mother-in-law and his wife's best friends (of whom there seemed to be rather a lot) telling him so quite often as well, and he knew he ought to believe it, and in fact he sometimes did, he managed to persuade himself that it was quite true; he would say yes, I am a very lucky man, very lucky indeed, and he would count his blessings again and yet again and congratulate himself upon them.

Since he counted them so extremely frequently, he knew exactly how many there were and the order in which they came: pretty, loving wife; three beautiful children; nice house (in a good area with good schools); good job in insurance, excellent prospects, fair salary; and then he was very healthy, he didn't have ulcers, and he could beat someone a fair bit younger than he was at squash; and he and Anne, as the pretty loving wife was called, had a very active social life, plenty of friends; and yes, he would say, pushing his rose-tinted spectacles more firmly on, yes, I am very lucky, most fortunate, and he would meditate upon his less fortunate friends and relations who had been made redundant or were getting divorced or who did have ulcers, and compare his lot most favourably with theirs.

It wasn't even as if he and Anne had a sterile or even a dull relationship. They talked and discussed a great deal, they were friends as well as lovers, as she liked to say, and in fact said quite often, and it was true of course, and they were lovers still after nine years, and every six days or so, Anne would turn the light out before he had finished reading, unbutton her Laura Ashley nightie and say 'James' in a particular tone of voice, that was an interesting hybrid of question and command. She always assumed he would be ready for her and of course he usually was, although there were times when he could have wished either for a variation in her approach or more sympathy with his own mood.

Anne had done a course in Self Awareness at the Adult Education Centre, and she knew that it was most important that women should take the initiative in sex whenever they so wished, and moreover that the woman had particular desires and needs of her own, as well as recognizing those of her man; and although she didn't actually feel the needs very strongly herself, she nevertheless wanted James to recognize their existence and how important they were, and not to regard their sex life as simply a gratification of his own.

And James knew, from listening to the coarse banter of his colleagues and squash opponents in various pubs and bars, that they would regard this attitude of Anne's as still further manifestation of his great good fortune, for many of them had to work quite hard to be allowed to gratify their desires, and they would have given their next promotion or place on the squash ladder in exchange for a wife who issued sexual invitations on a regular basis, however predictable they might be. And it wasn't even totally predictable really, James supposed; Anne was quite enthusiastic, just unimaginative, and afterwards, when she had climbed back into her Ashley nightie and was talking about her day, which was what she liked to do, he would stroke her hair tenderly and reflect on his fondness for her, and wrench his thoughts away from the disorder of desire and the flesh and back into the neat lines of the PTA, the babysitting rota, the children's progress with their reading and recorder playing, and the literary luncheon appreciation group which Anne had formed.

So there he was, very lucky, very lucky indeed. So how was it, he wondered, that so often, indeed with appalling frequency, depression would strike him in the stomach like a physical blow, the rose-tinteds would slither right to the end of his nose and fall off, and he would see his life for what it really was? And what it really was he knew he didn't really want. What he did want was slightly out of focus and very much out of reach; but he also knew that it was the real thing, not a fantasy, and that if it ever did come along, he would recognize it and reach out for it without hesitation.

It shimmered tantalizingly, both in his subconscious and the real world; but occasionally he would catch a fleeting glimpse of it, and it was like suddenly recognizing the beloved only just ahead, just out of reach, and his heart would thud, his knees jellify and he would reach forward, trying desperately to catch hold of it, to detain it before it was lost once more in the crowd.

The Glimpses, the fleeting glances, sometimes took the form of people, but more often they were an environment, an atmosphere, a feeling of being in the right place at almost the right time. And later, when the Glimpses had gone, and he sat eating Anne's cassoulets and crumbles in the warmth and mess of the family dining room, to the accompaniment of tales of the Suburban broods, and much interrupted by small pyjamaed figures, his mind would go back and try to analyse the substance of what he had seen. Gradually the formulation became more precise; what he was Glimpsing was beauty, and beauty of a very worldly kind. It was not sunsets or fireglow or the smile on the face of a little child that made him sick with longing (and indeed he had more than enough of all that sort of thing, particularly the smiles on the little faces), it was still, white rooms and sculptured furnishings, reedy music and diagrammatic paintings. And the people in the Glimpses were beautiful too: witty and stylish, their conversations designed as carefully as their clothes.

And as he began to know what he was finding in the Glimpses and why he liked them so much he was able to look out for them and so see more of them. He took to going to art galleries in his lunch hour, instead of walking in the park; he would wander through smart furniture shops, drinking in the chrome and the marble, so shiny, so perfect, so unsmudged; and as he grew bolder he would go into the most expensive and chic clothes shops and study not only the cuts and colours on view but the people buying and wearing them, all obviously rich and clever and successful and selfish, not a PTA member nor House Husband among them. And although he could not afford the pictures or the clothes or the coffee tables, he would occasionally buy a glass or a handkerchief and he would keep them in his wardrobe, or his desk drawer, as talismans, as living proof that there was another world somewhere, whose lifeblood was not Ribena and finger paints, but fine wine and beautiful books, and the air of which was not filled with action songs and arguments, but esoteric melodies and abstract-based discussions.

Once Anne found a pair of cashmere socks in his wardrobe that he had bought from Paul Smith; her indignation and wrath were more in proportion to the discovery of a batch of lurid love letters. 'Really James,' she said, hurling them on the bed, 'how could you, they must have cost a fortune, you know Dominic needs new dungarees, and your season ticket's about to expire, and you waste' – she looked at the ticket, quivering with rage – '£17 on a pair of socks. You must be mad, quite, quite mad, whatever is the matter with you, I bought you six pairs in Marks in April, it's not as if you need socks, I mean if it was a tie, I could understand a bit more, at least that would show, but socks, why socks?'

Useless to try to explain, James knew; sitting, head bowed with shame, clutching the socks, symbol of his profligacy and betrayal, he tried to form a coherent sentence about why socks; because they were a luxury, precisely because they didn't show, because they weren't functional, because only he knew that they were there on his feet: expensive, smooth, soft, unmatted from getting in with the nappies, un-stretched from being used as Christmas stockings. That was why socks.

Later that night, in bed, she was remorseful. 'I'm sorry darling I got so cross,' she said. 'Of course if you think you need some socks, then you should buy them. I don't suppose you realized how much more expensive they were. I'll get you some more tomorrow in Marks, I've got to get

Emma some tights, and maybe you could change those for a tie or something'

'No it's all right, I really don't need any,' said James with a sigh, turning over and deliberately choosing not to notice that she was unbuttoning her nightie, even though it wasn't scheduled for another two nights at least. 'I'm sorry too, but anyway, I couldn't change them for a tie, that would cost at least £35. Good night.' And as he lay awake in the dark, he drew some shreds of comfort from the fact that he knew exactly how much ties from Paul Smith cost, and Anne hadn't the faintest idea.

After that he kept all his trophies in the office.

Time passed and the summer holidays (camping in France) came and went as did Hallowe'en (Trick or Treating with the children) and Guy Fawkes (bonfire in their garden this year, with sausages, tomato soup and mulled wine for all the neighbours), and Christmas began to be heard in the distance.

Anne made puddings, cakes and sausage rolls endlessly ('for the freezer,' she explained, as if it was some kind of huge, hungry animal), sewed for the nativity play and planned carol singing; James worried about paying for it all, wondered whether his mother would actually come to blows with Anne's this year, and received an invitation to a Christmas party at one of the galleries where he had become something of a regular and had actually bought a couple of prints (hanging rather incongruously on his office wall, alongside his charts on pension schemes and his department's annual holiday rota).

He saw the Glimpses swimming suddenly and triumphantly into focus, accepted promptly, and then spent many hours worrying about what to wear; the socks of course would be ideal and needed an outing, but something more was needed. Nothing he possessed would be remotely suitable; his smartest suit was outmoded all over by inches, his jeans were over-washed and his casuals only just all right for family Sundays. Finally, feeling rather sick, he took his

Barclaycard to Simpsons and bought a light wool beige and brown jacket and some beautifully cut, slightly baggy beige trousers, and then feeling even sicker, a pale blue, faintly patterned silk shirt. It all cost him considerably more than the total allowance he gave Anne to clothe all the children for the winter.

Looking at himself in them though, it was worth the sickening guilt. In the mirror stood not the James he knew, solid reliable chap, faithful husband, selfless father, but someone else altogether. Smooth, handsome even, possibly unreliable, probably unfaithful and certainly selfish; a person in fact from the Glimpses.

He gazed and gazed, enraptured with himself, like an adolescent girl going to a party; then finally, and reluctantly, having taken the clothes off but with some of his new selfishness and style still hung about him, he went to Russell & Bromley and bought a pair of hugely expensive, soft leather loafers. He had thought his brogues would possibly do, but they stood, a sorry piece of sacrilege, beneath the trousers, betraying his homely roots; and besides, he felt he owed it to the socks to cover them with class.

Where to keep it all though? His small pen of an office was clearly unsafe, all he had was a coat hook behind the door, and home was hopeless; finally, in a flurry of inspiration, he thought of the left-luggage office at Paddington Station. He bought a cheap suitcase (totally unworthy of its precious contents but it couldn't be helped) and deposited the lot. He had not the faintest idea what he could do with them later, he didn't even think about it. He had an appointment with Destiny at the party, he felt; and Destiny could surely take care of a few articles of clothing.

'I'll be late tonight darling,' he said to Anne at breakfast on the morning of the party, 'Sales Department Booze Up. Don't worry about me, just go to bed.'

'But Jamie,' said Anne plaintively, 'you know I've got to rehearse the Carol Concert, and Sue can only stay till eight and I told her you'd relieve her then, I know I went through it all with you – Cressida don't put egg in your pocket – can't you possibly get out of it or at least come home early?'

'Sorry, no,' said James, amazed at his own firmness, and fixing his mind firmly on the suitcase at Paddington and its contents to lend him further courage. 'No I can't. Dominic stop that at once, I don't want your Ribena. You'll just have to get someone else to babysit for you, Anne, I'm afraid; I'm sorry.'

'But it's not for me, it's for us,' said Anne looking at him in astonishment at this piece of heresy. 'They're your children, not just mine.'

'True,' said James, picking up his briefcase and the paper, 'but it's your carol concert. Bye darling.'

Anne watched him going down the path and then started clearing up very slowly. He hadn't been the same since she had found the socks.

The clothes were a bit creased when he got them out of the suitcase but there was nothing he could do about that. He hung them up rather boldly behind his office door and hoped they would look better by six o'clock. They did.

He had his hair cut rather expensively at lunch time, feeling there was no point leaving the icing off the cake – or rather too much on it – at this stage; he promised Anne mentally as he paid the outrageous bill that he would go without lunch for two months to make up for it.

He waited until most people had gone home, changed in the men's cloakroom, put his own clothes back in the suitcase and took it back to the station. Then he took a taxi down to Sloane Street.

He was no longer nervous; he felt, in his new clothes, so different, so absolutely another person that what he was doing and where he was going seemed entirely right and appropriate, but he did feel an enormous sense of excitement and anticipation, as if he was off to meet some beloved person from whom he had been too long separated.

When he arrived the party was half complete. James stood in the doorway, holding the glass of champagne he had been handed, simply gazing into the room. Here surely was

Elysium, a glittering, glossy paradise: beautiful women, rich men (some of them beautiful too), fine clothes, brittle conversation. He caught snatches of it, as people passed him by: 'Darling . . . such heaven . . . you look marvellous, what have you been doing . . . did you see his last exhibition . . . frightfully overrated . . . Aspen for Christmas . . . new husband . . . absurd divorce case . . . with a wife like that who needs a mistress . . . absolutely broke . . . sold all his mother's shares . . . tiny house in Nice, do come . . . '

It was like the music of the spheres, and he would have stood there all evening, perfectly content, quite careless of the fact that he could not contribute even a note, had not someone suddenly pushed past him, trodden on his foot, and overbalanced, tipping the entire contents of a glass of champagne down his shirt. And then a voice: 'Oh God how absolutely ghastly, I am so sorry, how could I have done such a stupid thing, oh look at your shirt, and it's so beautiful too, what can I do to make amends? Come with me, come on, Jonathan Jonathan, where are you, look it's too awful, look what I've done to this poor man's shirt.'

James felt a hand on his arm, and then saw it sliding down to take his own: a small white hand, it was, with long red nails, and wearing a selection of fine gold twisty rings. Following the line of the hand up the arm, his eyes took in fine black crepe (cut away to show much fine white bosom), a mane of streaked blond hair, and a face which could only be described as beautiful, smiling at him encouragingly as its owner pulled him through the crowd.

'Now,' thought James, 'now if only I could die now, this instant, and I need never see this ending,' and afterwards, as he relived the evening a thousand, ten thousand, times, he pinpointed that moment as the one he became actually part of the Glimpses, albeit only as an associate member.

But he did not die; he found himself alive and rather wet in a small kitchen behind the gallery with the owner of the hand and the arm and the bosom and the face dabbing rather helplessly at his shirt and still shouting for Jonathan.

'Where is the silly sod?' she said crossly. 'Talking to some rich Arab, I expect. He's never around when I need him.'

'Er, who is Jonathan?' asked James thinking he had better at least test his voice and show that he was not actually mute.

'Jonathan, oh, he's my boyfriend,' she said, 'and he owns the gallery, don't you know him then, I thought everyone here did.'

'Well no, not really,' said James and then terrified lest his credentials weren't going to meet her scrutiny. 'I'm here because I bought a picture once.'

'Oh really, whose?' she asked, recommencing her dabbing. 'Oh, dear, this isn't doing any good, not this creep who's on now, I hope, terrible waste of money, Jonathan, oh there you are, what on earth have you been doing, look I've spilt champagne all over this poor man's lovely shirt, what can we do, is it covered by insurance, do you think?'

'I shouldn't think so,' said Jonathan, looking slightly coldly at James and his shirt. 'Awfully sorry about it of course, but it'll dry clean OK. You shouldn't have stood anywhere near Georgina, she's hopelessly accident-prone, she's always spilling something over somebody, last time it was best claret over me. At least champagne doesn't show.'

'Oh Jonathan, you are a bastard,' said Georgina, hurling the cloth at him. 'How can you be so unkind, you deserve to be sued. Now look,' she said to James, 'let me at least get you some more champagne. Actually Jonathan is right, champagne doesn't usually stain, but do get it cleaned and send him the bill. He's quite right, I am hopelessly accident-prone, you wouldn't believe the things I do, I drove my own car over my own bicycle the other night, which didn't do either of them much good. Now look here's some more champagne. What do you do? I mean, are you a writer or a collector or something terribly glamorous?'

13

'Er, not exactly,' said James, wondering wildly what he could claim, and settling for the near-truth. 'I'm in . . . well, finance.'

'Oh,' she said instantly losing interest, 'a banker. I thought you looked a bit different.'

'Well I'm not quite a banker,' said James eagerly and truthfully, 'it's more – well insurance in a way.'

In every way, he thought, and thought also that he could hardly have said anything more boring. But it seemed not: she brightened up at once. 'Oh,' she said, 'Oh, how wonderful. That's amazing, you might be able to help me. Listen could you possibly, do you think, spare an hour one day next week to come to my flat, I've just bought a pair of Victorian seascapes, and I'm desperate to get them valued and insured, I think I've been rather clever and they're a bit special, and Jonathan only knows about this sort of tricksy rubbish, he won't even look at them, and the man who usually insures my stuff won't have the faintest idea, he's an absolute philistine. I mean do you know anything about Victorian paintings at all, it's a new field to me.'

'Well, I do actually,' said James thinking there must be indeed a God and a good one moreover. 'Not a lot, but enough to – well advise you.'

'Oh marvellous,'she said clasping his hand (so that once again the contents lapped perilously near the edge of the glass. 'Wonderful. So would you, could you, come and have a look at them? Or I could bring them to you, to your office, only they're a bit delicate really, the frames are disintegrating. And I'd probably drop them on the way.'

'Oh no, I'll come to your flat,' said James, trying to sound as if he received such invitations every day, 'really I don't mind a bit.'

'You are simply too kind,' said Georgina, 'really I couldn't be more grateful. Now look I'd better go and circulate a bit or Jonathan will sulk all tomorrow, he's so bad-tempered. Have you got a card or anything so I know where to ring? No, look, it's you who's doing the favour, so you ring me, here's my number, whenever it suits you. I'm usually there till twelve, and then I go to my class, and then various other places, so it's best to ring early. But really any time will do, I'm sure you're in thousands of desperately high-powered meetings all the time, I do think it's so kind of you.'

'No, honestly,' said James, 'it's nothing, really, I'd like to do it.'

'You're sweet,' she said, standing on tiptoe and kissing his cheek. 'I'll wait to hear from you. And I really am so sorry about your shirt. All right, Jonathan, I'm coming . . .'

James left almost at once. He wanted to preserve the perfection of the evening, to place it in some untouchable place in his mind, before it became smudged or even blurred. He walked for hours; up Sloane Street, through the park, down Mount Street and into Bond Street, and he sat for some time on one of the seats near Asprey's, gazing at his expensive shoes and remembering with painstaking care every moment of the evening behind him. The Glimpses had been all, more, than he had ever dreamt; and he felt not as if he had been in some strange alien place but rather that he had come safely and at long last home.

And so his strange new life began. He replaced his clothes in the suitcase in the Gents at Paddington, replaced the case in the left-luggage office yet again, and then caught the 10.13 home. It seemed astonishing that he could have journeyed so far and so fast, and yet not even be on the last train. Anne was back from choir practice and whirring somewhat aggressively at the sewing machine.

'It's the angels' robes for the playgroup nativity concert,' she said slightly coldly when he asked her what she was making. 'I told you I had to make them all. Tomorrow I have to start on the halos. Nobody else was prepared to take them on, and there's only ten days to go. How was the party?'

'Oh fine,' said James, going quickly into the kitchen. 'You know what these things are like.'

'No actually I don't,' said Anne, and no actually, you don't, thought James and, as with the price of the Paul Smith tie, the thought gave him immense pleasure.

He telephoned Georgina on Tuesday rather than Monday, not wishing to appear gauche or even in possession of too much time.

'Hallo,' she said, when she answered the phone. 'Yes, who is this?

'Oh,' said James, 'it's the man from the party.'

'Which party?' she said, sounding puzzled and he realized that far from the party being the highest pinnacle of her social career, as it had been for him, it was probably one of many identical small mounds.

'Oh, you know,' he said, 'the one at the gallery. You spilt champagne down my shirt.'

'Oh, God yes, how kind of you to ring, you're going to insure my paintings. Wonderful. How's the shirt?'

'Oh, it's fine,' said James, thinking of it rather sadly as it lay, uncared for and slightly smelly, in the suitcase. 'Really, no damage.'

'Oh, good,' said Georgina, 'Jonathan was right; he usually is, it's such a drag. Now when can you come round?'

'Well, how's tomorrow?' asked James.

'Perfect,' she said. 'Come about eleven, and then I'll buy you lunch afterwards, to say thank you.'

'Oh, no you mustn't,' said James, horrified at the thought of more appalling sartorial shortfall. He could just about, he thought, get away with his very best suit for looking at the paintings, but there was no conceivable way he could wear it out to lunch in the Land of the Glimpses.

'Yes, I absolutely insist,' said Georgina. 'It's the least I can do. Now my address is 17 Boltons Grove. It's just off the Boltons, garden flat. See you tomorrow.'

An hour later saw James in a state of wretched ecstasy in Austin Reed, his Barclaycard growing very warm in his pocket, buying a suit. He did seem to have good taste, he thought, and more surprisingly, to be able to wear clothes well; in a dark-grey pinstripe, and a white-and-grey striped shirt, he could hold his sartorial own against Jonathan any day. These at least he would be able to take home, Anne would never know what they'd cost, and then he could smuggle the shoes in a month or so later. He was beginning to enjoy the whole thing.

'Oh, hallo,' said Georgina, dressed in a bath towel and looking slightly surprised as she opened the door to him next day (he had pleaded toothache in the office). 'Gosh, is that the time already? I've only just got up. Come in, would you like a coffee or something?'

'Yes please,' said James looking round him with interest. Georgina's flat was exactly as he had known it would be while being totally unpredictable (how uncomfortably well he understood this new world. It was as if he had been a changeling, stolen away at birth by the Suburban fairies. He liked that thought, it charmed him and made him feel less guilty). White everywhere, with high ceilings, and marble floors; in the drawing room an exquisite silk Indian carpet hung on one of the walls, two tall carved screens stood in either corner of the room, and a heavy wrought-iron chandelier with tall white candles in it hung from the ceiling; a slightly surprising raspberry pink sofa set in the window bay lent the room wit. There were two Chiparus bronzes, a Lalique brass lamp and an art nouveau rocking chair; two enormous ferns spilt out of a pair of pure white jardinières. James stood drinking it in, like a starving man; he could hardly tear his eyes from it even to go into the kitchen (all black and white, not a splinter of pine to be seen) where Georgina was calling him to fetch his coffee.

'Could you bear to wait just three minutes while I get dressed?' she said. 'And then I'll show you the pictures.'

'Yes that's fine,' said James. 'No hurry, really you go ahead.' He would have waited three hours and happily, but in almost exactly three minutes she was back, wearing jeans and a grey silk shirt. She really was most beautiful: quite tall and very slim, her eyes so dark blue they were

17

almost navy, her hair a wild blond mane. She could have been any age from eighteen to twenty-five; boldly he told her so, and she laughed.

'I'm just twenty-one, the flat was a birthday present, do you like it?'

'Very much, yes,' said James, anxious to appear as one to whom a flat in the Boltons was an absolutely standard birthday present. 'But where are the paintings?'

'Oh, they're here,' she said, and dragged them out from under one of the sofas. 'Now what do you think? More coffee?'

'No thank you,' said James, looking at the pictures. They were fairly ordinary seascapes: pretty and a little unusual, but not worth more than £300 the pair.

'Oh dear, I can tell, they're worthless aren't they?' said Georgina.

'Well not worthless, but not worth much,' said James truthfully, 'not worth insuring separately anyway, you should just get them included on your existing policy.'

'Oh, damn, and I was so sure I'd made a real find,' said Georgina. 'Now that bastard Jonathan will laugh at me. Oh well, back to the drawing board. Gosh, it's nearly time for my class.'

James had been wondering what the class could be; Anne was always attending classes, and as well as her course in Communications, she had done Upholstery, Child Development and Literary Appreciation, none of which seemed likely Glimpse studies; he noticed that Georgina had a leotard lying over one of the chairs.

'Are you a dancer?' he asked.

'Oh heavens no. I'm an art dealer very manqué. As you can see. No, I go to dance class every day to try to keep my weight down. Now I haven't forgotten about lunch, I still want to take you, could you meet me at San Freds at one fifteen? Please. Don't argue. Just come.'

San Fredianos was Glimpse country all right. Pretty, careless people sat at tables with other pretty, careless people, frequently darting across the room to greet, to kiss, to exclaim still more. James arrived deliberately early and sat at the table Georgina had thoughtfully booked, watching and absorbing. He was a quick study; in the twenty minutes he spent there he learnt a great deal about the group behaviour and sexual signalling of the breed he was studying. When Georgina arrived, he took her hand and kissed her cheek. 'I missed you,' he said.

'Do you know,' she said, sparkling up at him, 'I don't even know your name.'

'My name,' said James, sipping a glass of the champagne he had taken it upon himself to order, 'is James. What else would you like to know?'

Two hours later they were both rather drunk. Georgina had knocked over two glasses of wine and spilt her sauce down her silk shirt; she sat, her thigh pressed hard against James's, her hand moving rather agitatedly in his, and her dark blue eyes fixed on his grey ones with some degree of intensity.

'Tell me,' she said. 'Could your company manage without you for another hour or so? Because I don't think I can.'

'Oh yes,' said James, 'I'm quite sure it could. Let's get a taxi.'

In the taxi he felt suddenly nervous. The strictly paced, absolutely predictable routine he went through with Anne every six days was the only sexual experience he had known for many years; he did not feel it really equipped him to move the earth or even a tiny bit of the Boltons with this beautiful hungry person.

Undressing (and oh, dear, he thought, more anxiously wretched than ever, the shirt and suit might be Austin Reed, but the vest and Y-fronts were Marks and Spencer and a baggy three years old at that) he felt worse and worse, and became totally silent, feeling foolish.

But Georgina did not seem to be caring very much, either about the Y-fronts or the silence. She lay on her bed (even in his hour of trial he noticed that the head of it was cast iron, art nouveau and undoubtedly worth a fortune), her own slightly too skinny body absolutely naked; and she held out her arms as he lay down and kissed his forehead in a gesture of extraordinary sweetness. What followed was quite outside his experience in levels of passion and delight, but he did not feel clumsy or nervous, it was as if some powerfully invading sexual force had entered him that he might enter her. It was a triumph and a glory and afterwards he thought that for the first time he had truly understood what it meant to make love.

'Goodness me,' said Georgina, as they lay smiling at one another. 'I hope your company has a good policy out on you.'

'I'm afraid,' said James with perfect truth, 'that they wouldn't mind if I died tomorrow.'

'Oh, nonsense,' said Georgina, 'I'm sure they must be hugely dependent on you. Now listen, I have to go in about ten minutes, to the Gallery to see some idiot painter with Jonathan. And you, I suppose, have to go back to your important job and then home to your lovely kind maternal wife.'

'I'm afraid I do,' said James, thinking with some dread of the metamorphosis that had to be gone through before he got home; rather like a speeded-up film he watched himself phoning from a call box 'tooth out, really painful, going straight home', the tube journey to Paddington, the exchange of his new shoes for his old at the left luggage office (the suit was quite enough to explain for one week), the dreary trundle home on the 6.13 having killed a couple of hours in the buffet bar and then 'hallo-darling-had a good-day-need-any help-up-there' as he got into bath time, story time and babysitting while Anne went to fulfil her duties as treasurer of the Residents Association.

It was all right at first; he thought himself dutifully into his proper role – or rather improper as he increasingly felt it to be – towelled down small plump bodies (to the accompaniment of some disturbing images of a larger skinny one) read *Winnie the Pooh* and dutifully ate sausages and mash despite his tastebuds being still tuned to quails' eggs and champagne. Later he helped Anne make lanterns for the Shepherds in the Nativity Play, commiserated with her over being landed with making all the quiches for the PTA supper and barn dance, and fell asleep in front of the television while she was out. But later, when she had come back and was making their bedtime cocoa, he remembered with a thud of anxiety that this was the Sixth, if not the Seventh night and the Laura Ashley nightie would undoubtedly be unbuttoned. It was; he closed his eyes and thought of the Boltons and got through it somehow. Not splendidly but just about competently; afterwards he mumbled something about being tired and fell into a confused sleep. Life might be beautiful amongst the Glimpses, but it was dreadfully demanding.

And expensive too, he thought, looking aghast at his Barclaycard statement two months later. From a fairly respectable £162 at the beginning of December, it had now soared into a very nasty looking £1260 with a note at the bottom that said, 'Please send at least £90 to clear the excess over your credit limit. Do not use your card further without authority,' and a list of purchases that would have made a wonderful case for a prosecuting divorce lawyer. Clothes, meals, flowers and wine all sat upon it in extravagant splendour; the suitcase in the left-luggage office was bursting at its tacky seams.

He was worried all the time; he worried about money, worried about his job (which he was neglecting terribly) worried about his marriage; he was perpetually tired, chronically confused (who am I today, this morning, tomorrow night) and permanently and rapturously happy.

For the impossible had happened and he and Georgina had fallen in love. He had not known love before, he realized; had not experienced the delicate uncurling of tenderness, the steady powerful growth of joy, the insistent pounding of desire, the explosion of need to be with the beloved every available moment of every existing hour. What he had felt for Anne had been a decorous, carefully chosen piece of furniture for his life; what he knew for Georgina was a total demolition of everything that could be deemed right and proper and a restructure into new, beautiful, unrecognizable territory.

At first he had not been able to believe that she loved him in return, he had thought she must be simply amusing herself, but she did, she told him so day after dizzy day, and grew paler and even thinner, while assuring him of her happiness and her contentment with the way things were. She had given up Jonathan, she had stopped wanting to go to parties; she simply waited, infinitely patient, for the times they could be together.

James found the transition from one life to another more and more difficult to make, the contrast increasingly painful and sharp. Although he had stopped pretending totally to Georgina, had told her some of the truth (that he did not actually quite belong with the Glimpses, that he was not in fact very important or rich) he still felt and indeed became, metamorphosed when he was with her into somebody quite different and in whom he was beginning rather dangerously to believe.

Every meeting, every lunch, every rare outing put him further in love, but it did something else too, more insidious, less innocent: it made him more deeply committed to, more totally besotted with, Georgina's lifestyle. And he had no right to that; he had earned her, perhaps, by way of words and loving and lovemaking, but not the rest. He was helplessly, hopelessly in debt, and worse than in debt, in thrall. The Glimpses had become sorcerers, they had cast a spell on him, and he could not escape.

The crunch came of course, it had to, sneaking up on him like some sinister, predatory beast.

It was not a love letter that gave him away, as they do in books, nor a well-meaning friend as they do in real life; not even his Barclaycard statement, his diary, or even the labels on his new shirts. It was a ticket from the left-luggage office at Paddington Station.

The children found it; they were playing with his wallet one Saturday morning, as he tried rather wearily to concentrate on what Anne was telling him about the new Neighbourhood Watch Scheme, and he realized too late that they had actually extracted the ticket, along with a five-pound note and his driving licence and were playing a game of cards with them all on the table.

'Children give those to me, at once,' he said, just a little too sharply; Anne looked up, aware of the urgency in his tone, saw the expression on his face, and then looked down at the table.

'What on earth have you got in the left-luggage office?' she said.

'Oh, nothing. Nothing much,' said James. He was sweating; he reached out for the coffee pot and tried to control his shaking hand.

'What do you mean nothing. Why should you have anything there? Why can't you tell me?'

'Of course I can tell you. It's just – well my briefcase. With some rather important work in. There's nowhere I can keep anything safe in this bloody shambles. I put it there for the weekend.'

'James, don't be ridiculous. You've got the office. You're lying. What on earth is in the left-luggage office at Paddington Station that you can't tell me about.'

'Oh, darling,' said James, in a last desperate attempt to escape from the vice that was holding him. 'Just some work. And – and some wine,' he added, beginning to stammer, 'some wine for next Thursday, when your parents are coming round. I couldn't carry it, so I left it until I had the car. All right?'

'No,' said Anne. 'Not all right. You're lying. And if you won't tell me what's there, I want to go and see for myself.' She was flushed and breathing very heavily; her eyes were brilliant and fixed on his face.

'I'm going to Paddington,' she said, 'now. Do you want to come with me or not?' James nodded helplessly. 'Come along children, we're all going out.'

Penny Vincenzi

They drove to Paddington in silence. The children were quiet, sensing a drama. James felt terribly sick. There was nothing now that he could do. Anne was going to open Pandora's box in the middle of Paddington station and the demons inside were deadly indeed.

They didn't look deadly, just rather odd. Three silk shirts, two of them slightly smelly; a suit; two pairs of shoes; a jacket; a Gucci wallet and cashmere sweater. Anne looked at them, looked at him, and then picked out the wallet. Inside was a bill for lunch at the Savoy, and a note in Georgina's handwriting. 'Thank you for the best two hours of my whole life,' it said.

'You creep,' was all she said, and then walked away to the car and the children, leaving James to journey home alone on the train.

He did think of ringing Georgina, but it seemed a messy point to do it at. He preferred to wait until at least something had been resolved.

When he finally got home, Anne was making bread as she always did when she was worried or upset; indeed the smell of baking, far from typifying calm and comfort to James always meant trouble, ranging in severity from a difficult committee meeting to a bad attack of PMT. He stood silent, waiting for her to speak.

'I don't want to talk about it now,' she said, very cold and calm. 'We'll wait until the children are in bed.'

'The children?' he said, 'don't you think this is more important than the children?'

She looked at him with such dislike, such contempt that his knees literally gave way beneath him and he had to sit down. 'I personally don't think anything is more important than the children,' she said, 'and certainly not your squalid, well-dressed adultery.'

She had always had a way with words.

'I have decided,' said Anne, finally sitting down that evening with a glass of wine and a very determined expression, 'that the best thing is for you to stay, at least for a while, so we can work things out. There's no point acting hastily. Obviously I am partly to blame, this sort of thing is never just one person's fault. I am quite happy to talk it through and find out what's gone wrong, and see what we can do to put things right again.'

'I should be feeling grateful,' thought James, wondering why he wasn't. 'I should be kissing her feet, saying I'm sorry, begging for forgiveness. But I'm not.'

'I don't want to hear about her,' Anne went on. 'I can't see the point. In fact I'd rather not. As long as you promise me never to see her again, then that can be the end of her as far as I'm concerned. I've no wish to know what she looks like or does, or what she has to offer. I can't see what good it would do. Obviously it's been a difficult time for you, but we must just try to put it behind us. You can't undo the past, after all.'

James looked at her sitting there, smiling carefully, not crying, not applying emotional blackmail, in her cosy battered chair where she had breastfed and cuddled and comforted the children, and mended their clothes and made out lists for Sainsbury's and written minutes of meetings, good Anne, kind Anne, well organized, loyal blind Anne, and he knew that he had to tell her, that there was no point trying to be kind, at attempting to spare her, selling her a soft option. He had to dish up the truth, raw, unseasoned, unpalatable and force her to swallow it.

'I'm sorry,' he said, 'but you have to hear about her. About all of it. I just have to tell you. You have to understand.'

Anne stopped looking determined and started looking nervous. She had found a pink once-fluffy rabbit stuffed down her chair, and she started picking at its bare patches, making them bigger, less neat. James looked at it, and thought it symbolized their marriage, getting balder and more hideous every moment.

'To start with,' he said, 'I can't possibly promise never to see her again. I love her. I'm sorry and I can't help it, but that's the fact of the matter. And more important probably is for you to hear what she has to offer. That will do some good, because it will make you see why we can't put things right. What Georgina, that's her name, what she has to offer, is a way of life. The way of life I need, that suits me. The life we have been sharing, you and I, is not right for me. I know that now. And I can't stay in it. It's stifling me. I need something more – well more adult.'

'I see,' said Anne. She was looking at him with an odd expression that was half distaste, half something quite different. Had James been a little less overwrought he might have recognized it as humour.

'That is precisely what Georgina has to offer me, you see,' he said. 'An adult life. A life with some beauty in it. A selfish life if you like. And it is the only life I can bear to lead now. I am desperately sorry, I can see I must seem hideously ungrateful, and you shall have every penny I can possibly give you, I shall visit the children if you will let me whenever I can, but I can't go on living here.'

Anne gazed at him blankly for a while and then said 'I see' for a second time. That was the end of their marriage.

It was not that neat and tidy of course. The hostilities actually went on for some time; Anne's calm exploded into a noisy, anguished outrage, and James's cool reason deserted him from time to time; but at the end of it they met; they gazed at each other over the dreadful irony of the head of the youngest child, awakened by the noise and now asleep again on his mother's lap, and managed to smile, exhaustedly, weakly, but at least not entirely estranged.

Anne then took the child to bed with her, closing the door gently behind her; and so, his marriage seeming to him thus most poignantly epitomized, James walked very quietly out of the door, into the car and drove to Georgina's flat.

He stopped on the way to phone her, to tell her no more than that he was coming; she had some friends with her but promised to get rid of them before he got there, and he feasted his mind desperately on her, and how he would find her, how he needed to find her.

The journey he was making symbolized the whole of his past life; away from the laurel hedges, the gravel drives, the estate cars, the quiet safe streets, and into the dazzling, hustling busyness of Saturday night London. He had left the womb he had inhabited for so long, so warm, so cosy, so increasingly uncomfortable, and been thrust into a new, bright, hard-edged world where he might be fighting for his life, but where at least the life was what he wanted. He knew it wasn't going to remain so simple, so clear-cut; there would be endless journeys back to the womb, half-felt regrets. There would be dreadful financial difficulties, legal unpleasantness and sorrowing faces, and the loss of much love. But for this hour, this night, he allowed himself the luxury of seeing it simply, of having chosen what he wanted, done battle for it and won.

Tonight he would be where he belonged, cleaved finally to the Glimpses; in a white flat in Kensington with not a bottle of Ribena in a half-mile radius, where the Fisher Prices must be the nice new couple at number 92 and the only cries in the night were adult and orgasmic.

Exhausted and exalted, he reached the Boltons, parked the car, ran down the steps, rang the bell. Georgina fell into his arms; beyond her stood paradise, quiet, peaceful, beautiful . . .

'What is it?' she said, 'what has happened, tell me, tell me everything.'

'I've done it,' he said weakly, collapsing on to the pink sofa.

'I've left her. I'm here to stay. If you'll have me.'

'Oh, my darling,' said Georgina, 'as if I wouldn't.' She paused and looked at him, her navy-blue eyes huge and starry. 'I have some wonderful news too. I'm going to have a baby . . .'

Alice Walker

Olive Oil

Alice Walker is one of the most prolific and prized writers in the West. She won the Pulitzer for The Color Purple *(turned into the film by Steven Spielberg) and has received countless other awards and fellowships for short stories, poems, children's literature, essays and novels, to mention just a few of the genres she has made her own. Alice lives in California. She calls* The Temple of My Familiar, *her latest book, 'a romance of the last 500,000 years' which gives a small hint of her general scope.* Olive Oil, *by way of contrast, focuses on how massage can mend the mind, and put magic into relationships.*

She was busy cooking dinner, a nice ratatouille, chopping and slicing eggplant, courgettes and garlic. George Winston was on the box and the fire crackled in the stove. As she dripped olive oil into a pan a bit of it stuck to her thumb and she absentmindedly used her rather rough forefinger to rub it into the cuticle, which she noticed was also cracked. In fact, she had worked a lot over the last month putting in a winter garden; the weather most days had been mild, but it was also dry and occasionally there had been wind. Hence the extreme dryness of the skin on her hands.

Thinking of this, pottering about, putting a log on the fire and a pot of water for noodles on the stove, she touched her face, which, along her cheekbones, seemed to rustle it was so dry. Massaging the painfully dry cuticle, she swooped up the bottle of olive oil, sniffed it for freshness, and poured a tablespoonful into her hand. Rubbing her hands together she rubbed the oil all over her neck and face. Then she rubbed it into wrists, arms and legs as well.

When John came in from splitting wood he sniffed the air hopefully, wanting to enjoy the smell of the ratatouille, one of his favourite dishes. Putting the wood down and kissing Orelia on the cheek he noticed how bright, almost burnished her skin looked. He was sorry he had a cold and could not smell her, since her sweet fresh smell always delighted him.

'Still can't smell anything, eh?' she asked.

'Nope.'

To which she replied, emphatically, 'Good.'

One of the sad things about their relationship was that even though she loved John she was unable to expect the best from him. John sometimes thought this was solely his fault, but it wasn't. Orelia had been brought up in a family and a society in which men did not frequently *do* their best in relation to women, but rather a kind of exaggerated approximation to what their male peers told them was correct. Then, too, at a very young age, when she was no more than seven, her older brother, Raymond, gentle and loving, whom she had adored, had betrayed her. Her other brothers, insensitive and wild, had designated an ugly, derisive nickname for her, 'Rhino' (because even as a little girl dryness caused the skin on her elbows and knees to appear grey and thick), which she had borne as well as she could until one day he had called her by it. She was shattered and never really trusted a man not to unexpectedly and obliviously hurt her feelings no matter how much she loved him, again.

So John was not trusted, no matter what he did, and sometimes he pointed this out to her, but mostly he kept quiet. No matter how many times he proved himself different from other men, in her eyes he always seemed to measure up just the same, and this was depressing. However, he loved Orelia and understood many of the ways she had been hurt by society and her family, and he empathized with her.

While they were eating he mentioned how glowing she looked and she simply smiled and forked up bowls of salad. He was surprised she didn't tell him immediately what she had done to herself – that was her usual way.

That night before she went to bed she washed herself from face to feet in the tin washbasin he had bought; it was a feat that regularly amazed him because she did, indeed, manage to get clean in less than half a gallon of water, whereas John felt the need each night to fire up the woodburning water heater and luxuriate under a hot shower that used gallons. While he bathed in the bathhouse outside, she went wild in the kitchen with the olive oil, massaging it into her scalp, between her braids, into her face and body, into her feet. Glowing like a lamp she preceded a bewitched John up the narrow ladder to the sleeping loft.

Alas, the day must soon come when John got back his sense of smell: his colds rarely lasted longer than a week. Orelia thought about this every day as she slathered on the olive oil. She had grown to love the stuff. Unlike her various sweet-smelling oils and creams it really combated and won the battle over her skin's excessive dryness, and its purity brought the glow of honest health to her skin.

Orelia and John had been intimate for so long that any little secret kept from him was like a sharp piece of straw in his sock. One night when the worst of his cold seemed over, he took his shower early so that he could be in the room with her when she bathed. Over the pages of his *Natural History* he watched her peel the mauve-coloured thermal underwear from her dark, glowing body and fill the tin washbasin with hot water from the copper kettle, which was almost the exact colour of her face. He watched her soap her cloth and begin industriously, if somewhat bemusedly, washing her face, neck and ears. He watched her soap and palpate her breasts, and he longed to be where the soap was, covering her deep brown nipples with his tongue. She looked over at him as she moved down her body with the soapy cloth and finally squatted over the pan. John riveted his eyes, which he felt were practically steaming, on a story in his magazine about the upside-down eating habits of flamingos. By the time he looked up she was sitting decorously in a kitchen chair, her feet soaking in the pan. And while she sat, she was busily rubbing something into her skin.

'What's that?' asked John.

The sad truth is that Orelia considered lying to him. And a lot of memories and unpleasant possibilities went through her mind in a flash. She remembered being a little black girl with little skinny, knock-kneed ashy legs, and how every morning her mother had reminded her to rub them with Vaseline. Vaseline was cheap and very effective. Unfortunately Orelia almost always put on too much or forgot to wipe off the excess and so everything she wore and everything on which she sat retained a slight film of grease. This greasiness about herself and her playmates (most as ashy as she) eventually sickened her, especially when television and movies made it clear that oiliness of any sort automatically put one beyond the social pale. The best white people were never oily, for instance, and she knew they put down readily any poor whites and black people who were. So Orelia graduated to Pond's and Jergens, which did the job against her ashiness, but not nearly as well or as inexpensively as simple Vaseline.

She thought about men's need to have sweet-smelling women, too, while she waited to answer John. Of John's enjoyment of her body when it was perfumed, especially. Actually, as she thought about it, either of them was likely to come to bed in a cloud of Chanel.

Then she gazed into his eyes, veritable pools of trust. Whatever else John expected of her, he never expected her to lie. He expected the best.

'You got your smell back?' she asked, as she dried her feet.

'Yeah,' said John.

'Well, come here then.'

John came toward her, appreciating her glistening body with its full breasts that had nursed children and now gently sloped, and then stood in front of her. She raised herself against him.

'Smell,' she said. If he fails me it will be just as I expect, she said to herself. Waiting for Raymond's betrayal to be duplicated by John.

John sniffed her cheek and neck and rubbed his nose longingly against her shoulder. '*Um*,' he said, somewhat fervently.

She held up the bottle. 'It's olive oil.'

'Olive oil, eh?' he said, peering at the bottle and scanning its fine print. 'From Italy. It sure looks great on you.'

'What do you think of the smell?' she pressed.

'Earthy. Like sandalwood without the sweetness. I like it.'

'You do?' She was suddenly radiant. Her love of John flooding her heart.

He looked at her, puzzled. He never knew what was going to make her happy. Sometimes he felt he just blundered along by the grace of God and hit the jackpot.

'I can cure your dandruff problem,' she said briskly, picking up a comb. 'Sit here between my knees.'

'Which a way you wants me to turn my face?' said John slyly, sticking out his lips and grazing her belly button as he kneeled to put a pillow on the floor in front of her chair.

Orelia carefully covered John's shoulders with a towel and soon she was scratching huge flakes (embarrassingly-many and large, to John) off his scalp and explaining how dandruff, especially among black people, was caused not only by a lack of moisture, but a lack of oil. 'We're dryer than most people,' she said, 'at least in America we are. Maybe in Africa our diet takes care of the problem.' She advised that he throw his Head and Shoulders away.

As careful as a surgeon she divided his hair into dozens of segments and poured small amounts of oil between them. Then, using her fingers and especially her thumbs, she massaged his scalp vigorously, humming a little tune as she did so.

After she'd thoroughly oiled and massaged his scalp (which for the first time in months did not itch) she amused herself by making tiny corkscrew curls, 'baby dreads' she called them, all over his head. She explained that tomorrow he could wash out any excess (though surprisingly the oil seemed to have soaked in instantly and there didn't seem to be any) leaving his scalp comfortable and his hair shiny but without any resemblance to the currently fashionable 'jerri curl', which relied solely on harsh straightening chemicals and grease and which they both thought made black people look degraded. 'Hyena-like,' as Orelia described it.

It was all wonderful to John, sitting between Orelia's knees, feeling her hands on his head, listening to her hum and softly talk to him, an intimacy he'd longed for all his life, but one he had assumed would never be for him. His sisters, with their unruly locks, had enjoyed the haven between his mother's knees and between each other's knees, and between his aunt's cushiony knees, as they fiddled with each other's hair, but he, a boy, had been excluded. He imagined himself as a small child and how much he must have wanted to get between somebody's knees; he imagined the first few times being cajoled and then being pushed away. He knew that if he went far enough back in his memories he would come upon his childhood self weeping and uncomprehending over this.

But now, look.

John knew there was a full moon, he could feel it in the extra sensitivity of his body, and the fire made a gentle droning sound in the stove; the leaping of the flames threw heat shadows across his face. He felt warm and cosy and accepted into an ancient women's ritual that seemed to work just fine for him too. It turned him on and gave him an idea.

'Let's continue this on yet another plane,' he said.

'Say which?' said Orelia, smiling.

While Orelia sat with hair comb dangling John went and got the futon from the guest-room bed and flung it on the floor before the fire; he threw down pillows and covered everything with large towels. Throwing off his robe he entreated her to stretch out on the futon, where he immediately joined her, olive oil bottle in hand.

Soon they were oiling each other like children forgotten among the finger paints. Orelia oiled John's knees and elbows especially well, and as she did so she felt the hurt from Raymond's betrayal disappear from her heart. John, who had long ago learned that we massage the spot on other people that most hurts in us, went to work on Orelia's knees, rubbing a lot but then nibbling and kissing a lot too. Soon they were entwined, the olive oil easing the way to many kinds of smooth and effortless joinings. They laughed to think how like ratatouille and sautéed mushrooms they both tasted, and giggled to be slipping and sliding against each other's bodies like children in mud. And much, much later they fell happily asleep in each other's arms, as oily and contented as any lowlife anywhere. And she was healed of at least one small hurt in her life, and so was he.

Fay Weldon

Subject to Diary

Fay Weldon started as an advertising copywriter but swiftly moved on in the late sixties to become an enfant terrible *in the feminist corner of mainstream fiction, with novels like* The Fat Woman's Joke *and* Puffball. *Today her tragi-comic novels retain the Weldon bite but their powerful plots are as likely to be on television and film – most recently* The Life and Loves of a She Devil *became the controversial* She Devil *starring Roseanne Barr and Meryl Streep. Married, with four children, she lives in Somerset and London.* Subject to Diary *was inspired by a business tycoon who while trying to make a personal appointment said, 'Subject to diary, of course.' 'It seemed a sorry reflection on all our lives,' says Fay, 'and how very hard life is for women in business, whose "personal appointments" tend to be gynaecological.'*

If you do nothing unexpected, nothing unexpected happens.

Oriole Green gave her name to the clinic receptionist, an unsmiling girl with dark skin and blond hair and almost no eyebrows at all, who punched Oriole's name up on the computer and then asked her if she'd been to the clinic before. Oriole said yes, without thinking, for she was under considerable stress, and the girl with no eyebrows punched some more buttons and then said flatly,

'You're lying. You haven't.'

Oriole was on the eve of her fortieth birthday and for fifteen years had been spoken to, on the whole, and at least out of the bedroom, with politeness and respect. Though in the bedroom, she had noticed, men who were most – no, reverential was the wrong word, as was courteous – guarded was perhaps more accurate – were the ones who most wished to take her down a peg or so: called her names, slapped her around a little. Oriole didn't mind: it was a relief. It was the price, she reckoned, a woman paid for being successful. Nothing was for nothing.

But this was not a bedroom. This was not a suitor, an impregnator, an erotic hit-and-runner, this was a chit of a fat-faced girl behind a desk in the Serena Clinic for Women, a double-fronted house in a dusty suburban garden where pregnancies were terminated for money, and such a girl, who was doubtless paid twice what her equivalent in the public sector would be, should not feel entitled to be rude to clients. The girl wore a pink name tag on her white coat. It read 'Daisy'. Daisy should smile and be friendly and helpful; and out of human kindness, what's more, not merely in the interest of good public relations. Except, Oriole supposed, a girl in her early twenties who was not pregnant, who was not a supplicant for termination, would feel superior to her less fortunate sisters. Or perhaps, more likely, since the waiting list at the clinic was long, the problem was merely that no one had bothered properly to train the reception staff. Even in the private sector, termination came under the heading 'seller's market'.

'I must have made a mistake,' said Oriole, returning rudeness with courtesy, as one should. She had most certainly been to the Serena Clinic twice before, only of course, as she would have remembered sooner had she not been under stress, using another name on each occasion. On her first visit, when she was twenty-eight, she had given her married name, and on the second, when she was thirty-six, her boyfriend's surname, out of some kind of rivalry, she now supposed, with his wife. Though at the time she had just felt better using his name, not her own. But now she had given the clinic her own name, her school and professional name: as if finally she accepted responsibility, not of course for a child exactly, but at least for the non-event the child must of necessity be: and she felt somehow less hole in corner, in fact rather open and brave.

Even 'child' sounded wrong. A putative non-child perhaps: an alleged and accidental non-child. Of course this non-child, this growing cluster of cells, had, in a way, to be congratulated, inasmuch as, so successfully and so far, it had evaded all the powerful suggestions that it should not be, should not come into existence, egg and sperm by some miracle of happenstance colliding and joining, the two amongst millions not to succumb to the hazards set up by nature itself – a too acid, too alkali womb; a too early, too late arrival of the egg and/or delivery of the sperm; and so forth: oh, well done, well done! Not to mention the more considered incentives towards not-to-be: the contraceptive poisons, the rubber sheaths, the hormone-induced-non-receptivity, the other many traps and fail-safe devices invented by humanity to stop itself breeding itself out of existence. What, survived all this? Still living? And then, once fertilized, to have *clung on* satisfactorily; to have successfully set the welcoming mechanism of the host body into vigorous motion – oh yes, you had to congratulate this cluster of dividing cells, even as your own surging hormones sickened you. Well done, well done, you had to say, for having got so far! But also, so sorry, I do have to hit you on the head at this the last and greatest hurdle. I don't want you. You can't survive if I don't want you. You got it right, but in the wrong body. A factor beyond your comprehension: one you were too tiny to comprehend, let alone forestall. That the whole great intended unit should notice you as you grew, and turn against you. For now that your scale has changed other forces must come into play. Pipped at the post, oh brave and courageous one, the one amongst millions. What was the month now? June? Left to itself it would be born in November.

'Funny thing to make a mistake about,' said Daisy uncheerily. She had a hairy upper lip, and had bleached the dark hairs, which was a mistake. Why didn't she just tweeze them out? 'Sit down,' said fat-faced, greasy Daisy, as if Oriole's standing was in itself a nuisance.

Oriole sat down. There was one other person in the waiting room, which was painted pale pink and had pictures on the walls of pretty ladies in crinoline, in silhouette. She was a thin girl with a white face and red-rimmed eyes, who lowered her eyes to her copy of *House and Garden* rather than meet Oriole's. There was an article inside the magazine, Oriole knew, in the series 'Successful Women', featuring Oriole Green. Oriole had cut it out and pinned it on her kitchen wall. She was proud of it. The thin girl flicked past the page.

Oriole had been named for a bird, so her mother said: born to soar and fly. Of course you'll succeed, said her mother, proudly. Sometimes Oriole felt like a bird: she had a lean, small, muscly body covered by the finest designer feathers, a small beaky nose and bright sharp intelligent eyes, and a lot of reddish hair; she could feel herself sometimes hopping about: this appointment, that appointment, up those stairs, down that lift, pecking around, then soaring, soaring—

There was an uncomfortable silence in the waiting room. The thin girl snivelled.

Oriole took out her diary and looked through November. It was a busy month. Ex-king Alleyne of a minor Arab state had his book coming out: the Shrinks were making a comeback: there was the Head Office Conference in Reykjavik: all fourteen branches would be represented. She, Oriole Green, personnel manager, would be speaking. In December the company was going public. You had to prepare people for change; even if change was to their advantage people hated it. Hers was to be the keynote speech. How could you fit in having a baby with all that, even if you wanted one, loved the father? Neither of which she did, not for lack of trying. How could you find a man to love, a man who was altogether admirable and superior to yourself, once you were past, say, thirty, and earning well? And you didn't have babies by, marry or set up home with men you didn't love. Did you? Others seemed to, it was true, but only women with no standards, no expectations, no subtlety.

Oriole couldn't remember waiting like this, on previous occasions. She'd been shown immediately to her room, undressed, settled down, been weighed up by the anaesthetist and gone straight into surgery. She felt obscurely that the wait was Daisy's fault.

Oriole flicked through the current week. She had managed to adjust her appointments to keep not only this afternoon free but tomorrow morning as well. Body and mind might need a little time to recover, to adjust to a change in state. She reckoned to feel low for a week or so in any case. The sooner the operation was done the better. Hours counted. This one was somehow dripping uncontrolled out of her life, thanks to Daisy.

The pale girl and her suitcase were taken away by a nurse whose name tag said 'Audrey'. Daisy and Audrey, the girls who worked at the clinic. Audrey smiled a great deal, showing broken teeth. Audrey's smile was worse than Daisy's un-smile. Were the Serena Clinic forward-looking, it would have had Audrey's teeth capped. Or not employed her at all. The sense of things rotten or bad or missing in such a place as this surely had at all costs to be avoided.

'Will it be long?' Oriole asked Daisy, rashly.

Daisy looked back at Oriole and thought unspeakable things, or so it seemed to Oriole. Oriole was, quite determinedly, not looking her best. She wore no eye make-up. People went either way at funerals, she noticed. They either looked their best or their worst.

'Enjoy it while you can,' said Daisy.

Oriole had worn her best to her father's funeral: her worst to her mother's. She wondered why. She hadn't grieved over-much when either of them died; she thought perhaps it was because she loved them, and so felt little guilt, and their deaths were after all timely. Her father had gone suddenly, through a stroke. Her mother lingered on in a kind of passive shock for less than a year, then had cancer of the liver diagnosed, and died promptly and painlessly almost of her own volition. They'd been in their seventies, which neither had enjoyed. They were accustomed to being active, and were not so short-sighted that they couldn't see the litter on the floor, the bits of stick and wrappers that the dog chewed up, which they were now too stiff to bend to pick up, having to wait instead for the daily help to arrive to see to it. Old age was no way to end a life. If you had a diary for a whole life, all the appointments would be crammed near the beginning, getting fewer and fewer as you flicked through, until the pages were all but empty.

Oriole felt tears in her eyes. She knew Daisy would misconstrue them. Daisy did. Daisy said, 'Sometimes people change their minds—', but she said it unpleasantly, judgementally, Oriole thought, she who had been named after a bird, to soar and sing and rejoice. The kind of women who end up in this waiting room of mine are feckless and hopeless, Daisy implied: the kind who change their minds and put me and my computer to endless trouble.

Oriole smiled coolly at Daisy and made no reply.

Oriole thought, well, this is really not time wasted. Thank you, Daisy. This is thinking time, reflective time. Everyone needs this quality time. In progressive businesses such spare time is built into timescales, just as free periods were when we were at school. No doubt that particular free time was the result of timetabling inconsistencies and inadequacies. Never mind: we students, being ignorant, interpreted it as a gift, a kindness, from a benign authority, and were the happier for it.

Seven weeks from her last period. She looked that up in her diary too. There was the little tick. Regular as clockwork; predictable as the moon. Was the moon predictable? She supposed so. The moon came and went, waxed and waned, without Oriole noticing. What was the point of noticing the moon, if the moon took no notice of you? 'Oriole,' her mother once said, 'life is not all give and take, tit for tat: you do this and I'll do that, watch my back and I'll watch yours. Other factors intervene.' But what? Love? Her mother loved her father and she, Oriole, had intervened by being born. And even love ended in death, in silence. In strokes, and cancer of the liver.

So little time to think. Too tired to think when she got home: and for holidays she went to health hydros where she starved and exercised herself into somewhere between a stupor and a high. Too tired to talk. And who was there to talk to, even if you could formulate the right words to echo the bizarreness of your thoughts? By the time you'd said too often to too many friends, when they rang to suggest lunch, or an outing, or a holiday, 'just a moment, I'll get out my diary' and then, 'sorry, I can't make it', they'd lost patience, moved on, thought you valued something more than them. Which in a way you did, so you could hardly blame them. Men in business had wives to live their lives for them – remember birthdays, arrange dinners, have their children – Oriole only had herself. She'd been married once: but it hadn't outlasted a year. He'd been an air-traffic controller: he knew exactly where not only he but everything and everyone else would be, ought to be, at a certain time. In the end the uncertainty of her hours, the sudden crises, the middle-of-the-night phone calls – some of her clients were Australians, and just didn't seem to comprehend that their glorious midday was someone else's exhausted two in the morning – had defeated him. 'We're heading for a crash,' he'd said, panicky, and so of course they were. He wanted her to be at home when he was, waiting, coming into existence when he opened the front door, blanking out of it when he left. Well, of course, she wanted him to be the same. There when she wanted him: not when she didn't. Francis, her husband.

She'd been upset, guilty, tormented, confused by his demands and expectations. She couldn't concentrate, she quite forgot to look in her diary. Francis had been the one to point out that she hadn't bled for two months. She was three months gone by the time she got to the Serena Clinic. That had been really horrible. And when she got back four days later there were two significant messages on the answerphone: one on Monday asking her to be a fill-in speaker at the Toronto conference – and she knew her promotion depended upon it – and one on Wednesday from Francis saying he knew she would go to Toronto not stay at home, and so he was going off himself. Where? Anywhere, just somewhere else, away from her. And so he had. Now he was married to a nice boring little stay-at-home and had two children. The oldest had been born with some disorder which made its head swell up with water. Oriole somehow felt it was her fault, though of course that was absurd. But she'd been upset. She'd loved him, this man who had the flying machines within his care and control – this dextrous male. If he'd given her time she could have broken the addiction, because that was what it was, an addiction to her diary. Subject to diary. The diary that kept you forgetful, so busy were you being reminded. Forgetful of what?

She couldn't remember now why she'd felt obliged to get rid of the air-traffic controller's baby. Some necessity, some need, some fear? Perhaps his. Or had she just been putting motherhood off to some more convenient time? If that had been the reason, she'd been wise enough. If she looked through past diaries it was clear there never had been, never would be, a convenient time.

Speaking the unspeakable. Daisy was punching up names and numbers on her computer. She could say to her, 'Daisy,' – such an advantage to the anonymous, the habit of putting name tags on the humble – 'Daisy, why do you pluck out your eyebrows but leave your lip-hairs alone? Shouldn't it be the other way round?' But you couldn't say that. Not just because Daisy could pull a string or two, make sure Oriole's anaesthetic was too light, expose her to risk of septicaemia and other unforeseeable things as well. The humble had all kinds of amazing powers. She searched for something friendly and companionable to say to Daisy, but failed.

What could she say? 'I am an important person; please treat me with courtesy?' No. Any woman with her legs apart and some tearing, rending instrument up inside her as she slapped nature in the face was pretty much of a muchness with the last one on the table, the next one to come.

'You are here on the computer,' said Daisy, 'if Green's your maiden name?'

'Yes,' said Oriole. Maiden name. How sweet and naïve it sounded. She wondered what kind of girl she'd been. How could one ever know: you could only see yourself from the inside out. She thought she probably hadn't ever had much brain, only competence and a kind of soaring sensuality. So how had it gone wrong? Was it mood, a kind of generalized feeling tone, or nature, or just the chance events of a certain day which had led her to this point: forty, childless, unmarried. Not a bad point to be. Nothing wrong with being forty, or childless, or unmarried, except that spoken all together they sounded too final, too unwanted for comfort.

'The first time you were here you had let it go three months,' observed Daisy, 'and there were complications. Still, it hasn't affected your fertility.'

'Clearly not,' said Oriole. The second time she'd been only six weeks pregnant: that was Hassan's baby. She remembered well enough why she'd let that one go by. Hassan had been beautiful, beautiful, but married; he didn't think, or reason, or plan; he couldn't organize anything; he was a gardener; he loved all living, growing things except, it seemed, Oriole's baby. She didn't want to lose him so she'd lost the baby instead: she never even told him. She lost him anyway. He worked for the Parks Department, nine to five, and the complications of her unsocial hours and him getting away in secret from his wife had quite worn out the romance. Lovers looked silly in diaries, their initials softly pencilled in. 'I will meet you, my darling, my darling, subject to diary!' Men could do it: women couldn't – that was the truth of it.

'An expensive form of contraception, if you ask me,' said Daisy.

'I didn't,' said Oriole.

She could see this was her last chance. But how did you have a baby by your PA and go on working in the same office with him? Stop work and live off what? With him? Off him? On his lower salary? He wouldn't get much further up the ladder. She wrote his annual report, she knew it well enough. Oriole Green, a source of scandal and mirth! Oriole? Oh, Oriole the high-flyer: flew over a volcano, got her wings burned, plummeted, died. Babies got into your heart and twisted knives of guilt and obligation. Babies killed you: everything in you that wasn't totally female, at any rate. That flourished.

'Sorry I spoke. No need to snap,' said Daisy. 'Everyone snaps in here. It's the stress.'

And what you knew you grew to need, couldn't do without. The luxury of her bedroom, with its view over the city: the sense that it honoured her, found her special. The routine of early morning: the private, leisured silk, carefully chosen, against the skin, the softness of pale carpet; again yet softer, paler feet as you searched with your toe for your slipper, warm and safe inside while wind and rain and nature pattered against the pane. She didn't *want* to give it up. Other people – men, babies – intruded into the eroticism of solitude. Perhaps you had to get married before you were twenty, have babies before you were twenty-five, before you knew what there was to miss.

'Are you really nearly forty?' asked Daisy, looking across from her computer screen. 'Because you don't look it.'

Oriole smiled coldly; perhaps this impossible Daisy was a temp: filling in for someone who must surely know how to behave, and understood without being told that the personal information now freely available about everything and everyone to any girl with a computer at her fingertips, had somehow, in the interests of the social niceties, to be referred to but at the same time tactfully overlooked.

'Mind you,' said Daisy, 'we get people in here up to fifty, but mostly they've got six already and it's medical. Lots of women have babies at forty.'

'More fool them,' said Oriole shortly. She would have stayed silent, other than that the sudden flow of words from Daisy's hairy mouth filled the pale-pink room in a dangerous way, and might break the silence for ever, if they were not somehow stilled. It didn't work.

'There are tests for Down's Syndrome,' went on Daisy, 'if that's what you're worrying about.'

'I hadn't even considered it,' said Oriole. Nor had she. A non-child cannot have Down's Syndrome or, if it does, can hardly suffer from feelings of inadequacy on that account; not during its brief putative existence.

'Lots do,' said Daisy. 'You'd be surprised. It isn't a nice job, this; but if I don't do it someone worse will.'

'It seems perfectly reasonable work to me,' said Oriole. 'I imagine there is a high degree of job satisfaction. You're working in the community, with people, in a healing environment, meeting very important human needs.'

'Is that what I'm doing?' asked Daisy. 'It seems to me I'm working for a crew of murderers and not even getting danger money.'

'What sort of danger?' asked Oriole, startled.

'Being hated,' said Daisy. 'People just sit where you're sitting, waiting, beaming out their dislike.'

'Perhaps it comes from the babies,' said Oriole, before she had time to think. 'Perhaps the hostility comes from them. They can hardly thank you for what you're doing. Well, not doing. But helping organize the doing thereof. That is to say the doing-away-with.'

'Oh thank you,' said Daisy. 'That's a real help. Ta very much.'

She swung her swivel chair so that her back was to Oriole. Her hair was greasy. There was a yellowy stain down the back of her white coat.

Oriole thought, this is me, Oriole Green, sitting in a female clinic having a spat with a greasy girl at a computer. This is where love leads you – or sex, while it lasts. And of course it wouldn't last, couldn't. The gap between affairs lengthened: she noticed it. Once the arrival of one lover trod hard upon the heels of the last. Now years could intervene: the diary of love which had long, long stretches of nothingness. Last chance, last chance. She might still find someone like herself, intolerably busy, to settle down with, subject to diary, to provide a baby with a proper home but, come to think of it, she doubted it. Last chance!

'Daisy,' said Oriole, 'there's a yellowy stain down the back of your overall. I only mention it because you can't see it, and I expect your employers put quite a price on smartness.'

'They put a price on murder,' said Daisy, 'nothing else. I could wear a butcher's overall for all they cared. Bloodstains and all. How much are they asking you, Oriole?' She consulted the screen. 'Eight hundred and twelve pounds plus anaesthetic fees. Wow! Of course, you are forty. That puts the insurance premiums up. Most women get out at about six hundred. No reduction for quantity, it seems, or you'd be less. And the stains down the back of my overall will be baby sick. And my own view is, if you have a baby you should stay home and look after it, but chance would be a fine thing, wouldn't it?'

'Chance,' said Oriole, wings healed, spirits soaring, 'is a very, very fine thing,' and when the smiling nurse with broken teeth came in to take her and her overnight suitcase up to her room, she said she'd changed her mind.

'You'll lose your deposit,' said the nurse, her smile simply blanking out, not even fading, 'your room being booked, and the operating theatre too. We can't rebook at this late stage. These last minute changes of mind are very inconsiderate of others. And we've had a whole spate of them lately.' The nurse looked very hard at Daisy, knowing perfectly well whose fault it was, but Daisy had fallen sullen and silent again and didn't so much as raise her eyes from the screen.

As for Oriole, she asked for a year's leave of absence on full pay and got it, with no argument from anyone. If you do the unexpected, unexpected things happen.

Louise Erdrich

The Leap

Louise Erdrich started writing in her diary at the age of 19, then graduated to poems, short stories, then finally novels including Beet Queen *and* Tracks. *Part native American Indian, and now aged 35, she works very closely with her husband Michael with whom she is currently writing a new love/adventure novel. Between them they have six children aged 2 to 22, which must have some bearing on the unusual mother/daughter relationship in* The Leap. *'This story is a fantasy: I want to save my children that way. It's also tied in with an old-fashioned circus that comes to town every year. So much is untold about the relationships in the background of each performer . . .'*

My mother is the surviving half of a blindfold trapeze act, not a fact I think about much even now that she is sightless, the result of encroaching and stubborn cataracts. She walks slowly through her house here in New Hampshire, lightly touching her way along walls and running her hands over knick-knacks, books, the drift of a grown child's belongings and cast-offs. She has never upset an object or as much as brushed a magazine on to the floor. She has never lost her balance or bumped into a closet door left carelessly open.

It has occurred to me that the cat-like precision of her movements in old age might be the result of her early training, but she shows so little of the drama or flair one might expect from a performer that I tend to forget the Flying Avalons. She has kept no sequined costume, no photographs, no fliers or posters from that part of her youth. I would, in fact, tend to think that all memory of double somersaults and heart-stopping catches had left her arms and legs, were it not for the fact that sometimes, as I sit sewing in the room of the rebuilt house in which I slept as a child, I hear the crackle, catch a whiff of smoke from the stove downstairs, and suddenly the room goes dark, the stitches burn beneath my fingers, and I am sewing with a needle of hot silver, a thread of fire.

I owe her my existence three times. The first was when she saved herself. In the town square a replica tent pole, cracked and splintered, now stands cast in concrete. It commemorates the disaster that put our town smack on the front page of the Boston and New York tabloids. It is from those old newspapers, now historical records, that I get my information. Not from my mother, Anna of the Flying Avalons, nor from any of her in-laws, nor certainly from the other half of her particular act, Harold Avalon, her first husband. In one news account it says, 'The day was mildly overcast, but nothing in the air or temperature gave any hint of the sudden force with which the deadly gale would strike.'

I have lived in the West, where you can see the weather coming for miles, and it is true that out here we are at something of a disadvantage. When extremes of temperature collide, a hot and cold front, winds generate instantaneously behind a hill and crash upon you without warning. That, I think, was the likely situation on that day in June. People probably commented on the pleasant air, grateful that no hot sun beat upon the striped tent that stretched over the entire centre green. They bought their tickets and surrendered them in anticipation. They sat. They ate caramelized popcorn and roasted peanuts. There was time, before the storm, for three acts. The White Arabians of Ali-Khazar rose on their hind legs and waltzed. The Mysterious Bernie folded himself into a painted cracker tin, and the Lady of the Mists made herself appear and disappear in surprising places. As the clouds gathered outside, unnoticed, the ringmaster cracked his whip, shouted his introduction, and pointed to the ceiling of the tent, where the Flying Avalons were perched.

They loved to drop gracefully from nowhere, like two sparkling birds, and blow kisses as they threw off their plumed helmets and high-collared capes. They laughed and flirted openly as they beat their way up again on the trapeze bars. In the final vignette of their act, they actually would kiss in midair, pausing, almost hovering as they swooped past one another. On the ground, between bows, Harry Avalon would skip quickly to the front rows and point out the smear of my mother's lipstick, just off the edge of his mouth. They made a romantic pair all right, especially in the blindfold sequence.

That afternoon, as the anticipation increased, as Mr and Mrs Avalon tied sparkling strips of cloth on to each other's face and as they puckered their lips in mock kisses, lips destined 'never again to meet', as one long breathless article put it, the wind rose, miles off, wrapped itself into a cone, and howled. There came a rumble of electrical energy, drowned out by the sudden roll of drums. One detail not mentioned by the press, perhaps unknown – Anna was pregnant at the time, seven months and hardly showing, her stomach muscles were that strong. It seems incredible that she would work high above the ground when any fall could be so dangerous, but the explanation – I know from watching her go blind – is that my mother lives comfortably in extreme elements. She is one with the constant dark now, just as the air was her home, familiar to her, safe, before the storm that afternoon.

From opposite ends of the tent they waved, blind and smiling, to the crowd below. The ringmaster removed his hat and called for silence, so that the two above could concentrate. They rubbed their hands in chalky powder, then Harry launched himself and swung, once, twice, in huge calibrated beats across space. He hung from his knees and on the third swing stretched wide his arms, held his hands out to receive his pregnant wife as she dived from her shining bar.

It was while the two were in midair, their hands about to meet, that lightning struck the main pole and sizzled down the guy wires, filling the air with a blue radiance that Harry Avalon must certainly have seen through the cloth of his blindfold as the tent buckled and the edifice toppled him forward, the swing continuing and not returning in its sweep, and Harry going down, down into the crowd with his last thought, perhaps, just a prickle of surprise at his empty hands.

My mother once said that I'd be amazed at how many things a person can do within the act of falling. Perhaps, at the time, she was teaching me to dive off a board at the town pool, for I associate the idea with midair somersaults. But I also think she meant that even in that awful doomed second one could think, for she certainly did. When her hands did not meet her husband's, my mother tore her blindfold away. As he swept past her on the wrong side, she could have grasped his ankle, the toe-end of his tights, and gone down clutching him. Instead, she changed direction. Her body twisted towards a heavy wire and she managed to hang on to the braided metal, still hot from the lightning strike. Her palms were burned so terribly that once healed they bore no lines, only the blank scar tissue of a quieter future. She was lowered, gently, to the sawdust ring just underneath the dome of the canvas roof, which did not entirely settle but was held up on one end and jabbed through, torn, and still on fire in places from the giant spark, though rain and men's jackets soon put that out.

Three people died, but except for her hands my mother was not seriously harmed until an overeager rescuer broke her arm in extricating her and also, in the process, collapsed a portion of the tent bearing a huge buckle that knocked her unconscious. She was taken to the town hospital, and there she must have haemorrhaged, for they kept her, confined to her bed, a month and a half before her baby was born without life.

Harry Avalon had wanted to be buried in the circus cemetery next to the original Avalon, his uncle, so she sent him back with his brothers. The child, however, is buried around the corner, beyond this house and just down the road. Sometimes I used to walk there just to sit. She was a girl, but I rarely thought of her as a sister or even as a separate person really. I suppose you could call it the ego-centricity of a child, of all young children, but I considered her a less finished version of myself.

When the snow falls, throwing shadows among the stones, I can easily pick hers out from the road, for it is bigger than the others and in the shape of a lamb at rest, its legs curled beneath. The carved lamb looms larger as the years pass, though it is probably only my eyes, the vision shifting, as what is close to me blurs and distances sharpen. In odd moments, I think it is the edge drawing near, the edge of everything, the unseen horizon we do not really speak of in the eastern woods. And it also seems to me, although this is probably an idle fantasy, that the statue is growing more sharply etched, as if, instead of weathering itself into a porous mass, it is hardening on the hillside with each snowfall, perfecting itself.

It was during her confinement in the hospital that my mother met my father. He was called in to look at the set of her arm, which was complicated. He stayed, sitting at her bedside, for he was something of an armchair traveller and had spent his war quietly, at an air force training ground, where he became a specialist in arms and legs broken during parachute training exercises. Anna Avalon had been to many of the places he longed to visit – Venice, Rome, Mexico, all through France and Spain. She had no family of her own and was taken in by the Avalons, trained to perform from a very young age. They toured Europe before the war, then based themselves in New York. She was illiterate.

It was in the hospital that she finally learned to read and write, as a way of overcoming the boredom and depression of those weeks, and it was my father who insisted on teaching her. In return for stories of her adventures, he graded her first exercises. He bought her her first book, and over her bold letters, which the pale guides of the penmanship pads could not contain, they fell in love.

I wonder if my father calculated the exchange he offered: one form of flight for another. For after that, and for as long as I can remember, my mother has never been without a book. Until now, that is, and it remains the greatest difficulty of her blindness. Since my father's recent death, there is no one to read to her, which is why I returned, in fact, from my failed life where the land is flat. I came home to read to my mother, to read out loud, to read long into the dark if I must, to read all night.

Once my father and mother married, they moved on to the old farm he had inherited but didn't care much for. Though he'd been thinking of moving to a larger city, he settled down and broadened his practice in this valley. It still seems odd to me, when they could have gone anywhere else, that they chose to stay in the town where the disaster had occurred, and which my father in the first place had found so constricting. It was my mother who insisted upon it, after her child did not survive. And then, too, she loved the sagging farmhouse with its scrap of what was left of a vast acreage of woods and hidden hay fields that stretched to the game park.

I owe my existence, the second time then, to the two of them and the hospital that brought them together. That is the debt we take for granted since none of us asks for life. It is only once we have it that we hang on so dearly.

I was seven the year the house caught fire, probably from standing ash. It can rekindle, and my father, forgetful around the house and perpetually exhausted from night hours on call, often emptied what he thought were ashes from cold stoves into wooden or cardboard containers. The fire could have started from a flaming box, or perhaps a build-up of creosote inside the chimney was the culprit. It started right around the stove, and the heart of the house was gutted. The babysitter, fallen asleep in my father's den on the first floor, woke to find the stairway to my upstairs room cut off by flames. She used the phone, then ran outside to stand beneath my window.

When my parents arrived, the town volunteers had drawn water from the fire pond and were spraying the outside of the house, preparing to go inside after me, not knowing at the time that there was only one staircase and that it was lost. On the other side of the house, the superannuated extension ladder broke in half. Perhaps the clatter of it falling against the walls woke me, for I'd been asleep up to that point.

As soon as I awakened, in the small room that I now use for sewing, I smelled the smoke. I followed things by the letter then, was good at memorizing instructions, and so I did exactly what was taught in the second-grade home fire drill. I got up, I touched the back of my door before opening it. Finding it hot, I left it closed and stuffed my rolled-up rug beneath the crack. I did not hide under my bed or crawl into my closet. I put on my flannel robe, and then I sat down to wait.

Outside, my mother stood below my dark window and saw clearly that there was no rescue. Flames had pierced one side wall, and the glare of the fire lighted the massive limbs and trunk of the vigorous old elm that had probably been planted the year the house was built, a hundred years ago at least. No leaf touched the wall, and just one thin branch scraped the roof. From below, it looked as though even a squirrel would have had trouble jumping from the tree on to the house, for the breadth of that small branch was no bigger than my mother's wrist.

Standing there, beside Father, who was preparing to rush back around to the front of the house, my mother asked him to unzip her dress. When he wouldn't be bothered, she made him understand. He couldn't make his hands work, so she finally tore it off and stood there in her pearls and stockings. She directed one of the men to lean the broken half of the extension ladder up against the trunk of the tree. In surprise, he complied. She ascended. She vanished. Then she could be seen among the leafless branches of late November as she made her way up and, along her stomach, inched the length of a bough that curved above the branch that brushed the roof.

Once there, swaying, she stood and balanced. There were plenty of people in the crowd and many who still remember, or think they do, my mother's leap through the ice-dark air towards that thinnest extension, and how she broke the branch falling so that it cracked in her hands, cracked louder than the flames as she vaulted with it towards the edge of the roof, and how it hurtled down end over end without her, and their eyes went up, again, to see where she had flown.

I didn't see her leap through air, only heard the sudden thump and looked out my window. She was hanging by the backs of her heels from the new gutter we had put in that year, and she was smiling. I was not surprised to see her, she was so matter-of-fact. She tapped on the window. I remember how she did it, too. It was the friendliest tap, a bit tentative, as if she was afraid she had arrived too early at a friend's house. Then she gestured at the latch, and when

I opened the window she told me to raise it wider and prop it up with the stick so it wouldn't crush her fingers. She swung down, caught the ledge, and crawled through the opening. Once she was in my room, I realized she had on only underclothing, a bra of the heavy stitched cotton women used to wear and step-in, lace-trimmed drawers. I remember feeling light-headed, of course, terribly relieved, and then embarrassed for her to be seen by the crowd undressed.

I was still embarrassed as we flew out the window, towards earth, me in her lap, her toes pointed as we skimmed towards the painted target of the fire fighter's net.

I know that she's right. I knew it even then. As you fall there is time to think. Curled as I was, against her stomach, I was not startled by the cries of the crowd or the looming faces. The wind roared and beat its hot breath at our back, the flames whistled. I slowly wondered what would happen if we missed the circle or bounced out of it. Then I wrapped my hands around my mother's hands. I felt the brush of her lips and heard the beat of her heart in my ears, loud as thunder, long as the roll of drums.

Penelope Lively

Crumbs of Wisdom

Penelope Lively is a writer for both children and adults. After publishing a number of children's books, her first novel for adults was published in 1977 and shortlisted for the Booker prize. Several novels and ten years later, Penelope won the Booker prize with Moon Tiger, *and has continued writing brilliantly ever since. She is married and lives in Oxfordshire and London.* Crumbs of Wisdom *features all the observation and wit for which Penelope is known. 'I was looking at a dismal bungalow beside a petrol station and wondered what sort of person could live there. And, nothing in this world being what it seems, I decided probably a retired romantic novelist . . . and the story arose from that.'*

'I've never heard of Ruth Harrap,' said Clive Morland.

Elaine, the tutor, laughed. 'Of course you have, Clive. All those lovely romantic historical novels one read when one was fifteen. Not up-market literary stuff, I know, but real craftsmanship. We can all learn from a writer like that.'

'I read animal books when I was fifteen.'

The members of the Creative Writing Group were a disparate lot, united only in their resentment of the tutor. Elaine was a published writer, and her two novels, long out of print, could occasionally be tracked down in public libraries. The only member of the group who had achieved print was Clive, a retired teacher, who had two articles in professional journals and a piece in the *Guardian*, some years ago. There was a tacit acknowledgement, though, that papers and magazines did not really count. It was only a real book that signified. There was a splinter movement among the younger members of the group who had their sights on television and fought a relentless battle for more discussion of drama and situation-comedy writing. The age range ran from the three sixth formers to a group of over-sixties who had long since abandoned any desire or intention to publish and specialized in destructive criticism of anything that anyone else wrote.

'I don't see why we can't try Martin Amis,' said Lucy, one of the sixth formers.

It had been Elaine's proposal that they should vary their usual routine of fortnightly discussion meetings with an annual visit to an author.

Sylvia, one of the over-sixties, a founder member of the group who long pre-dated Elaine herself and hence was accustomed to pull rank, had pointed out that traditionally the group always made its annual outing to a famous literary house. 'We're due for Chawton again this year.'

But Elaine, in the event, had won the day. The argument switched to which writer should be visited. Interest mounted. Names were bandied around. Fay Weldon? Anita Brookner? Len Deighton? Controversy raged, with literary affiliations pitilessly exposed. The group became polarized between those lobbying for names of popular acclaim and those sternly determined on established quality. Jeffrey Archer was set against Iris Murdoch. The young proposed figures unheard of by the rest of the group. Clive Morland suggested J.B. Priestley; when it was pointed out that Priestley was no longer alive he retired into a sulk from which he emerged only to rubbish other nominations.

They reached tentative decisions. Elaine was deputed to ring up the publishers of a popular crime writer, and reported that they had not been at all helpful. She wrote to a well-known woman novelist, and received no reply. It was at this point that she began to press for Ruth Harrap.

'I've heard of her,' said Sylvia. 'I've read her. She's like Barbara Cartland, only less so, if you see what I mean. You used to see hundreds of her on station bookstalls.'

'She'll be dead, I don't doubt,' said Clive.

Elaine smiled sweetly. 'As a matter of fact she isn't, Clive. She's getting on, but that's no crime, is it? Actually she wrote me a rather nice letter once, years ago, after I'd written to tell her what pleasure her books gave me when I was a girl.'

The group eyed her, stonily.

'Actually I suppose you could say that in a way she was a sort of influence. When I started writing seriously myself my early work owed quite a bit to her style. Of course I was doing something rather more complex – more ambitious, I suppose you might say, and when *Tigers of the Night* came out I can see that not many readers would have seen any connection but . . . '

'Pity there wasn't,' said Sylvia. 'Or you'd have been selling in hundreds on station bookstalls.'

The teenagers giggled. Elaine, with difficulty, maintained her smile. 'If indeed one had been aiming at that sort of market.'

'I want to go and see the Barbara Cartland lady,' said Lucy. 'If we can't have Martin Amis. She'll wear pink ostrich feathers and diamond rings like knuckledusters. And there'll be blue satin sofas and pomeranians. It'll be hilarious.'

And so it was decided. A few weeks later Elaine announced with satisfaction that she had a reply from Ruth Harrap. 'She'd love us to come. Isn't that marvellous! Tea, she says. At about four.'

'That's a let-down,' said Lucy. 'I thought we'd get pink champagne.'

Elaine ignored this. 'Her house is called Foxdene. I think that's after one of the books. *Foxdene* was the eighteenth century one, I'm sure, with the consumptive heroine and the mad poet. Aren't we lucky! She remembers me, I imagine – I sent her a copy of *Tigers of the Night*, actually, when it was first published. One of the things you must all remember, if and when you publish, is the importance of complimentary copies. Bread upon the waters, you know.'

'Let's see her letter,' said Sylvia. A forthright retired librarian, her principal activity as a member of the group nowadays was to query Elaine's leadership and refer obliquely to the superior skills and status of previous tutors. The group regarded this running warfare as good spectator sport; the honours were usually about even.

Elaine handed over a single sheet of paper, with a touch of reluctance. Sylvia studied it.

'She doesn't say she'd love us to come. She says bring your group to see me if you wish. She doesn't say anything about remembering you.'

'The letter was presumably dictated to her secretary,' returned Elaine. 'One doesn't go on at great length in an official letter.'

'If that's the case she needs a new secretary. There's two mistakes there. And the typewriter's out of the ark.'

Elaine sighed. 'We don't all of us share your passion for technology, Sylvia. It's not what you write *with* that matters,

65

as I'm forever saying, it's what you write. And I think we're very privileged to be making this visit. Now, let's get on, shall we? We've all been reading Keith's story and we're going to discuss it. Clive, would you like to start?'

'I counted five sentences ending with a preposition. He can't spell pyjamas or marmalade. A short story should be three thousand five hundred words long and by my reckoning this is all of five thou. He's got this bloke driving from London to Cheltenham on the M4 and I can tell you for a fact . . .'

The group braced itself for action.

On the day appointed for the visit to Ruth Harrap they assembled at Elaine's house. Despite the steadily falling rain there was a festive atmosphere and an exceptional camaraderie. Outfits appeared that had never been seen before. A couple of the older women wore hats; several of the men had put on suits. The sixth formers were tidier and more scrubbed than usual. Elaine herself was resplendent in lilac with a general effect of trailing chiffon and tinkling costume jewellery. She was in a state of exhilaration in which bossiness combined with slightly manic arguments about the route and who should go in which car.

'Now listen, everybody, do remember that this isn't just a fun occasion, there is a serious purpose as well. We're going to have the chance to talk to a very celebrated, very successful author, even if she's not as well known just now as she once was, and it's the most marvellous opportunity to pick up a few tips. Crumbs of wisdom. So do . . .'

'If we don't get moving soon we're not even going to get crumbs of chocolate cake,' said Clive. 'Come on. Marching orders.'

'All right, all right. Now I think if I go with Keith, in front plus Lucy and the other girls and if Sylvia . . .'

Arguing, clutching hats and umbrellas, the group piled into the cars.

Two hours later the leading car came to a halt. The others drew up behind. Everyone got out and gathered around

Elaine, who seemed perturbed. They were on the outskirts of an undistinguished small town, beside a petrol station. Traffic flashed along a by-pass.

'Lost, are we?' said Sylvia with satisfaction. 'Wouldn't you know it!'

'We're not lost,' said Keith, a normally unshakeable VAT inspector who appeared at this moment to be on the brink of some kind of outburst. He had, of course, just experienced two hours of Elaine. 'We're not bloody lost at all. This is what the directions said, to a T. That's got to be the house.'

He pointed. The group stared doubtfully at the building next to the petrol station, a large dour box-like bungalow guarded by a rigid square of conifers. There was a pervading smell of petrol, and the relentless shush-shush of traffic. Rain fell. A cedarwood sign beside the front gate said 'Foxdene'.

'So here we are!' cried Elaine, pulling herself together. 'All present? Right, then!'

She marched up the concrete path to the front door, with the group straggling behind, and rang the bell.

There was a pause. The group dripped. 'I'd imagined something rather different,' said Sylvia. 'Regency mansion, that sort of thing. Or a nice Georgian rectory, even.' Elaine glared.

The door was opened, at last, by an elderly woman in a shapeless tweed skirt and grubby sweater. Elaine smiled uncertainly: 'Miss Harrap is expecting us.'

'Come in.'

The group shed coats and umbrellas in a dark hallway smelling of yesterday's dinner. They were ushered into a sitting room where those who could sat, and the rest perched on the arms of sofas. Their guide inspected them for a moment and then dumped herself down in the desk-chair. It occurred to everyone that this was, in fact, Ruth Harrap.

The group dealt with the situation in various ways. The sixth formers nudged each other and tried to stifle their reactions. There was an outbreak of that sudden searching for handkerchiefs and fervent inspection of surroundings that indicates collective embarrassment. Elaine launched into a hectic account of their drive. '. . . but as it turned out Keith was absolutely right, I *had* muddled up the two roads, so we doubled back and here we are! I can't tell you how thrilled we feel, Miss Harrap! But let me introduce everyone . . . '

Ruth Harrap listened impassively. When Elaine was through she spoke at last: 'If anyone wants the doings it's along the passage and turn left.'

The group rustled and cleared throats. 'Not right now thank you so much,' said Sylvia.

'What we're longing for is to pick your brains a bit,' said Elaine. 'May we? Can I start? For instance, do you like to write in the morning, or are you a night person?'

Ruth Harrap considered. She had straggly white hair of the kind that has yellowed in places, and wore a hearing-aid. At last she said, 'I don't like to write. Never did. Gave it up years ago, thank God.'

Elaine smiled indulgently. 'Oh, of course we realize you're not doing as much as you used to. But writers never really retire, do they? I mean, I'm mostly tutoring these days myself but one is always first and foremost a practitioner, even if one's output slows up.'

'Elaine wrote a book called *Tigers of the Night*,' offered Lucy. Innocently, or so it seemed.

'Haven't heard of it,' said Ruth Harrap.

'Bread upon the waters . . . ' murmured Sylvia, *sotto voce* but not quite *sotto* enough.

Ruth Harrap rose and left the room, without explanation.

'Do you think she's gone to get tea?' said Elaine wildly. 'Maybe we should offer to help. Lucy, why don't you . . . '

There was a disturbance among the occupants of the sofa. A dog, in appearance like a decaying bath-mat, and evidently of great antiquity, had emerged from beneath and was making a tour of people's legs, snuffling.

'Pomeranians,' said Lucy. 'Blue satin.' The sixth formers collapsed into giggles.

'Oh, for goodness sake . . . ' snapped Elaine.

At this moment there came the unmistakable sound of a lavatory being flushed. Ruth Harrap re-entered the room, adjusting her skirt, and sat down again without a word. The group fidgeted uneasily.

'Have a look round the garden if you like,' said Ruth Harrap.

The group gazed out of the window, beyond which the conifers and a rectangle of lank grass were almost obscured by a curtain of drizzle.

'Well . . . ' murmured Elaine. 'What we're all wondering', she went on brightly, 'is . . . what advice would you give to the aspiring writer?'

'The who?'

'Aspiring writer. The . . . you know . . . person who wants to write.'

'You needn't spell it out,' said Ruth Harrap tartly, displaying her first sign of animation. 'I couldn't hear you, that's all.' She paused. 'Don't. That's what I'd say.'

Elaine laughed merrily. 'Oh, I do understand. I mean, in my humble way I've toiled in the vineyard as well. I *know*. It's gruelling. Punishing. But the rewards, Miss Harrap! And I don't *of course* mean financial rewards. The artistic satisfaction. All that.'

There was a silence. The author stared at Elaine, her face knotted in disapproval. 'That may be your experience, for what it's worth. It's not mine. I never wrote but for cash. I wanted to be a buyer in a department store. Never got promotion. Ten years in china and gifts, I was, and then all those books, and I don't know which was worst.' She heaved herself to her feet again. 'You'd better have some tea before you go. How many with sugar?'

'Lucy, perhaps you girls could go and help Miss Harrap,' said Elaine, in a strangled voice.

The group sat in silence. From the kitchen came the clatter of crockery, and, surprisingly, sounds of merriment. Elaine sat studying a picture above the mantelpiece, wearing a pinched expression. The others took turns rebuffing the dog. Their hostess and the three sixth formers returned, bearing a tray with mugs of tea and plates of Jaffa cakes and Tea-time Fancies. 'Pass the plates round, dear, will you,' said Ruth Harrap to Lucy. It was clear that some kind of accord had been established.

They drank, and ate. Their hostess had a conversation with the girls about the dog's ancestry: she demonstrated how he could sit up and beg for a biscuit. Sylvia made an enquiry about the name of a plant on the window sill, which prompted a desultory horticultural exchange. Cups and plates were gathered up and returned to the trays.

Elaine rose. She had recovered her composure. 'We really mustn't trespass on your time any longer, Miss Harrap. This has been so kind. I know we're all tremendously thrilled – it's an experience we shall treasure.' She smiled graciously.

Ruth Harrap surveyed her visitors. She appeared to be making some kind of assessment. 'That's forty pounds,' she said. 'Three pounds a head and half price for schoolchildren. I'll knock off the odd fifty pence.'

There was a stunned silence. 'I'm sorry?' faltered Elaine.

'You wanted to come and see me. I didn't particularly want to see you. It seems to me fair enough.'

Elaine gaped. Then she forced a laugh. 'Of course. I take the point entirely. She delved in her bag. 'I haven't actually got . . . Will a cheque be all right?'

'A cheque will do,' said Ruth Harrap.

They collected their coats and umbrellas. They filed out on to the pavement again. Elaine brought up the rear, her head held high, her face wearing once more the pinched expression. Everyone avoided her eye.

'Poor old soul,' said Sylvia.

Clive snorted. 'Poor old soul nothing. Sensible lady, and good luck to her.'

'She can't ever have been the type for ostrich feathers anyway,' said Lucy. 'Actually she was rather nice.'

Elaine rallied, with an effort. 'What you all have to remember is that art and eccentricity often go hand in hand. Artists are unpredictable people. Writers come in all shapes

and sizes.' She began to perk up, warming to her theme.
'And of course a true professional, like our good hostess, is
not going to reveal the mysteries of her craft just like that, is
she? There's a certain sense of privacy. Not to mention the
difficulty of actually communicating the essence of . . . '

The other members of the group were already sorting
themselves out into the cars. 'Come on, Elaine,' said
someone, briskly.

No one said very much, on the return journey. The sixth
formers were especially quiet, busy planning for themselves
careers in merchant banking, computer programming or the
fashion industry.

Tim Parks

The Room

*Tim Parks was born in Manchester in 1954 and grew up
in Blackpool and London. Today he lives in Italy with his
Italian wife Rita and their two children. His prizewinning
novels include* In Tongues of Flames, Loving Roger, Home
Thoughts *and* Family Planning. The Room *is part of a
planned collection of stories on sex and relationships, and was
triggered off by an overheard conversation between two lustful
business men: 'They were lamenting the cost of hotel rooms
and discussing the possibility, finances permitting, of renting
a bedsit together in which to spend lunch breaks and stolen
weekends with their mistresses. I imagined the ladies meeting
for the first time . . .'*

This afternoon she didn't go straight to the room. Instead she mooched for half an hour, first in a record shop, then looking through posters in a place that mainly sold bric-à-brac for tourists. She imagined the posters on the wall opposite her bed, each one changing the colour and flavour of her life. Then she imagined buying one for the room. Apparently this was a strange thought, for she stood there frowning at a boldly painted naïve image of man, woman and child against a post-modern backdrop. What sense would there be in hanging this in the room?

And she decided not to buy fruit today. Today would be different. Perhaps this was what had been disturbing her. Sameness. Or, more specifically, lack of progress. Looking at her watch, seeing she was going to be late, she very deliberately did not quicken her pace. And this perhaps was a far greater change than anything that might be worked by the purchase of a poster or the non-purchase of fruit.

Life. Walking past dreary boarding houses in Earl's Court, this young woman was very beautiful, though she herself did not believe so. Her camellia-coloured skin had the faintest soft freckling below wide, plum-dark eyes. She walked too quickly in flat shoes and loose, casual clothes, hiding everything, one among so many on these pavements. Essentially she was a happy person.

Arriving at the famous 69 (trust him to remark on its appropriateness), she let herself in, discreetly obeying all the rules they had established: a light but not hurried pace along threadbare carpeting, softly down the stairs with the creak where they turned, almost silent insertion of the key. She opened an old brown London door on to the familiar stale smell.

The room. It was untidy, for today was Monday and the others always left it like that. There was the bed to be made up, a bit of clearing away to be done. These were tasks she would normally tackle brightly, lowering shabby, drape curtains over the legs of passers-by, lighting the spots, finding music on the radio. Today she swung her shoulderbag on to an armchair that no charity shop would accept and lay down on the bare mattress. The mattress was new. Sweet Dreams it was called. Nobody, so far as she knew, had ever slept on it.

And how odd that today of all days, with her feeling the way she did, he was late. She remembered a recent conversation. Since he taught statistics, since she had studied with him, it was not unusual for them to talk about chance, probability and coincidence, though usually jokingly. ('Assuming a man comes once in every bout of lovemaking and a woman twice, and given a mean copulative frequency of the population as a whole, pensioners, infants and war-wounded included, of once a month, what is the probability that the total number of achieved, non-masturbatory orgasms, of a randomly selected sample, will, etc., etc.' They used to laugh about this kind of thing.) But it must have been last week he had said quite seriously that he had noticed that when he was feeling different sometimes, different things happened; a curiously inarticulate proposition, coming from him, as she had swiftly, joyfully pointed out, as he had freely acknowledged, and yet he honestly had noticed it, as if there were such a thing as premonition after all. But not in the classic sense. More a sort of extraordinary subterranean process by which one's feelings were already attuned to an eventuality before it happened. So intriguing if one could think of a way of analysing it statistically: frequency, circumstances. Yet he himself could hardly offer one concrete example. Something was going on, but so elusive.

Lying on the superior sprung surface manufactured by Sweet Dreams Ltd, the only significant investment in this shabbily furnished room, Alice observed that she was not crying, nor especially sad. Yet by that curious process he had spoken of she realized that she was already prepared for what would happen. She knew they would not make love today. Nor ever ever again perhaps. Those terrible words.

Then she was just thinking of where she, Alice Morton, had come from, where she might be going to and what place this room might have in her life between these two distant points, when the scratching of a key in the door appeared to belie her melancholy. He was here. Immediately she was on her feet, pulling the clean bed linen out of the bag by the dresser. Bustle, bustle. Spread the sheets, pull on the pillow slips, mix a drink perhaps if the others had left any. They would only have an hour or so at max. Glasses. Those bastards hadn't even washed the glasses.

'Sorry,' a woman's voice spoke behind her.

She turned in shock. For heaven's sake, could this be the wife?

The woman by the door was older, a shade thick about the middle, but very fashionably dressed in skirt, silk blouse, a light jacket around her shoulders. Her face was at once authoritative and friendly, the skin only faintly tired about cheeks, the corners of the mouth.

'I'm sorry,' she repeated with a full, strong voice. 'I really didn't mean to disturb. Just that I left my watch here I think. I'd hate to lose it.'

They looked at each other. Alice understood and relaxed. She must be Jonathan's friend's woman, the other couple who used the room. She smiled broadly, almost burst out laughing, the release from tension generating a sense of hilarity, naughty children getting away with things. So when the other woman had found her watch on the floor by the bed, she suggested: 'Why don't you stay and have a cup of tea till he gets here? It's so odd actually seeing you after all this time. You must be Christine, right?'

Smiling, somewhat wry, the woman agreed. They sat at the table with its sticky wooden surface, below light filtering through the curtains. It was early afternoon.

'Oh, by the way,' Alice began, 'now I've got the opportunity, can I make a complaint? You never clean up properly. I mean, the dishes and crumbs on the carpet and stuff. Even the loo's dirty sometimes. I don't want to be a bore but it is rather a drag us having to do it on Monday.'

The woman was straightforward, unembarrassed: 'I'm sorry. You're right. Jack's always in such a hurry. You know. He tells his wife he's playing football, so he only has a couple of hours, and if I stayed on behind I'd have to get the tube and bus home, and there's my boy waiting for me. We always mean to clean up,' she added, 'but Jack's so impulsive. We end up making love right to the last minute. We only have the once a week, you know.'

'Jonathan's incredibly orderly,' Alice said. 'He always says we should leave it tidy for you.'

For a moment both women, one old enough to be the other's mother, laughed. The afternoon ticked by in this small quiet run-down room in London which two lovers had rented to pleasure their mistresses. Alice looked at her watch: 'He's disgustingly late, he's never been late before.' She laughed again. 'We should really get them to put a phone in here to make communications a bit easier. Perhaps with an answering machine, you know, so that when you arrive you could check to see if the other had left a message.' Then, barely pausing and only realizing the truth of her words as she spoke them, this beautiful young woman said: 'Though I was meaning to tell him it was over today.' No sooner was it out than she felt that dazed surprise that comes with the realization of the glaringly obvious.

'What? Why?'

'Oh I don't know.' Alice stood up and ploughed a hand into the jet black hair he raved about so much. 'It's become such a ritual. Okay, he loves me so much, he really does. He's so passionate about me and everything and we make love so well. I've never made love like with him. I'm so happy with him. But in the end, there's his wife, there's his children. He's never going to leave them. If it were just his wife he says he'd leave her and I believe he would. The letters he writes me. The way he is with me. I'm sure he would. But not the kids. I've seen him with them. We went out for the day once with his boy. He'll never leave them. They're so lovely.'

Sipping her tea, the older woman asked: 'How old are you?'

'Twenty-one.'

'And Jonathan?'

'Thirty-four.'

'Like Jack.' She smiled. 'I'm forty-one.' Then merely added: 'I wonder if he'll be able to afford to keep the room on his own if you two drop out. Perhaps we'll have to sort out some other arrangement.'

For a few moments neither spoke, apparently stilled by the dustiness of this small sad space, usually so alive for both of them with the intensities of erotic pleasure. Straight-backed, dignified, a definite air of careful preservation about her, Christine sipped her tea. Alice paced about the room. Then the girl said, 'Oh shit,' and plumped herself down on the edge of the Sweet Dreams mattress. 'At the beginning it was so wonderful. We even managed to go on holiday together. To Paris. And of course I half believed then something might come of it. You know how you do. Just that now it's such a ritual. We come here. We mix a drink, put the radio on. We make love, gloriously. We smoke, we eat grapes or kiwis. We talk about the same old things. And we can never be seen out together, because all my friends know him as the Statistics Prof. and of course all his friends know his wife. So we can never grow together or become anything different or hope for anything.' Very determinedly she finished: 'Well, I get my degree next month and that's it. I'll break it off. Start a new life.'

To hear her speak, she gave the impression of talking to one who didn't believe her. But the older woman nodded her comprehension: 'I've never met him, but Jack told me something about him, that he'd leave home and live with you, but for the kids.' She shrugged her shoulders in an expression that told the younger woman: '*C'est la vie.*' It wasn't perhaps quite the sort of elder sisterly comfort Alice had been expecting, and now she asked almost abrasively, 'And Jack?'

'What?'

'Your one. Is he planning to leave his wife?'

'Good heavens, no.'

'So he has children too. They seem to be a universal curse. Or an excuse.'

'No, he doesn't actually. The wife wants kids, but it seems they haven't been able to have them.'

'So he could leave her tomorrow if he wanted! He has no excuse at all!'

'I suppose he feels sorry for her. If he left her now she'd be nearly forty with no kids, nothing. She's older than him.'

'But feeling sorry for someone's hardly a good reason for staying with them, is it?' Alice was growing indignant.

'No, but probably he's not that unhappy with her or the whole arrangement anyway.' She laughed quite cheerfully. 'He always says: "Inertia will pull me through in the end." ' Still chuckling, this older woman, who Alice now found time to notice was heavily though tastefully made up, began to hunt for and eventually found a packet of cigarettes in her handbag.

'But you, wouldn't you be better off with someone who could give you everything? You know, if you're already forty-one you . . . '

'Oh, he has a fine line in dirty talk, I like that. He's good company, lusty in bed. He knows how to give me what I want.'

'But that's an awful thing to say.'

Her tea finished, the mature woman held up a hand, then ducked a little out of habit to light her cigarette. She tossed her hair back with simple, stylish self-assurance: 'Sweetheart, I was actually married for fifteen years. I have a twelve-year-old son. After what, about ten years, first Phil, my husband, and then I were unfaithful, and after a while we both found out. But we never split up. I don't know why. It wasn't just Mikey, my boy. More a feeling that, well, that life went that way, that that was the direction. You know?' And now she added, as if inconsequentially: 'A couple of years later he died in a car crash.'

'I'm sorry.'

'Oh you don't have to be. All I'm saying is that one learns, I suppose, to separate passion from the mainstream of your life.'

Taking this in, Alice said intelligently: 'I think that's awfully sad.'

'Well, maybe at first.'

Alice stood up again and went to look in a foggy mirror which showed her full length and tomboyish in jeans and yellow T-shirt. Her movements as she swayed there, then swung away on one heel, were so much those of a girl doing some sport, rather than a woman who knows how to wear clothes and hold her body. Which curiously made her seem vulnerable in her very vitality. With sudden fervour, she said: 'Well, I don't accept it. I won't. I'm going to tell him, either he leaves his wife, or it's over.'

'You're not of an age to accept it.'

'I hate it,' Alice snapped, raising her voice and rounding on her lover's friend's lover, 'I absolutely hate it when people try to circumvent any proper argument by simply saying I'm too young. As if the old couldn't talk to the young. It's terrible.'

'It is terrible,' the other equally agreed with one raised eyebrow. For a moment the two women stared at each other, then Alice laughed bitterly: 'Anyway, he'll understand. He's idealistic too. I mean, he suffers this separation of his love life from his family life, coming here to this squalid little hole to have sex, never being able to go out together in company. He's always saying, either he'd like to fall in love with his wife again or somehow substitute me for her. Only the problem is she'd get the kids. Which is understandable of course, though I'd be perfectly willing to look after them, and from what he says she's not a very good mother either.' The girl hesitated, emotion had brought quite bright spots of colour to her cheeks: 'All I'm saying is, he understands perfectly well that the situation's not ideal. He'd never ask me to accept it permanently.'

For all reply the older woman pulled a mirror from her handbag and scrutinized her face as one who is preparing to leave.

'Whereas this Jack of yours is just in it for fun and sex, I gather.'

But this deliberate provocation drew only a broad smile which the woman exchanged with herself in her compact.

'Oh, I'm sorry,' Alice said. 'What a stupid little girl I'm being.'

'Not at all. You're perfectly right. He's in it for sex, fun, excitement, to relieve the boredom of his happy marriage. I'm in it for the same reasons to relieve the boredom of my pleasantly humdrum existence with son and sister. What's the fuss? Neither of us really want to change anything I shouldn't imagine. And if this Jonathan's got any sense,' she added, 'nor would he.'

'Well I think that's awful. It may be okay as a temporary arrangement, but as something permanent it's dishonest. To others and to yourself.'

The older woman put her mirror back in her bag and began to edge out from behind the table, dusting cigarette ash from her jacket sleeve. And again Alice had that fleeting sense of careful, cosmetic preservation. 'Dishonest,' she repeated, almost in tears now.

'I can understand why you would think so.'

'I mean, there must be happy marriages, relationships, which have no need of outside entertainment, which contain everything.'

After a moment's pause, straightening her jacket, the older woman looked up and said: 'Yes, I think you're right. There must be. Certainly that would be the best thing.'

'Well, I think Jonathan and I could do it. I really do. And that's why I'm going to tell him it's over. To force him into action. One thing or the other.'

There was a challenge in Alice's voice. Checking her watch, Christine said: 'Do you know that old joke about asking an Irishman the way somewhere and he scratches his head and says, oh, if I wanted to go there I wouldn't start from here.'

Alice said yes. She'd heard it before. 'So?'

'So, if I wanted to go where you do, love, I wouldn't start from where you are now. That's all.'

To which the younger woman came back with a student's sharpness: 'I don't care how rough the ground is, you can always draw a line between two geographical coordinates.' But then quite suddenly she burst into tears. Throwing herself face down on the bed, she sobbed so fiercely her sharp shoulder blades seemed to leap up inside her T-shirt. The other woman came over to sit by her side, though without touching her. She asked:

'Do you love him, then?'

The girl moaned, 'Terribly. I only think of him. All day every day.'

'And he tells you he loves you?'

'But he does, I know he does.'

'That's not exactly the point.' And then she said: 'Look, if he was supposed to be here an hour ago, he's obviously not coming now. Why don't we nip out together and grab a sandwich or an ice-cream or something. Cheer you up. Then I'll have to get back to work.' When the girl went on crying, this fashionable, carefully dressed, middle-aged woman, put a hand on her back and caressed her lightly. Speaking softly, she said: 'Alice, Alice, why don't you think of him as just a good lay. No, no, listen, I don't mean in a crude way at all. I mean as something you enjoy, someone you like to be with, an adventure that satisfies one part of you. But not the centre of your plans, your work, your home. You know? You've done a degree, haven't you, you're starting out in life, you don't want to look after his children, iron his shirts. OK, you love him, but there's no need to wrestle with words like temporary and permanent. Let things take their course.' Half laughing, but still soft, she added, 'London's teeming with rooms like this, you know, teeming, but they're never really part of anybody's home, are they? Come on. That's the way to see it.'

'No! No! No!' the girl suddenly shrieked, loud and quite

frighteningly, as if some spirit threatened with exorcism were clutching at her throat. 'No! No! No! I won't!' The older woman was clearly shocked by the wild energy of this refusal, for she immediately jumped up and backwards, as if scorched, or genuinely shaken, as when a memory is too sudden and searing to allow any defence. She stood staring at the girl, struggling to regain composure.

'Oh, I'm sorry,' Alice said, calming as suddenly as she had lost control a moment before. 'I don't know what's come over me today, I'm such a misery. I don't usually cry. I'll just wash my face a minute, then I'd love to come out with you.'

She got up and padded to the tiny bathroom where you could more or less flush the loo simply by changing the angle of the showerhead; and so at last she found his note. Taped to the mirror. Obviously he had supposed she would, as always, make straight for the bathroom to prepare herself, not imagining that her mood might mysteriously have attuned itself to this event beforehand in the very way he had himself observed. She had not gone to the bathroom because she had known there would be no sex today. And she had told herself she was fed up with sameness because in some remote part of herself she had known things would never be the same again.

The note said:

'Dearest, my dearest Alice. I know this is no way to announce things. I do know. It's cowardly. It's mean. But I can't face telling you in person. I would simply burst out in howls and sobs. I love you so dearly. Our times together have been so precious. But I feel constantly pulled in two directions, the object of some vicious tug of war. God knows we've talked about it often enough, and as you yourself suggested once, seeing you makes it impossible for me to act normally at home and be a good husband and father. At the same time I know now that I will never have the courage to leave my family for you and am plagued by guilt at the thought that I am wasting your life, your marvellous capacity for love and tenderness.

Oh Alice, my beauty, my dark eyes, my endless little giggler, I think of you so constantly, of your extraordinary capacity to be cheerful and make others so. I think of how happy, how light-hearted I have always been with you, and the idea that all this must end is torture.

Please, please remember me with affection.

Your truly loving,

Jonathan'

With turning on the taps then to wash her face, Alice did not hear the sound of the room's main door opening, but catching just the vaguest tremble of its slamming shut on its spring as it always would, imagined that the older woman must have decided to leave alone. So, with towel in hand, she slipped quickly out to catch up with her, not wanting to be left without company at this unhappy moment; and was thus able to cover her face a moment with the red cloth to hide the inevitable shock when she saw what she saw.

'Jack,' the woman who called herself Christine beamed. 'This is Alice, Jonathan's girl.'

There he was.

And in an extraordinary act of generosity, or perhaps contempt, and anyway with that apparent gaiety he had always most appreciated in her, and most misunderstood, she managed to ask, appearing from her towel and even offering a hand: 'Oh, have you forgotten something too? What a day!'

'My diary,' he invented, as promptly as he must often have been obliged to with his wife.

'Is this a page from it?' The paper was in her hand. But his eyes were imploring. What? Forgiveness? Or more? Clearly his only reason for arriving like this must have been to revoke the contents of that note.

'I'll leave the field to you then,' she said very practically, 'since Jonathan's obviously not coming.' For indeed the other woman was at this moment kicking off her high heels as she rapidly made up the bed. He stared at her but nothing more. Almost expressionless. She felt his eyes follow her out.

And emerging a few moments later into a grey afternoon light, walking by the curtains drawn over their pleasure (so dusty from this side), finding the note still crumpled in her hand, it occurred to Alice very lucidly that perhaps he had been entirely sincere in what he said there. Why not? She was worth so much more than the older woman, she had so much further to go. Let them keep their squalid room.

Georgina Tisdall

Princess Harafa's Revelation

Georgina Tisdall won the New Woman, New Fiction Competition 1990 – open to all previously unpublished writers – with this sparklingly simple and witty story. Aged 28, she is currently studying mime and believes this has influenced her writing. 'In mime you learn to practise the extremes of emotion, and I think that gives you greater control of the more everyday nuances of happiness, anger or whatever.' Georgina went to university for one year, then did a variety of jobs. It was while decorating a house with her mother, a muralist, that Georgina got the idea for Princess Harafa's Revelation.

Once upon a time there was a princess who lived in Chelsea. She was an Arabian princess and she was quite attractive, but unfortunately rather vain and haughty. Her name was Harafa. Being a modern princess, she had a live-in lover called Lord Plumbrain, who suited her very well. He had a lot of money, which Harafa liked spending; and Harafa liked hosting lavish meals which Lord Plumbrain liked eating. However, Harafa's real passion in life was for beautiful things. She searched far and wide to find the most exquisite objects for her home, and with every new object that she bought she felt a quiver of excitement. She dreamt that one day her house would be a work of art, admired by many.

However, everything is relative, and although Harafa was quite rich, she wasn't rich enough to buy rare and exotic woods or real marble. Instead, she hired the best artists she could find to paint the walls to look like exotic woods and real marble. The dining room walls were painted to look like real walnut panelling, and those of the drawing room like Chinese silk, while the stairs were painted like polished marble, inlaid with precious stones. For three years these craftsmen and women worked patiently on the house, and when it was finally completed Harafa was delighted, and invited all her friends and important acquaintances round to tea.

Tales of the elegance of her residence spread in all directions at once, and many people longed to receive an invitation to dine there. Harafa was pleased to have a home which she felt reflected so admirably her good taste and fine sensibilities. Lord Plumbrain said that he liked it too.

It was not long, however, before Princess Harafa began to feel pangs of dissatisfaction. She began to suspect that people were only friendly to her because she was a princess and gave lavish dinner parties. She was dimly aware of a deep emptiness inside her which all her style and wealth could not fill. It was at about this time that she began to notice cracks in the walls.

There were, it is true, some tiny hairline fractures in some of the walls, but in her anxiety Harafa seized upon them with relish, and so nurtured and nursed them in her mind that they appeared to grow to enormous proportions. At first, Harafa tried to rearrange the furniture so that the cracks could not be seen, but new ones appeared every day. The cracks became an obsession and the greater the obsession became, the more cracks appeared.

Harafa felt that the beautiful house she had worked so hard to create was now crumbling around her. She feared what other people might say, feared that her enviable reputation as connoisseur and art lover would be ruined. She spent all her waking hours hunting for cracks and then trying to disguise them in a variety of ways. At night she slept fitfully, and awoke feeling as tired as when she had gone to bed.

One night, Harafa had a vivid dream: she was giving a dinner party, when suddenly a small crack appeared in the wall behind her. As the very important guests chatted serenely together Harafa watched the crack growing deeper and wider. Before her eyes it developed into a gaping fissure, and then, to her horror, a huge abyss. Before the open-mouthed Harafa, the whole table, guests and all, was suddenly engulfed by the black hole. Harafa screamed, and sat bolt upright in bed. Her scream woke Lord Plumbrain.

Now, Plumbrain was a man with a keen interest in international affairs – that is, things that happened a long way away – and the further away they happened the more he was interested in them. Needless to say, he had noticed no cracks in the walls. Harafa recounted her dream in tears.

These cracks are terrible, she cried. 'They are everywhere, and I know that people are laughing at me. How can we possibly have anyone else round to tea? Oh, what am I to do?'

'I can't see any cracks,' muttered Plumbrain. 'Far more important things to worry about.' So saying, he rolled over and went back to sleep.

Finding no sympathy in her lover, Princess Harafa prayed to Allah instead. She asked him politely if he would please rid her house of these horrid cracks and restore her to the original state of happiness that she imagined she enjoyed before the cracks appeared. For several days Harafa prayed, but still the cracks jeered at her from the nooks and crannies of the house. 'How can Allah be so callous?' she thought. Surely He should understand her love of art and her desire for perfection?

The princess was not the only person praying that evening. Not very far away, in a leaky old barge on the river, a penniless house painter was also down on his knees. He had not had any work for months, and was feeling hopeless. 'Dear God,' he began (for he was Church of England), 'if you are there, please, please, send me some work, or I shall starve to death.' The Supreme Being (who goes by many names and answers to them all to avoid disappointing anyone) felt quite sorry for this man, so while he slept He wove new ideas into the dreams of the painter.

The next morning, Bill (for this was his name) awoke with a start. 'Well, I never,' he said, rubbing his eyes. 'I've had such amazing dreams. Something tells me I should go back to Chelsea one more time to look for work. I just have a feeling about it.' And so saying, he unchained his rusty old bicycle with rattling mudguards and squeaky brakes and set off.

The first house he tried was very grand but had seen better days, and Bill thought that it could probably do with a spot of paint. He straightened his jacket and combed his hair before knocking at the door. The old lady who answered the door said nothing. She looked him up and down suspiciously several times, then without even stopping to hear what he had to say, said, 'No, thank you' very firmly and closed the door in his face. Bill tried many more houses with the same result. He was beginning to feel very tired and disheartened, and was just about to give up and go home, when he found himself in front of a very grand seven-storey mansion. 'Well,' he said to himself, 'this seems like a very grand house . . . there's no reason why they'd want a simple painter like me, but who knows?' So saying he straightened himself up and knocked boldly on the door. Princess Harafa herself answered, and when she saw Bill she felt immediately that her prayers had been answered, and ushered him in eagerly.

For a while he was overwhelmed by the splendour of his surroundings, and stammered badly. 'H-h-how can I h-h-help you Ma'am?' he began, but the Princess, overcome with relief, led him directly into the first room. 'Look,' she cried throwing her hands up in a gesture of despair. 'See how many cracks there are in my beautiful walls. These used to be the envy of Chelsea, but now . . . ' Bill looked but saw nothing. He rubbed his eyes for he had noticed no cracks in the walls at all. Gradually, as he followed Harafa round the room and he became accustomed to her way of seeing things, small cracks did indeed begin to appear in the seams and joints of walls and woodwork. Harafa looked long and hard at Bill. 'Well Mr . . . ?' she began.

'Everyone calls me Bill, Ma'am,' said Bill.

'Well, Bill,' continued Harafa, 'as you can imagine all these cracks are becoming a terrible worry to me. The place is a mess. I feel too embarrassed to ask anyone round to dinner any more. I have been praying to Allah every day, and now you have arrived, so I'm sure that you can help me. Will you?'

Bill felt that his prayers had been answered too. 'I can start tomorrow morning, Ma'am,' he replied, and so saying jumped on to his bicycle and pedalled homewards whistling cheerfully.

The following day he arrived at the house at eight o'clock promptly. He had with him all his tools and brushes, ladders and paints, scrapers and sanders and fillers, and he began work in the dining room. At first the work absorbed him.

He was a fine craftsman who took time over his work and pride in a job well done. If the princess wanted the house perfect he would make it perfect.

However, as the weeks passed he grew tired of filling all these tiny cracks. It seemed to him that the more cracks he filled, the more cracks there seemed to be. Indeed he began to suspect that the very act of filling some cracks opened others, as if the room could not contain so much perfection. He began to feel that the room itself was straining to breathe. He developed contradictory feelings towards the cracks. Finally, he went to Princess Harafa and told her that the task was impossible.

'Er, Your Highness,' he began, rather sheepishly. 'I'm having problems with the cracks. You see the more cracks I fill in, the more appear. Indeed it seems to me that the room has a human quality. It needs the cracks to breathe.'

'Ridiculous,' fumed the Princess. 'Whoever heard such rubbish . . . a room needing to breathe? This is just an excuse because you are taking so long with your work.'

'Well I'm sorry,' said Bill, 'but it just feels wrong . . . and I can't go on with it.'

'Stupid man,' screamed Harafa. 'Here take your money and go. Now!' and she stamped her feet (very prettily) and stomped upstairs to find Lord Plumbrain. Bill picked up all his brushes and paints and ladders and scrapers and sanders and fillers and loaded everything carefully on to his bicycle. He was not sorry to go, and he was certain that as he left, he could feel the house breathe a huge sigh of relief. Harafa had paid him well for the work that he had done, so at least he wouldn't have to worry about where the next meal was coming from.

He had always felt that painting and decorating was a very straightforward job, but now he was not so sure. And as he cycled across the bridge his wonder intensified. By the time he arrived at his leaky old barge with the grass growing on the roof, he had resolved to do something different with his life. It was time for a change. He would make his barge seaworthy again and set off for an adventure, and as he made this resolution it was as if a huge burden was taken from his mind. With joy in his heart he made himself ready for bed.

Lord Plumbrain was watching television when Harafa stormed furiously into the room. 'The cracks are worse than before,' she wailed, 'I thought that man was the answer to my prayers but Allah has deceived me . . . and now everything is worse than ever.' Lord Plumbrain focused even more intently on the television. 'The house is a complete mess,' howled the Princess. 'Oh how could Allah treat me like this? If people knew the house was in such disarray I would be the laughing stock.'

'Terrible, terrible,' muttered Plumbrain, 'wars going on everywhere. Famines, violence . . . It's terrible.'

'Oh the cracks, the cracks,' wailed the Princess.

'Trees being cut down. Wasting the world's resources. Shocking,' Plumbrain continued, eyes glued to the television.

As it was obvious that none of the tears were having an effect, Harafa stopped crying. She would have to do something herself, but what? At that moment her eyes fell upon an advertisement on the back of an old newspaper. 'Botchit and Cuverup: Professional Decorators,' she read, and then, 'Long established Firm: Fast and reliable. Just ring 773 3337.'

'Well,' thought the Princess (not spotting the danger signals), 'they seem as good a place to start as any.'

Meanwhile, in a dingy warehouse in Wapping, Botchit and Cuverup were counting the takings from their most recent job. Botchit was tall and thin and rather yellow in complexion, and Cuverup was small, plump and balding. Botchit was the one with the brains. 'Three for me. Two for you,' counted Botchit.

'Hey,' cried Cuverup, 'How come you get three and I only get two?'

'Well, I was the one who arranged the job wasn't I?'

'Yeah, but I did most of the work,' growled Cuverup.

'Call that work!' cried Botchit. 'You'd be nothing without me, right?'

Before Cuverup had time to disagree, the phone rang. Botchit picked up the phone gingerly. 'Botchit and Cuverup at your service,' he said as brightly as he could manage.

'Good morning,' said Princess Harafa politely. 'My name is Princess Harafa and I live in Chelsea.'

'Well I never,' said Botchit, his eyes widening, 'it's a Princess.' Cuverup straightened his tie and ran his hand through his imaginary hair.

'I have a problem with my walls,' continued the Princess. 'They are meant to be perfect, but there are cracks everywhere and no one seems to be able to do anything about it. Can you help me?'

'I'm sure we can help you with your walls,' was Botchit's oily reply, 'although it will of course be necessary for us to see the job before we can discuss prices, Madam.'

The following day, Botchit and Cuverup arrived outside the Princess's house in Chelsea. 'This is a bit grand isn't it,' observed Cuverup. 'Yeah,' whispered Botchit, 'we should make a big wad from this one.' And they grinned broad toothy grins at each other.

The Princess, even more elegantly dressed than usual, showed them around the house. As each crack was viewed and inspected, Botchit and Cuverup heaved deep sighs, and made tut-tutting noises. Occasionally, they looked at each other and shook their heads wisely. This only confirmed the Princess's worst fears, so that by the time the tour of the house was completed she was very nervous indeed.

'Well, do you think you can do it?' she enquired cautiously.

'Well,' sighed Botchit, winking at Cuverup, 'it's not easy. You see where you've got so many cracks in one panel, like here for example.' He reached out and touched the nearest wall. 'It would be easier to replace the whole panel.'

'That's right,' agreed Cuverup, 'and where you've got so many cracks in the doors, it would be better to put new doors in.'

'You need new wood, you see,' enthused Botchit.

'Old wood isn't elastic enough,' continued Cuverup, 'and it doesn't matter how hard you sand and scrape, you'll never get the same finish on the old wood, as you will on the new.'

'Oh dear,' sighed the Princess, 'I suppose that's true,' and as she looked around her, it did seem to her that the wood was too old and the paint too thin, and that a completely new finish was needed. Finally it was agreed that Botchit and Cuverup should begin the next day at eight o'clock prompt. Everybody was delighted, and that night Botchit and Cuverup, feeling very proud of themselves, went out to celebrate with a few drinks.

Two days later, Botchit and Cuverup turned up at the house muttering something about a hangover and the work began. Quickly scaffolding was erected, and the whole building swathed in polythene. There was banging and crashing everywhere, and a continual low humming noise which was impossible to trace.

As time went on, the Princess became even more peevish than usual. She couldn't find anything, and hadn't seen Plumbrain for weeks. The bath was full of wooden planks, and the kitchen full of bricks. 'Really,' thought Harafa. 'This is ridiculous. I'm a prisoner in my own home,' and she set off to find Botchit and Cuverup, who had long since disappeared under a fine layer of masonry dust. She found them in the cupboard under the stairs. 'This has been going on for too long,' she moaned, 'and nothing to show for it. Everything just seems even worse. When will it all be over?' Botchit explained patiently that he was doing his best, and if things were to be kept to a high standard, they would take time. Cuverup added that the only way the job could be done faster would be to bring in more people to do the work.

'Yes indeed,' added Botchit slyly. 'We know a few people in the business, if you're interested.' Harafa was interested in anything that would finish the ordeal as quickly as possible, and wearily agreed.

The next day a dozen more painters, carpenters and builders arrived at the house, and Botchit and Cuverup decided to move in so that they could supervise better the work that was now going on night and day. No longer could anyone say that cracks were visible, because no walls were visible, nor come to think of it was anything else. A fine mist of wood and brick dust filled the air, so that it was impossible to see more than a yard in front of you. The Princess retreated to the top of the house and began praying furiously. 'Dear Allah,' she began, 'Author of all Perfection. What kind of a game are you playing with me? I was so distressed when the cracks appeared that I prayed to you, and asked you to take them away. All I wanted was peace of mind, but everything is worse now than ever before.'

Suddenly there was a low rumbling sound like distant thunder, and Harafa felt the walls trembling all round her. Paintings came crashing to the floor, and priceless vases fell off priceless furniture and smashed on the ground. The windows burst in a cascade of rainbow fragments. Finally, with dramatic restraint, the once sumptuous residence of the Princess crumbled slowly to the ground, all seven floors collapsing one on to another like a fairground concertina. All that remained was a huge pile of rubble decorated by a faint halo of dust.

For a while there was total calm.

The minutes passed and there began a gentle scrabbling in the rubble. Wearily, Harafa pulled herself out from a pile of wooden joists and gazed at the destruction around her. She stared around her in disbelief . . . her home, her beautiful home, with all the priceless works of art, the beautiful furniture and family heirlooms, was no more. None of these things were replaceable.

Lord Plumbrain, who had just been to the local super-market to buy some recycled toilet paper, was most surprised on his return. What confronted him was a dirty and haggard-looking Harafa gazing abstractedly at him from the top of an enormous pile of rubble. 'Goodness me,' he said after a stunned pause. 'Looks like a bomb's hit it.' He skimmed his eyes across the scene from the rubble to Harafa and back to the rubble (which was considerably easier on the eyes).

Superimposed images of Beirut and Vietnam, Hiroshima and Nagasaki came into his mind. 'Couldn't be war,' he puzzled, 'there wasn't anything in the papers about war.'

Harafa glowered at him from her dusty heap and tears welled up in her eyes.

'Something really ought to be done about this,' continued Plumbrain, doing nothing himself, but waving his arms about a lot. 'Why I'll . . . I'll . . . write a report immediately.' It then dawned on him that as his office was no longer an office as such, writing a report would not be so easy. He started hopping agitatedly from one leg to another. Harafa cried and cried copious tears of self-pity.

'The people responsible for this must be brought to justice,' asserted Lord Plumbrain enthusiastically. Gazing blurrily at the rubble, Harafa thought that the people responsible probably had already been brought to justice.

'Harafa darling,' enquired Plumbrain nervously, 'are we insured for this?'

Harafa said nothing but cried even more. She cried until she was worn out with crying. Then she stopped. She felt no more fear or anger or shock: nothing – only an awareness of great calm within. With shiny eyes she surveyed her kingdom of rubble once again, and as she did so she remembered Bill's words: 'It needs the cracks to breathe.' A smile flickered across her face. For years she had clung to her house and her possessions, had tried to create a perfect world around herself so that she could feel secure and happy, but now that all these things were gone she felt only a great weight lifted from her shoulders. She breathed deeply, a huge sigh of relief, and as she did so she felt the tension in her chest melting away and the breath loosening the muscles around her shoulders. She had never realized before quite how tense and stiff she was and this sudden relaxation after so many years made her feel happy in spite of herself, as if a small summer breeze was blowing through her body, taking with it all her old fears and anxieties. She breathed again and felt a surge of energy into her limbs, and with it the sudden uncontrollable urge to laugh. As the oxygen coursed through her passages and cavities, she threw back her head and erupted in laughter.

'Are you all right darling?' asked Plumbrain anxiously.

'I'm fine,' laughed Harafa, 'absolutely fine.' And so saying, she picked herself up and clambered rather unsteadily down from the rubble. Harafa's laughter worried Plumbrain, and the more she laughed, the more worried Plumbrain became, and the more worried Plumbrain became the more Harafa laughed.

She didn't know what she was going to do, but one thing she felt certain about: it didn't matter. Dusting herself down, she turned her back on the remains of her house and of Plumbrain, and walked determinedly towards the river. She felt only tremendous relief, and an urge to listen to the swirling waters of the river. She was free. As she leant over the stone parapet, the inevitability of the water's endless race to the sea comforted her, and the gentle bobbing up and down of boats at their moorings eased her mind. One boat in particular caught her attention: a rather charming, leaky old barge with a grassy roof. As she watched it slowly chugging down river towards the sea, she had the feeling that in some strange way, in some sense still impossible for her to grasp, Allah had indeed heard her prayers.

Douglas Kennedy

En Route to Algiers

When he first approached me, I was sitting in a café on the Boulevard Mohammed V, attempting to fish a drowned wasp out of my glass of mint tea. He was a tall, narrow, loose-jointed chap in his early thirties, with an unfortunate moustache and pale sunstruck skin that wasn't coping too well with the North African light. But it was his eyes that initially commanded my attention. They were a curious mixture of melancholy and bemusement – the eyes of someone who was always eager to please; who tried his best to be at ease with the world, yet inevitably ended up feeling awkward and out-of-step with everyone and everything around him. The eyes of the sort of person I didn't expect to meet in a nowhere town on the Moroccan/Algerian border.

'Hey, do you speak English?' he said.

The accent was American – a flat, unvarying American voice that conjured up the flat, unvarying topography of the Midwest. And though I was tempted to answer his question with some wise-guy retort like, 'Yeah, for thirty-three years', I simply nodded a reply, waiting to see why he wanted to know.

'Am I glad to hear that,' he said, dropping himself into the chair opposite mine. 'Haven't spoken English to anyone in weeks. Anyone except my wife, that is.' He proffered his hand. 'The name's Ed Dunne.'

'Nick Hamilton,' I said.

'Don't mind if I join you, Nick, do you?'

'I don't mind,' I said.

'What sort of accent is that?' he said.

'American.'

'Doesn't sound it to me.'

'I've been away a long time,' I said.

'Me too. Eight months to be exact. But, I tell you, it seems like ten years in this place.'

He paused for a moment, his eyes nervously darting between our table and a nearby congregation of Berber men sharing a hookah. And then, leaning across the table to me, he whispered, 'Can I give you a piece of advice, Nick?'

'Sure,' I said.

'Uncross your legs.'

'Why?'

'Because when you cross your legs like that, the sole of your shoe is pointing at those guys over there.'

'Big deal,' I said.

'It's gonna be a big deal when they see the sole of your shoe. Don't you know it's a helluva insult in Morocco to point the sole of your shoe at someone?'

'Who told you that?'

'My company. They gave me a training course in stuff like that before they sent me out here.'

'You working here?'

'Yeah, I'm working here,' he said, a tinge of jailbird resignation entering his voice. And he told me that he was a telecommunications engineer, dispatched from his home state of Indiana to oversee some new exchange system which the big multi-national he worked for was installing for the Moroccan government.

'My first time living outside of the States and I get sent to this dump,' he said, gazing out at the grey breeze-block buildings which fronted the Boulevard Mohammed V, and the piles of festering fruit which clogged the nearby kerb, and the street butchers peddling lengths of intestine, and the pair of undernourished German Shepherds arguing over an unplucked chicken carcass nearby. 'A real beauty spot, isn't it?'

'I only pulled in around an hour or so ago on the 12.06 from Casablanca,' I said. 'But from what I've seen so far, I don't think I'm going to be hanging around town for very long.'

'Consider yourself lucky. I've got twenty-eight months to go here. That is, if I don't shoot myself first. What the hell possessed you to visit this joint?'

'I'm en route to Algiers. The train passes through here, so I got off for the night. That's all.'

'What are you going to do in Algiers?' he said.

'I don't know really.'

'What do you mean, you don't know? You gotta be going to Algiers for some reason.'

'No, no reason. I'm just travelling around.'

'Why you doing a thing like travelling around?' he said.

Why you doing a thing like travelling around? Only a fellow compatriot of mine could have asked a question like that. Because only a Yank could have possessed the combination of neck and ingenuousness needed to demand that a stranger explain his motives for knocking about North Africa. And I knew that his question warranted the sort of confessional answer for which we Americans are justifiably famous. He wanted the story of my life in five minutes or less, because then he could tell me the story of his life in five minutes or less, and by the time ten minutes had elapsed, we would've known where we stood with each other – 'knowing where you stand with someone' being what so much of American life is really all about.

And I probably could have summed up my life in five minutes or less. I could have told him that, fourteen years ago, I landed in Dublin as a university student, and was immediately smitten by the boggy bohemianism of the place. So smitten, in fact, that I lingered on after getting my degree and fell into a job teaching English at some questionable language institute; a job I took to support myself while I wrote The Novel which just about every idiot American who comes to Dublin talks about writing. And now, over a decade later, I was still teaching English to Arab students, but had long since relegated my literary ambitions to that circular file which the local dustmen collect once a week.

I could have also mentioned that, though I'd never married, I was the veteran of twenty-eight separate romantic disasters. Granted, most of these liaisons were nothing more than brief skirmishes – with an average lifespan of around seventeen days each – which means that I could easily stand accused of being an emotional fly-by-night. And I'd probably plead guilty to such charges because (as I've been told far too often) I am one of those people who simply find it difficult to commit themselves to anything; who avoid lingering in any situation for too long out of the fear that it will inevitably lead to entanglements, demands, pain. Maybe that's one of the reasons why I spend all my holiday time away from Dublin, jumping on trains in foreign climes. Because a train journey is, to my mind, the ultimate form of transience. It pulls you slowly through an alien landscape, allowing you the chance to stop and momentarily engage in the world you're passing through. Yet it also gives you an escape route out of that world whenever you feel the time has come to leave town. Whenever the dread of staying too long begins to hit.

So, yes, I could have condensed all that personal information into one tight five-minute soliloquy. But if my years in Dublin have taught me anything, it's this: as soon as you reveal anything about yourself to a passing acquaintance, you're up for sale and going cheap. For if you want to travel lightly through life, you must never give too much of your game away – especially when you find yourself cornered by another countryyman in some Moroccan backwater. And therefore, when this guy Ed hit me with the question, *Why you doing a thing like travelling around?*, I dodged it by saying:

'Because I like trains.'

This bemused him further. 'Because you *like trains*? I don't get it.'

'There's nothing to *get*,' I said. 'I'm travelling around North Africa by train because I simply enjoy travelling around by train. That's all there is to it.'

'But don't you have a job or something?'

'Yes. I teach at a school in Dublin. But this is my spring break.'

'You're a schoolteacher in *Dublin*?' he said. 'That's a kinda unusual occupation for an American.'

'Kinda,' I said. And to get him off the subject of me, I said, 'Is your wife from Indiana too?'

'No, she's actually from your neck of the woods,' he said.
'She's Irish?'
'Welsh. From Cardiff, to be exact.'
I asked him how a telecommunications engineer from
Indiana had come to marry a woman from Cardiff. His
answer sounded like an instruction manual in courtship.

'Well, I was doing this postgraduate engineering degree at
the University of Indiana, and I was sharing this apartment
with this guy, and one night he said, "You want to go to a
party?" And I said, "Sure." And then he said, "You mind
if I bring this girl along?" And I said, "Okay by me." And
then he said, "This girl's got a friend – an undergraduate
exchange student from Wales. Mind if I bring her along
too?" And I said, "Sounds good." And that girl – the
exchange student from Wales – was Wendy. So we went
to the party, and we danced and we talked. And at the end
of the night, I said, "Can I see you again?" And she said,
"Yes." So we saw each other again, and again after that, and
pretty soon it became a love relationship, and about a year
after that we got married.'

I've heard more passionate accounts of courtship in my
time. But passion was evidently not one of Ed's strong
points. He was the new breed of expatriate who lived
in North Africa – the technological emissary from the
West. Unlike the past generation of foreigners who came
to Morocco in search of sensual pleasures, I sensed that he
dwelled here in a self-contained world of microchips and
solid-state circuitry, maintaining a *cordon sanitaire* between
himself and the grubby realities of life on the wrong side
of the Mediterranean. And the more he talked about his
homelife and his three-year contract in Morocco, the more he
made it clear that he saw his existence as a complex software
system he was determined to master.

'You wouldn't believe the infrastructural deficiencies of
this country,' he said, his voice dropping down octaves
into conspiratorial tones. 'Bad roads. Bad sewage system.
Bad water pressure. Bad television reception. Plus the fact
that you really can't get through to the people here. Really

Douglas Kennedy

can't get them on the same wavelength as you, if you see what I mean. Tell you true, I'd go straight back to Indiana tomorrow if I could. But if I told my bosses I wanted out of here, I know they'd tell me to kiss my job goodbye. Which is something I cannot afford to do. 'Course the big problem I have at the moment is that Wendy really hates the place. Can't blame her. I mean, she's not working – not that there'd be anything for her to do out here – and there's no foreign community in this town to speak of. Only about three other couples, and they're all . . . well, *Belgian*. So she's got a whole lot of free time on her hands. And that's kinda getting her down, if you see what I mean.'

'I see what you mean,' I said.

He suddenly gave me one of those playful, fraternal pokes in the shoulder for which Americans are also justifiably famous, and said, 'Hey Nick, I just got a great idea. You got any plans for dinner this evening?'

'Not exactly.'

'Well then, you've just got yourself an invitation for supper at our place.'

I hemmed, I hawed, I made the usual protestations about not wanting to impose, but he was adamant. 'I'm telling you, Nick, Wendy'll love the surprise. It'll make her day.'

I seriously doubted that, but I also figured that I had nothing to lose by accepting his offer of an evening's hospitality. Especially since the train to Algiers was leaving tomorrow morning at seven, and I was going to be on it.

So I threw a couple of dirhams down on the table to pay for my tea, and I followed him home. It was only a short walk from the Boulevard Mohammed V to the modern block of apartments where he lived. The building itself was a squat concrete cube which urgently needed a whitewash. So did his flat. It was spacious, yet spartan, with little in the way of personal touches to convince me that two people were actually living there. Lightbulbs had been left bare, no pictures hung on the badly blemished walls, and the furniture was Early Bedsitter. It was the flat of a couple

108

who were still trying to convince themselves that they were just passing through town.

The woman who greeted us at the door of this flat was a one-time resident of the County of Fetching, now tired and brittle. Wendy couldn't have been more than twenty-five but she had a pair of dark crescent moons etched below her eyes, and a taut mouth that was almost always in possession of a cigarette. As we crossed the threshold, she gave Ed a perfunctory peck on the cheek and then reached for a packet of Benson and Hedges.

'Meet Nick,' Ed said. 'I got talking with him downtown and dragged him back for a bit of chow.'

She nodded and gave me a slight smile.

'I hope you don't mind me landing on you like this,' I said.

'I don't mind,' she said.

'Whatcha up to, honey?' Ed said.

'Making carrot juice,' she said flatly.

'Hey Nick, come on into the kitchen. Got to show you this nifty little gadget I just bought.'

On the kitchen counter sat a high-speed juice extractor that looked like it ran on nuclear fuel, and basically atomized any fruit or vegetable you subjected to it.

'Bought this to beat the high price of fruit juice in Morocco,' Ed said. 'I mean, they're asking four bucks for a quart of fresh O.J. in the local grocery store, so I figured there's gotta be a better way of getting my daily dose of Vitamin C. Which is why I bought this baby. Best juice extractor on the market. Only problem is, you gotta be real careful about washing the fruit, since everything that's grown out here is fertilized with human dung. Which means that you first gotta wash the fruit in potassium concentrate, then soak it in fresh water. Isn't that right, honey?'

'Tell me about it,' Wendy said. 'I've just spent two hours treating these carrots.'

'Yeah, and you're using the wrong carrots as well.'

'What?' Wendy said.

'You're using *small* carrots,' Ed said, and then turned to me. 'I keep telling her, don't use small carrots – use large ones. But *she* never listens.'

Wendy smiled thinly and lit a fresh cigarette.

'How 'bout getting Nick a drink?' Ed said. We adjourned to the sitting room, and Wendy brought out a tray of salads and hors-d'oeuvres, as well as a bottle of vodka, a bottle of Scotch, and a pitcher of carrot juice. She poured a large Scotch for me, and then mixed herself a vodka and carrot juice. Ed restricted himself to water.

'If you need anything else, Nick, just ask and she'll get it for you.'

Ed had this habit of referring to his wife as *she*. When I asked Wendy whether she'd enjoyed living in Indiana, Ed jumped in:

'*She* really hated it there too.'

'That's not true,' Wendy said. 'What I didn't like was your circle of business friends.'

'What you didn't like was their wives,' Ed said.

'All right. I didn't like their wives. And I especially didn't like the women's club they all belonged to, and which *you* wanted me to join.'

'But it was something for you to do.'

'Sitting around with a group of Valium-soaked corporate wives, comparing notes on whether your husband's stock was rising or falling within the company, raising money for charity . . . '

'Hey,' Ed interrupted, 'what's wrong with raising money for charity?'

'It is boring.'

'Well, you're one to talk. I mean, what do you think you were doing back in Indiana? Nothing but paid charity.'

I winced. Wendy stared at her husband coolly and stubbed out her cigarette. 'I know you never thought that working at a soup kitchen was much of a job,' she said. 'And I also know that you thought the pay was nothing. But at least it was a job – a job which I found myself. A job which did some good. A job which *I* happened to enjoy.'

Ed quickly backpedalled. 'Look, honey,' he said, trying to sound conciliatory. 'I know just how hard you worked to find that job, and I mean, even though it was only a part-time job, it was terrific. Just terrific. But all I was saying was, you shouldn't knock those women back in Indiana. I mean, if you'd *had* your way, you could've sat at home too . . . '

'But I didn't sit at home,' Wendy said, the anger now showing.

'I'm not saying that you *did* sit at home. What I'm trying to say is that those women in Indiana didn't sit around either. They did significant stuff too.'

'You call their amateur dramatics group "significant stuff"?'

'I see nothing wrong with amateur dramatics in Indiana,' Ed said.

Wendy poured herself another vodka and carrot juice and reached again for the packet of Benson and Hedges. I tried to shift the conversation by asking if they'd gotten friendly with any Moroccans.

'I've basically met the local engineers working on Ed's project,' Wendy said, 'but I can't say that I've taken much to them. Especially since they have this habit of undressing me with their eyes any time I meet them. Though I suppose that's preferable to being touched up by them. Which I have been once or twice.'

Ed suddenly sat up. 'Hey, thanks for telling me. I mean, this is the first time I've ever heard about it.'

'It was all quite innocent, darling.'

'There's nothing innocent about guys touching up my wife . . . '

I excused myself and went to the loo. When I returned a few minutes later, I overheard Wendy saying, 'Don't tell me you're jealous again?'

More drinks were poured and Ed kept going on about the 'guys who've chased my wife'. I sat back and sipped my Scotch and listened, silently congratulating myself for stumbling upon such an excellent evening's entertainment – Strindberg in the armpit of Morocco. And though I felt marginally shameless about relishing this display of marital fireworks, I decided I could live with the guilt. Anyway, what is travel but a form of voyeurism which allows you to loiter with intent in other people's lives before hitting the road again? And if Ed and Wendy wanted an audience for their verbal punch-up, I was very willing to assume the role of the crowd. As long as I wasn't pulled into the ring with them.

'. . . Then there was this newspaper photographer in Indianopolis who took a shine to Wendy,' Ed said. 'He was some kind of Arab immigrant, wasn't he?'

'He was Lebanese,' Wendy said. 'And very sweet.'

'Oh yeah, very sweet. So sweet he kept plaguing you . . . '

'He meant no harm.'

'Meant no harm? You know what this guy did, Nick? He kept coming over to our house. Bought Wendy this négligé which he wanted her to model for him. Even started calling me up at the office, asking me where my wife was.'

'He was just a child, Ed.'

'We had to change our phone number. Twice.'

'All men are children when it comes to women.'

'Lebanese guys particularly.'

Around eleven, Ed looked at his watch and said that it was his bedtime. 'I get up to go to work every morning at five-thirty, so I'm not too big on late nights,' he said. 'But don't let me break up the party. And if you want to spend the night, we've got a spare bedroom. *She'll* give you sheets and stuff.'

He went off without saying goodnight to Wendy. When he closed the bedroom door behind him, she exhaled loudly.

'He's so bloody protective. And now he's going to get worried every time he sees a Moroccan man look at me. I'll never hear the end of it.'

Another large vodka and carrot juice was poured. Another cigarette lit.

'I keep thinking, maybe I should just leave. Go back to Britain or the States or just travel for a while. I've decided I don't really believe in this marriage any more.'

'You must've believed in it at one time.'

'I was twenty then. In Indiana on this student exchange programme. And Ed was the first person I met who ever took a relationship with me seriously. So when my year was up, and I had to go back to Cardiff, marriage seemed like a practical decision. I could finish my degree in the States, then get work there. But around four months after the wedding Ed landed this job with the phone company, and they immediately sent him off on a training course in Seattle. Which meant I was left behind in Indiana to complete my course work and cram for my finals.'

'How long were you apart?' I said.

'Six months. A very long six months.'

She drained the glass and lifted the vodka bottle. It was dead, so she switched to Scotch. And said that three weeks after Ed left for Seattle, she began to feel lonely. So lonely, in fact, that she sought out company. But when Ed paid her a surprise visit in Indiana three months later, and she gave him a rundown on her extracurricular activities, he became volatile. 'I told him about the other men because I don't believe in hiding things. But it got very destructive between us after that.'

However, they did manage to patch things up before he returned to Seattle. But then, two months later, 'I met this English bloke at the airport.'

'What airport?' I said.

'Indianapolis Airport. I was going out to visit Ed, and I met this bloke from Southampton who was a graduate student at Indiana University. Doing a doctorate in . . . oh, I forget now. But he was on the same flight as me to Seattle, and we got talking in the departure lounge, so we decided to sit together on the plane. And before we landed, he asked me for my phone number. When I got back to Indiana, he called me up, asked if we could meet for a drink.' She took a large gulp of Scotch. 'It happened after that.'

It was like getting drunk with an expatriate Madame Bovary. And when she talked about the series of marriage counselling sessions that Ed had dragged her to in Indiana,

I pleaded exhaustion and said that I really should be staggering back to my hotel.

'You're tired?' she said, the words slurring.

'Dead tired,' I said.

'Not as tired as me,' she said bleakly. 'You can't be as bloody tired as me.'

Her hand reached out for me and I took it. When she pulled me towards her, I didn't put up much of a struggle. Nor did I protest too much when our lips touched, and her mouth opened and closed deeply around mine. But as I bit into her, and tasted a curious combination of vodka, carrot juice, Scotch and tobacco, an even stronger flavour began to make its presence known – the tang of mutual despair, mutual melancholy. And for one brief instant I thought: will it always be like this? Will I always be a hit-and-run merchant? Will I never stand still? Yet I didn't dwell on these thoughts for too long, as I allowed them to be muffled by a sodden voice within my brain which said: 'Forget the introspection. Get on with it. You've got a train to catch in a few hours.' And I heeded the voice's advice.

But that voice was soon replaced by another, more malevolent, voice; a voice which roared at me in rage and informed me that I was going to die. It was the voice of Ed. I didn't catch much of what he was saying, because as soon as I vaulted up from the sofa, he caught me with a ferocious right-hand jab to the mouth, and followed that up with a rapid salvo of punches against which I had no defence. I sank to my knees, but was quickly hauled off them, as Ed grabbed me by my hair and collar and sent me on a trajectory towards the front door. Wendy let out a scream that could be heard in Algeria, but what happened after that remains a little blurry, since the next thing I remember was that I was in the street, running. Running for my life and telling myself: 'You've got to get on that train.'

I didn't get very far, as my legs buckled and I collapsed on the ground next to a burnt-out car. When I tried to pull myself back up by grabbing on to the car's side-view mirror, it came away in my hand, and I held it close to my face and inspected the damage. A bad gash over my right eye. A nose that haemorrhaged blood. A lip split in two. A grotesque gap in my mouth where a front tooth used to live.

I threw the side-view mirror away, and lay slumped in the soft Moroccan clay, the desert wind sending a chilly gust of panic through me. Down the road, a police car on patrol stopped and trained its searchlight on me. I listened as the car engine was silenced, as a door opened, as a pair of boots crunched towards me.

And when the beam of a hand-held torch hit my face, I looked up into its harsh, clear light and said:

'Good evening, officer. Could you tell me the way to the railway station?'

But I knew that I wouldn't be leaving town for a while.

Anne Tyler

Teenage Wasteland

Anne Tyler is one of the most honest, and quietly funny, writers alive. Born in 1941, she lives in Baltimore with her psychiatrist husband and two daughters. Hardly stirring from there, she writes perceptively of everyday life in which private hopes and fantasies are depicted as clearly as thought bubbles above her innocent characters' heads. The Accidental Tourist *was turned into a successful film starring William Hurt and Kathleen Turner; her latest book is* Breathing Lessons. Teenage Wasteland *is an ironic tale of parents who have done nothing wrong — although not everyone agrees . . .*

He used to have very blond hair – almost white – cut shorter than other children's so that on his crown a little cowlick always stood up to catch the light. But this was when he was small. As he grew older, his hair grew darker, and he wore it longer – past his collar even. It hung in lank, taffy-coloured ropes around his face, which was still an endearing face, fine-featured, the eyes an unusual aqua blue. But his cheeks, of course, were no longer round, and a sharp new Adam's apple jogged in his throat when he talked.

In October, they called from the private school he attended to request a conference with his parents. Daisy went alone; her husband was at work. Clutching her purse, she sat on the principal's couch and learned that Donny was noisy, lazy and disruptive: he was always fooling around with his friends, and he wouldn't respond in class.

In the past, before her children were born, Daisy had been a fourth-grade teacher. It shamed her now to sit before this principal as a parent, a delinquent parent, a parent who struck Mr Lanham, no doubt, as unseeing or uncaring. 'It isn't that we're not concerned,' she said. 'Both of us are. And we've done what we could, what ever we could think of. We don't let him watch TV on school nights. We don't let him talk on the phone till he's finished his homework. But he tells us he doesn't *have* any homework or he did it all in study hall. How are we to know what to believe?'

From early October through to November, at Mr Lanham's suggestion, Daisy checked Donny's assignments every day. She sat next to him as he worked, trying to be encouraging, sagging inwardly as she saw the poor quality of everything he did – the sloppy mistakes in maths, the illogical leaps in his English themes, the history questions left blank if they required any research.

Daisy was often late starting supper, and she couldn't give as much attention to Donny's younger sister. 'You'll never guess what happened at . . . ' Amanda would begin, and Daisy would have to tell her, 'Not now, honey.'

By the time her husband, Matt, came home, she'd be snappish. She would recite the day's hardships – the fuzzy instructions in English, the botched history map, the morass of unsolvable algebra equations. Matt would look surprised and confused, and Daisy would gradually wind down. There was no way, really, to convey how exhausting all this was.

In December, the school called again. This time, they wanted Matt to come as well. She and Matt had to sit on Mr Lanham's couch like two bad children and listen to the news: Donny had improved only slightly, raising a D in history to a C, and a C in algebra to a B-minus. What was worse, he had developed new problems. He had cut classes on at least three occasions. Smoked in the furnace room. Helped Sonny Barnett break into a freshman's locker. And last week, during athletics, he and three friends had been seen off the school grounds: when they returned, the coach had smelled beer on their breath.

Daisy and Matt sat silent, shocked. Matt rubbed his forehead with his fingertips. Imagine, Daisy thought, how they must look to Mr Lanham: an overweight housewife in a cotton dress and a too-tall, too-thin insurance agent in a baggy, frayed suit. Failures, both of them – the kind of people who are always hurrying to catch up, missing the point of things that everyone else grasps at once. She wished she'd worn nylons instead of knee socks.

It was arranged that Donny would visit a psychologist for testing. Mr Lanham knew just the person. He would set this boy straight, he said.

When they stood to leave, Daisy held her stomach in and gave Mr Lanham a firm, responsible handshake.

Donny said the psychologist was a jackass and the tests were really dumb; but he kept all three of his appointments, and when it was time for the follow-up conference with the psychologist and both parents, Donny combed his hair and seemed unusually sober and subdued. The psychologist said Donny had no serious emotional problems. He was merely going through a difficult period of his life. He required some academic help and a better sense of self-worth. For this reason he was suggesting a man named Calvin Beadle, a tutor with considerable psychological training.

In the car going home, Donny said he'd be damned if he'd let them drag him to some stupid fairy tutor. His father told him to watch his language in front of his mother.

That night, Daisy lay awake pondering the term 'self-worth'. She had always been free with her praise. She had always told Donny he had talent, was smart, was good with his hands. She had made a big to-do over every little gift he gave her. In fact, maybe she had gone too far, although, Lord knows, she had meant every word. Was that his trouble?

She remembered when Amanda was born. Donny had acted lost and bewildered. Daisy had been alert to that, of course, but still, a new baby keeps you so busy. Had she really done all she could have? She longed – she ached – for a time machine. Given one more chance, she'd do it perfectly – hug him more, praise him more, or perhaps praise him less. Oh, who can say . . .

The tutor told Donny to call him Cal. All his kids did, he said. Daisy thought for a second that he meant his own children, then realized her mistake. He seemed too young, anyhow, to be a family man. He wore a heavy brown handlebar moustache. His hair was as long and stringy as Donny's, and his jeans as faded. Wire-rimmed spectacles slid down his nose. He lounged in a canvas director's chair with his fingers laced across his chest, and he casually, amiably questioned Donny, who sat upright and glaring in an armchair.

'So they're getting on your back at school,' said Cal. 'Making a big deal about anything you do wrong.'

'Right,' said Donny.

'Any idea why that would be?'

'Oh, well, you know, stuff like homework and all,' Donny said.

'You don't do your homework?'

'Oh, well, I might do it sometimes but not just exactly like they want it.' Donny sat forward and said, 'It's like a prison there, you know? You've got to go to every class, you can never step off the school grounds.'

'You cut classes sometimes?'

'Sometimes,' Donny said, with a glance at his parents.

Cal didn't seem perturbed. 'Well,' he said, 'I'll tell you what. Let's you and me try working together three nights a week. Think you could handle that? We'll see if we can show that school of yours a thing or two. Give it a month; then if you don't like it, we'll stop. If *I* don't like it, we'll stop. I mean, sometimes people just don't get along, right? What do you say to that?'

'OK,' Donny said. He seemed pleased.

'Make it seven o'clock till eight. Monday, Wednesday, and Friday,' Cal told Matt and Daisy. They nodded. Cal shambled to his feet, gave them a little salute, and showed them to the door.

This was where he lived as well as worked, evidently. The interview had taken place in the dining room, which had been transformed into a kind of office. Passing the living room, Daisy winced at the rock music she had been hearing, without registering it, ever since she had entered the house. She looked in and saw a boy about Donny's age lying on a sofa with a book. Another boy and a girl were playing ping-pong in front of the fireplace. 'You have several here together?' Daisy asked Cal.

'Oh, sometimes they stay on after their sessions, just to rap. They're a pretty sociable group, all in all. Plenty of goof-offs like young Donny here.'

He cuffed Donny's shoulder playfully. Donny flushed and grinned.

Climbing into the car, Daisy asked Donny, 'Well? What did you think?'

But Donny had returned to his old evasive self. He jerked

his chin towards the garage. 'Look,' he said. 'He's got a basketball net.'

Now on Mondays, Wednesdays, and Fridays, they had supper early – the instant Matt came home. Sometimes they had to leave before they were really finished. Amanda would still be eating her dessert. 'Bye, honey. Sorry,' Daisy would tell her.

Cal's first bill sent a flutter of panic through Daisy's chest, but it was worth it, of course. Just look at Donny's face when they picked him up: alight and full of interest. The principal telephoned Daisy to tell her how Donny had improved. 'Of course, it hasn't shown up in his grades yet, but several of the teachers have noticed how his attitude's changed. Yes, sir, I think we're on to something here.'

At home, Donny didn't act much different. He still seemed to have a low opinion of his parents. But Daisy supposed that was unavoidable – part of being fifteen. He said his parents were too 'controlling' – a word that made Daisy give him a sudden look. He said they acted like wardens. On weekends, they enforced a curfew. And any time he went to a party, they always telephoned first to see if adults would be supervising. 'For God's sake!' he said. 'Don't you trust me?'

'It isn't a matter of trust, honey . . . ' But there was no explaining to him.

His tutor called one afternoon. 'I get the sense,' he said, 'that this kid's feeling . . . underestimated, you know? Like you folks expect the worst of him. I'm thinking we ought to give him more rope.'

'But see, he's still so suggestible,' Daisy said. 'When his friends suggest some mischief – smoking or drinking or such – why, he just finds it hard not to go along with them.'

'Mrs Coble,' the tutor said, 'I think this kid is hurting. You know? Here's a serious, sensitive kid, telling you he'd like to take on some grown-up challenges, and you're giving him the message that he can't be trusted. Don't you understand how that hurts?'

'Oh,' said Daisy.

'It undermines his self-esteem – don't you realize that?'

'Well, I guess you're right,' said Daisy. She saw Donny suddenly from a whole new angle: his pathetically poor posture, that slouch so forlorn that his shoulders seemed about to meet his chin . . . oh, wasn't it awful being young? She'd had a miserable adolescence herself and had always sworn no child of hers would ever be that unhappy.

They let Donny stay out later, they didn't call ahead to see if the parties were supervised, and they were careful not to grill him about his evening. The tutor had set down so many rules! They were not allowed any questions at all about any aspect of school, nor were they to speak with his teachers. If a teacher had some complaint, she should phone Cal. Only one teacher disobeyed – the history teacher, Miss Evans. She called one morning in February, 'I'm a little concerned about Donny, Mrs Coble.'

'Oh, I'm sorry, Miss Evans, but Donny's tutor handles these thing now . . . '

'I always deal directly with the parents. You are the parent,' Miss Evans said, speaking very slowly and distinctly. 'Now, here is the problem. Back when you were helping Donny with his homework, his grades rose from a D to a C, but now they've slipped back, and they're closer to an F.'

'They are?'

'I think you should start overseeing his homework again.'

'But Donny's tutor says . . . '

'It's nice that Donny has a tutor, but you should still be in charge of his homework. With you, he learned it. Then he passed his tests. With the tutor, well, it seems the tutor is more of a crutch. "Donny," I say, "a quiz is coming up on Friday. Hadn't you better be listening instead of talking?" "That's OK, Miss Evans," he says. "I have a tutor now." Like a talisman! I really think you ought to take over, Mrs Coble.'

'I see,' said Daisy. 'Well. I'll think about that. Thank you for calling.'

Hanging up, she felt a rush of anger at Donny. A talisman?

For a talisman, she'd given up all luxuries, all that time with her daughter, her evenings at home!

She dialled Cal's number. He sounded muzzy. 'I'm sorry if I woke you,' she told him, 'but Donny's history teacher just called. She says he isn't doing well.'

'She should have dealt with me.'

'She wants me to start supervising his homework again. His grades are slipping.'

'Yes,' said the tutor, 'but you and I both know there's more to it than mere grades, don't we? I care about the *whole* child – his happiness, his self-esteem. The grades will come. Just give them time.'

When she hung up, it was Miss Evans she was angry at. What a narrow woman!

It was Cal this, Cal that, Cal says this, Cal and I did that. Cal lent Donny an album by the Who. He took Donny and two other pupils to a rock concert. In March, when Donny began to talk endlessly on the phone with a girl named Miriam, Cal even let Miriam come to one of the tutoring sessions. Daisy was touched that Cal would grow so involved in Donny's life, but she was also a little hurt, because she had offered to have Miriam to dinner and Donny had refused. Now he asked them to drive her to Cal's house without a qualm.

This Miriam was an unappealing girl with blurry lipstick and masses of rough red hair. She wore a short, bulky jacket that would not have been out of place on a motorcycle. During the trip to Cal's she was silent, but coming back, she was more talkative. 'What a neat guy, and what a house! All those kids hanging out, like a club. And the stereo playing rock . . . gosh, he's not like a grown-up at all! Married and divorced and everything, but you'd think he was our own age.'

'Mr Beadle was married?' Daisy asked.

'Yeah, to this really controlling lady. She didn't understand him a bit.'

'No, I guess not,' Daisy said.

*

Spring came, and the students who hung around at Cal's drifted out to the basketball net above the garage. Sometimes when Daisy and Matt arrived to pick up Donny they'd find him there with the others – spiky and excited, jittering on his toes beneath the backboard. It was staying light much longer now, and the neighbouring fence cast narrow bars across the bright grass. Loud music would be spilling from Cal's windows. Once it was the Who, which Daisy recognized from the time that Donny had borrowed the album. '*Teenage Wasteland*,' she said aloud, identifying the song, and Matt gave a short, dry laugh. 'It certainly is,' he said. He'd misunderstood; he thought she was commenting on the scene spread before them. In fact, she might have been. The players looked like hoodlums, even her son. Why, one of Cal's students had recently been knifed in a tavern. One had been shipped off to boarding school in midterm; two had been withdrawn by their parents. On the other hand, Donny had mentioned someone who'd been studying with Cal for five years. 'Five years!' said Daisy. 'Doesn't anyone ever stop needing him?'

Donny looked at her. Lately, whatever she said about Cal was read as criticism. 'You're just feeling competitive,' he said. 'And controlling.'

She bit her lip and said no more.

In April, the principal called to tell her that Donny had been expelled. There had been a locker check, and in Donny's locker they found five cans of beer and half a pack of cigarettes. With Donny's previous record, this offence meant expulsion.

Daisy gripped the receiver tightly and said, 'Well, where is he now?'

'We've sent him home,' said Mr Lanham. 'He's packed up all his belongings, and he's coming home on foot.'

Daisy wondered what she would say to him. She felt him looming closer and closer, bringing this brand-new situation that no one had prepared her to handle. What other place would take him? Could they enter him in public school? What were the rules? She stood at the living-room window, waiting for him to show up. Gradually, she realized that he was taking too long. She checked the clock. She stared up the street again.

When an hour had passed, she phoned the school. Mr Lanham's secretary answered and told her in a grave, sympathetic voice that yes, Donny Coble had most definitely gone home. Daisy called her husband. He was out of the office. She went back to the window and thought awhile, and then she called Donny's tutor.

'Donny's been expelled from school,' she said, 'and now I don't know where he's gone. I wonder if you've heard from him?'

There was a long silence. 'Donny's with me, Mrs Coble,' he finally said.

'With you? How'd he get there?'

'He hailed a cab, and I paid the driver.'

'Could I speak to him, please?'

There was another silence. 'Maybe it'd be better if we had a conference,' Cal said.

'I don't *want* a conference. I've been standing at the window picturing him dead or kidnapped or something, and now you tell me you want a —'

'Donny is very, very upset. Understandably so,' said Cal. 'Believe me, Mrs Coble, this is not what it seems. Have you asked Donny's side of the story?'

'Well, of course not, how could I? He went running off to you instead.'

'Because he didn't feel he'd be listened to.'

'But I haven't even —'

'Why don't you come out and talk? The three of us,' said Cal, 'will try to get this thing in perspective.'

'Well, all right,' Daisy said. But she wasn't as reluctant as she sounded. Already, she felt soothed by the calm way Cal was taking this.

Cal answered the doorbell at once. He said, 'Hi, there,' and led her into the dining room. Donny sat slumped in a chair, chewing the knuckle of one thumb. 'Hallo, Donny,' Daisy said. He flicked his eyes in her direction.

'Sit here, Mrs Coble,' said Cal, placing her opposite Donny. He himself remained standing, restlessly pacing. 'So,' he said.

Daisy stole a look at Donny. His lips were swollen, as if he'd been crying.

'You know,' Cal told Daisy, 'I kind of expected something like this. That's a very punitive school you've got him in – you realize that. And any half-decent lawyer will tell you they've violated his civil rights. Locker checks! Where's their search warrant?'

'But if the rule is —' Daisy said.

'Well, anyhow, let him tell you his side.'

She looked at Donny. He said, 'It wasn't my fault. I promise.'

'They said your locker was full of beer.'

'It was a put-up job! See, there's this guy that doesn't like me. He put all these beers in my locker and started a rumour going, so Mr Lanham ordered a locker check.'

'What was the boy's name?' Daisy asked.

'Huh?'

'Mrs Coble, take my word, the situation is not so unusual,' Cal said. 'You can't imagine how vindictive kids can be sometimes.'

'What was the boy's *name*,' said Daisy, 'so that I can ask Mr Lanham if that's who suggested he run a locker check.'

'You don't believe me,' Donny said.

'And how'd this boy get your combination in the first place?'

'Frankly,' said Cal, 'I wouldn't be surprised to learn the school was in on it. Any kid that marches to a different drummer, why, they'd just love an excuse to get rid of him. The school is where I lay the blame.'

'Doesn't *Donny* ever get blamed?'

'Now, Mrs Coble, you heard what he —'

'Forget it,' Donny told Cal. 'You can see she doesn't trust me.'

Daisy drew in a breath to say that of course she trusted him – a reflex. But she knew that bold-faced, wide-eyed look of Donny's. He had worn that look when he was small, denying some petty misdeed with the evidence plain as day all around him. Still, it was hard for her to accuse him outright. She temporized and said, 'The only thing I'm sure of is that they've kicked you out of school, and now I don't know what we're going to do.'

'We'll fight it,' said Cal.

'We can't. Even you must see we can't.'

'I could apply to Brantly,' Donny said.

Cal stopped his pacing to beam down at him. 'Brantly! Yes. They're really on to where a kid is coming from, at Brantly. Why, *I* could get you into Brantly. I work with a lot of their students.'

Daisy had never heard of Brantly, but already she didn't like it. And she didn't like Cal's smile, which struck her now as feverish and avid – a smile of hunger.

On the fifteenth of April, they entered Donny in a public school, and they stopped his tutoring sessions. Donny fought both decisions bitterly. Cal, surprisingly enough, did not object. He admitted he'd made no headway with Donny and said it was because Donny was emotionally disturbed.

Donny went to his new school every morning, plodding off alone with his head down. He did his assignments, and he earned average grades, but he gathered no friends, joined no clubs. There was something exhausted and defeated about him.

The first week in June, during final exams, Donny vanished. He simply didn't come home one afternoon, and no one at school remembered seeing him. The police were reassuring, and for the first few days, they worked hard. They combed Donny's sad, messy room for clues; they visited Miriam and Cal. But then they started talking about the number of kids who ran away every year. Hundreds, just in this city. 'He'll show up, if he wants to,' they said. 'If he doesn't, he won't.'

Evidently, Donny didn't want to.

It's been three months now and still no word. Matt and Daisy still look for him in every crowd of awkward, heartbreaking teenage boys. Every time the phone rings, they imagine it might be Donny. Both parents have aged. Donny's sister seems to be staying away from home as much as possible.

At night, Daisy lies awake and goes over Donny's life. She is trying to figure out what went wrong, where they had made their first mistake. Often, she finds herself blaming Cal, although she knows he didn't begin it. Then at other times she excuses him, for without him, Donny might have left earlier. Who really knows? In the end, she can only sigh and search for a cooler spot on the pillow. As she falls asleep, she occasionally glimpses something in the corner of her vision. It's something fleet and round, a ball – a basketball. It flies up, it sinks through the hoop, descends, lands in a yard littered with last year's leaves and striped with bars of sunlight as white as bones, bleached and parched and cleanly picked.

Lisa St Aubin de Terán

The Bolshybally

Lisa St Aubin de Terán has a wanderlust, instilled in her from childhood, that propels her stories along with a restless, yet dreamy, energy. Three times married, with three children and now living in Italy, Lisa exploded into the literary world with two prizewinning novels: The Slow Train to Milan *– about travelling through Europe with her first husband, Jaime; and* Keepers of the House, *based on seven years with Jaime on his decaying South American plantation. Romance surrounds all her characters like a cloak that alternately reveals and conceals the truth about them, and the heroine of* The Bolshybally *uses this magical trick to her own advantage.*

It pleased La Rusa to surround herself with mystery. She had furnished her sitting room with it, knotting the drapes in such a way that the twisted folds seemed to conceal secrets that La Rusa wasn't telling. It was rumoured that the hollow ring that gave the style its bulk when she had finished pinning and poking her thin chestnut hair into place was filled with gold and diamonds. No one had ever been close enough to her to rummage through her hair, though. Mealtimes all over the town were spent discussing where the Russian lady kept her hoard, and where she came from. The general consensus of opinion was that she was not Russian at all. Yet, despite twenty years of interest in her origins and her affairs, no one had managed to bring up any conclusive proof against her.

Judge Gomez swore that he had known La Rusa carnally in a whore-house in Bogotá many years before. But Judge Gomez had been known to mistake his own daughter for the old laundress who pressed his wife's linen, so his evidence had to be dismissed as unreliable. Word had it that La Rusa came from a backstreet of Maracay. She was also said to have grown up in a corrugated shack by the curves of San Pedro on the desert road that led to Barquisimete. A German girl who worked shifts for La Rusa claimed that the boss was a German from the Colony Tovar. Whatever the truth might be about La Rusa's nationality, it was clear that she herself was never going to enlighten either her clients or her girls. She spoke a smattering of French, and she cursed in an unrecognizable language. There was a photograph of the late Tsar and Tsarina over the grand piano in her room, together with a page from a magazine with a picture of the grand Duchess Anastasia.

In her youth, La Rusa had liked to let slip hints and remarks about the missing Anastasia, as though to imply that by some miracle she had been resurrected to run an elegant brothel in the Andes. She had seen the film at least a dozen times, and she had adopted a number of mannerisms from the screen, together with a soft throaty way of rolling her rrr's. For years it had thrilled her to be taken for the royal refugee, and she would have continued to fantasize had not some interfering pedant worked out the ages and asked her point blank if she could really be nearing sixty. If only they knew, all those people struggling on their anthill of a town, how much she did have in common with the famous Anastasia. For she too had the whole world against her, needling to uncover her identity; and she was friendless, despite her wealth and her position as empress of the red light zone. Each of her girls had more friends than she. Sometimes it seemed that she was doomed to be a female Judas of prostitution, predestined to take the silver and be shunned. Sometimes she felt quite sad and bitter about her lot, but not so bitter that a drop of rum mixed with lemon and honey could not ease the thoughts away.

The sun would work its way around her yard with tyrannical indifference every day. The mornings would begin to throb with the gathering heat, and flies and mosquitoes would try to squeeze through the protective mesh that veiled every window of the house. The afternoons would swelter, slowly unravelling the tapestry of her life. It was hard to be elegant in such heat. The silk around her body crumpled and her hair mutinied in sticky wisps. The afternoons were a time for vigilance, the sentry duty that led up to the ritual opening of her court. At half past six sharp the painted carousel that gave La Rusa's 'Rainbow' so much of its character began to turn, rising and falling to the hurdy gurdy underneath its maypole centre. Side-saddle on each multicoloured horse sat one of her girls.

It was a privilege to work for La Rusa. The money was good and the prestige was important. Anyone who had sat for more than six months on the carousel could be sure to find another job anywhere within a radius of two hundred miles. And it was a fact that it was easier to marry out of La

Rusa's than it was to marry off the street. It was true, too, that no one really knew her, or particularly liked her, but she showed no weaknesses and therefore gave no hold for anyone to understand or care for her as a person. Hundreds of girls were grateful to her for giving them the social education that would otherwise always have remained out of their reach. La Rusa might have been a leading lady in many of the not-so-local weddings where girls from the Rainbow married into respectable families; yet the very nature of her business excluded her from such social gatherings. She would have given the game away to the other side. Her own secrets were enclosed in a kernel in the centre of a nut of other secrets. La Rusa was not just a famous madam, she was also an enigma.

She ruled her world without any potions or visible spells. While her girls spent their free afternoons roaming through the covered market looking for persuasive roots and herbs, La Rusa would stay at home playing one of the three tunes she knew on her tarnished piano. Although the entire neighbourhood was sick of these hammered tunes, La Rusa never was. On the days when her self-administered tots of honeyed rum were most generous, she would arrange herself in a certain position on the faded gold brocade of her *chaise-longue*, and summon one of her minions to her as though she were the grande dame of Hollywood she felt she might have been had circumstances been otherwise. Her girls came to her by rota, carrying an old-fashioned usherette's tray laden with emery boards and oils. Then, while her nails were manicured, La Rusa would tell of her night of glory.

She liked the prettiest girls best. She liked them to kneel at her feet while she unwrapped her story. There were always girls who wanted to get close to her, either to share her business or to steal it. There were girls who were bribed by clients to discover her secrets. Within the hierarchy of the Rainbow it would have been worth a lot to have been La Rusa's confidante. There was power and security in her friendship. But no one ever managed to become her friend. They were all called in, in their turn, to her festooned chamber on the ground floor, yet the web that she spun was too frail for any of them to grasp and her gossamer was wasted. She listened to the mixture of relief and mockery that followed each manicurist out of her silken trap. There was usually a huddle of girls waiting on the galleried landing.

'What did she tell you? What did she say?'
'Just the bolshybally.'

The ripples of laughter drifted down to her backstage door.

'Not again! Didn't you ask her about the matinée?'
'Why didn't you ask her something new?'

The day's manicurist would put her tray away in the small cupboard at the top of the stairs and say, 'So what's new? You know she's got bally on the brain. She just keeps you away with it.'

Back in one of their tightly shuttered bedrooms the girls held an emergency meeting. Behind La Rusa's back, they decided their every action at these summits, pooling their thoughts so as to undermine her own.

It was a small room with a mosaic tiled floor and whitewashed walls. In one corner there stood an iron-framed washbowl and jug and a large bar of soap. In another corner there was a small plaster of Paris madonna propped against a crudely painted black-faced Saint Benito. Both of them were peeling from the heat of the fat votive candle that flickered at their feet. Beneath a plastic crucifix, the metal bed bulged and rippled under puce satin flounces chequered with sombre linen embroidery squares that were herringboned on to its slippery surface. La Rusa encouraged the girls to do needlework during the dead hours of the afternoon. She said it calmed them down while training them in a lady-like skill. It was, at least, a useful way for the girls to cover up the unsavoury stains that were part and parcel of their profession. Some of the girls were nearly forty now, and had worked for La Rusa for the best part of their lives. One or two of them were on their second layer of linen squares, and had long since passed the marriageable age. They were desperate to share in La Rusa's secrets and profits before old age robbed them of their work. Of these such girls, Angelica with her dark brown eyes and thick, ready fists was the leader.

'Listen, I worked in a lot of places before I came here, and I tell you it is not natural. You can't have a madam and no favourite. You just can't have that; it isn't right. La Rusa has told me that she doesn't care for me or any one of us more than another. And that is not right. She calls it fair. Well life isn't fair. And when things aren't natural then they're not safe either. That old bitch is killing this town with curiosity.'

'Angelica, what's the matter with that? It's too hot to get bothered. We get our money, we're happy here and I bet we do get to see the matinée, too.'

'For the love of God, can't you see we're in danger? What will happen here if La Rusa runs out to her bolshybally. She's capable of it, she goes on about it enough; "If I could have leapt as I saw them leap that night I would never have been a whore. I would have leapt, Angelica, leapt through the air like time itself in suspension. . ." So, girls, what happens here if the old bat disappears?'

Sofia, the girl who had answered before, spoke again, curling her legs up under her with a languorous slither that seemed to imply that any movement at all was an effort too great for her pale pampered limbs.

'If La Rusa bales out, Angelica, you can run the show together with a junta, and we'll all make heaps of money; but bags I don't have to do any more work.' Maria Eugenia, who had joined the Rainbow during the rainy season and so was the newest of them all, had a habit of watching everyone with an air of wounded innocence which made her very popular with the older clients. She was watching now, turning her tawny wide-open eyes from one speaker to the next.

'I agree with Angelica. We do the work here. They all use us, but they come for La Rusa. She's the main attraction.

Trade would fall off, you'd see, if it weren't for her and her bally secrets.'

'What's so urgent about now, though. What's new?'

'She's getting restless, that's what. She's lonely. She's calling us down more. Her fingernails are nearly worn away.'

Downstairs a giant insect began to buzz and shake and hum before settling into the rhythmic beating of the generator.

'Good God, it's nearly time to start; quick, get dressed, and get the rooms cleared.'

Downstairs, La Rusa was marking time with her fingertips on the carved back of her throne. This half hour before opening was her favourite time. The organ would begin to play soon, tantalizing the men in the streets. In the time waiting for the curtain to rise and the show to begin she could imagine herself in another place waiting to see another stage. Or maybe tonight would be the night the girls and the music made that magic in her brain. It had happened before, only once before, on the night of the Bolshoi Ballet.

From the corner of her eye she saw a mosquito caught in a new spider's web, and she sighed. There was intrigue in the air again. There would be another attempt, no doubt, at a palace revolution soon. It was silly for the girls to try. Surely they knew that she had more to her than they, she had survived the cold winds of the Steppes and wolves, wild Tartars and Cossacks' swords. She had held on to life by its claws through war and famine. She too had lain injured under trucks of straw and been smuggled through the plains. Well, Angelica knew, but maybe the others didn't, because she didn't talk about that part of her life so much any more; not since they'd started selling the 'Great Book of Facts' from door to door in the town and some of her details had become blurred, it seemed. It was such a long time ago She was a mere child then. It was even before she saw the ballet and discovered the secret of life.

Julie Burchill

Baby Love

Julie Burchill grew up in Bristol and at sixteen ran away to London where she became a reporter at the NME. *There she became famous for her ferocious rock reviews, and left to pursue a freelance career of being shocking in print. She has produced several non-fiction books and one steamy novel,* Ambition. *Of* Baby Love *she says, 'I got the idea after reading some interviews with middle-aged male writers in which they all claimed to be little boys at heart. When I thought about it, this apparently innocent statement began to seem rather dangerous; how can ickle boys take responsibility for their actions?'*

'There there,' she said, stroking his bulging brow. 'Poor baby. Brave little soldier. Who's a brave little soldier for Mama?'

Baby pointed a wobbly finger at his chest, not trusting his quivering lips to transmit the message. He lay across the bed, damp and distressed, a casualty of his own luxuriant daring.

Baby had been showing off when disaster struck; bouncing on the bed before attempting a death-defying leap on to the sofa. He had slipped and hurt his ankle; she had bestowed a magic-mend kiss. Baby had been well pleased.

'Baby have new hurt,' he announced now. 'Kiss better.'

'Oh? Where?'

Baby laughed; not his normal shrill squeal but a deep, dirty cackle, a dead ringer for those of the departed Sid James contemplating Barbara Windsor's bosom. He lowered his pyjama bottoms to display a fully erect nine-inch penis, looking like something matrons from Montana would ooh and ahh over at Stonehenge.

'There!' Baby cackled, grabbing her head and thrusting it against his groin.

Maria awoke to the wonderful world of Disney blaring from the cable channel. Daniel lay on the sofa on his stomach, naked, a joint dangling from his lips and a can of cola fizzing in his hand, sniggering at the antics of a posse of unlikely mice.

She groaned, pulling the pillow over her head. Then peeping out, she cased the room in one short guilty sweep, like a shoplifter sizing up his prey. My God, she thought, what a *mess*.

Now they were on the point of packing up and checking out, she could visualize the room as it had been the day they arrived; with cleanliness crackling like static from its fittings and fixtures, a room which seemed to hum, smug with satisfaction at its own ersatz elegance. It now looked as if a legion of Roman emperors, pursued by a package tour of heavy metal groups, had passed through it within the space of a week.

It had been a whole seven days ago when Maria and Daniel had arrived in Brighton; it now seemed like nothing more than a slice of morning, a scoop of afternoon and a creamy dream topping of night. They had dropped their suitcases and sat bouncing on the big bed, inarticulate with glee at having escaped London – she exclaiming over the delights of room service, he in ecstasy over the offerings of the twenty-four-hour cable TV. Soon two separate tables groaned 'Enough!' under the weight of their very different K.P. rations: champagne and cola, smoked salmon and Smarties, Camembert and crisps, Rioja and Ribena, hot black coffee in silver pots and a rainbow of Italian ice-cream in silver dishes. The TV stared blankly at the food.

Out came the cocaine; on went the DO NOT DISTURB sign; off came their clothes. Everything else could wait.

On the train back to London he was silent. Sulkiness thickened the air like pollen, making her feel sleepy. He sighed ceaselessly and kicked his feet against the opposite seat.

She didn't ask what the matter was; she knew the answer.

Last night as they had walked back from the South Pier to the Grand, he had said, 'Maria – I don't want to go home. Let's stay here. We could, you know. Just stay. Just carry on having fun. There's a million things we haven't done yet.'

She hugged him. She adored his enthusiasm.

'I'm not joking. We could have a brilliant time.'

This was Daniel's holy grail; the ultimate Brilliant Time. She felt like a wet blanket being thrown on the bonfire of his hedonism as she recited the rules and regulations of adulthood – work, money and mortgage. Daniel considered her answer thoughtfully for a moment. Then he puckered up the lips that had made grown men plead and beg on two continents, and, having carefully weighed the two viewpoints, he replied with a measured, moist raspberry.

On the mat Maria found a welcome home present: a letter confirming her promotion to the post of editorial director of Metro Books, plc. GOTCHA! she snickered to herself, not wanting to flaunt her triumph in mixed company. For she was successful, and Daniel was unsuccessful; and that was about as mixed as it got these days.

Her success could so easily remind him of his latest failure. Only a month ago he had auditioned for a part in a prime-time hospital drama that would have taken his career off the critical list once and for all. When the bad news came, he simply shrugged. 'That's cool. Something will turn up.'

It did: a demand from the Inland Revenue for forty thousand pounds in back taxes.

Daniel's past was forever on his trail, like David Janssen chasing the one-armed man in *The Fugitive*. It sniffed after him like a bloodhound after a bitch or a burglar. After many false leads, letters were constantly scratching at the door of Maria's flat, addressed to Daniel: unpaid parking tickets; overdue library books; determinedly cheerful postcards from old girlfriends. He looked at them all with the same absent-minded frown; as though *someone else* should have taken care of it.

'You're the most babyish man I know,' she teased him one night in bed.

'Babyish, moi?' he said, taking her nipple into his mouth.

In the beginning it had been part of his charm. But now she couldn't help wondering if it had all gone a bit too far.

It was she who had started it, calling him Bad Baby in affectionate recognition of his inability to function outside of the plush playpen of her apartment. The way the label always hung out of his sweaters; the way she couldn't take him out to dinner without taking his clothes to the dry cleaner the morning after; the way his attempts at DIY turned the air blue and his thumbs purple. He called her Mama because of the effortless efficiency with which she did everything; she made life look like ice-dancing, a smooth glide to a full-marks finish. She was the grown-up he would never be – even though he was thirty-one, and she was twenty-six.

Mama and Baby games became a way of erasing their separate pasts, whose very existence they found too painful to contemplate, being freshly in love. It also smoothed out the difference between them in the here and now. Only by shedding their old selves could they be born again with each other, tender enough to touch.

Men were all big babies anyway, reasoned Maria as they went deeper into their private world. It was just that Daniel was more honest than most. He could laugh at himself.

Soon after he moved in with her, they stopped seeing people. Every night when she got home from work at seven, he'd be in bed. She would drop her clothes on the floor and join him. After three hours of sex they would order in pizza, open a good red, play board games, watch TV with the sound off and the Velvet Underground blasting, smoke dope and snort coke till around three, all the while singing their own songs and speaking their own language. Maria was mystified as to why everyone didn't live this way, just pigging out on pure pleasure; mystified as to why she had spent so many evenings standing up in crowded rooms with a glass of cheap white wine in her hand, being bored by masters of the art, when she could have been staying in, enjoying herself. But then, how could she have done it before she had Daniel? He had given her back her youth, helped her shut out the dreary adult world of dinner parties, blind dates, barbecues, house prices and holiday plans – all those sad adult pleasures, all those envious adult responsibilities which tried to make their love sit up straight, stop playing with itself and *behave*.

On her first day at her new job, he called her at work. 'I just called to say I love you,' he sang.

'OK, Baby, that's enough,' she said on the third call.

When he called again demanding that she sing him his favourite song 'You Must Have Been A Beautiful Baby', she hung up.

When she returned from lunch, her secretary Jill said, 'Oh, Maria – you had six calls. From a Mr Bad Baby.'

'Oh? And did Mr Bad Baby leave any message?' Maria asked, trying to sound as cool and casual as was humanly possible for one covered from head to toe in a scalding red stain of agony.

'Yes. He said—' Jill consulted her scratch pad, making no attempt to hide her relish. 'Ah, here it is. He said, "Tell Mommy Bunny that Bad Baby doesn't love her any more." '

'Thank you, Jill,' said Maria calmly.

She was just about to gain sanctuary behind the safety of her own door when Jill said clearly, 'If Mr Bad Baby phones again, should I give him a message from Mommy Bunny?'

'Yes,' said Maria, turning to face her tormentor. 'Tell Mr Bad Baby to grow up.'

At her desk, Maria tossed a coin to decide between sobbing and screaming. She should have pretended that Mr Bad Baby was just some unknown pervert! In ten minutes, the story would have plummeted down from her penthouse through the building like an elevator out of control.

As it happened, she was wrong. The coin fell to the floor and she was on her knees under her desk peering at it when Suzy from Publicity popped her head round the door, only five minutes later. 'Hi. Has Mommy Bunny got a minute to discuss publication scheduling?'

Daniel was in bed when she got home. The room was strewn with cola cans, sweet wrappers and comics. 'Mama!' he cried, holding his arms out for a hug.

'Don't you ever do that to me again!'

'Why?' he squealed, panic pinging across his face and voice like a ping-pong ball across a table.

'Because it's bloody embarrassing!'

'But why?'

'Because it bloody is!'

'But . . .' He burst into tears. She was horrified. 'Can't you take a joke any more? Can't you?' he shouted defiantly.

'Yes. But not in public. Do you understand that there is a difference?'

'Yes!' he snapped back, and went into the sitting room to play with his train set.

Sometimes Maria wondered whether he was waving or drowning. It was so very hard to tell. He didn't *seem* to be worried about his life; that he was now grid-locked in the outer suburbs of youth, that his trust fund was drier than a good martini and that he hadn't worked in six months.

He'd been born into a minor showbiz dynasty and been a hot child movie star for a season during one of their temporary moves to Los Angeles. After a string of flops, his family returned to England.

In the mid-seventies, the teenage Daniel was considered by the *demi-monde* to be 'the most beautiful boy in London'. The capital was a soft city then, and a boy with his beauty and charm could ride the perfect pleasure wave of parties and premières and people for a thousand and one crazy nights, working now and then – a play on the fringe one year, a film on the Riviera the next. For years he was considered 'a promising actor' – though one jealous wag said this was 'because he's always promising to sleep with directors'. Some also muttered that he was 'a fag of convenience'. But his beauty and charm were enough to lift him up above such pettiness.

Until the eighties, that is. In the eighties, something happened.

Slowly but surely, all his crazy actor friends were cleaning up their acts: quitting drugs, drinking spritzers, marrying pretty young Born Again Christians, having children, moving to smallholdings in Surrey – *working hard*. They gave him big hugs, but little time. Only the unemployable had time to play these days.

He had never been a fireball of blind ambition, and Maria liked that. Men on the make repelled her; their passion went into their projects, rendering them humourless and diminishing their capacity for extracurricular fun. She was ambitious – but only because of the freedom success could buy.

At first they tried functioning in the grown-up world, but it didn't work; they sat at dinner tables in Islington and Chelsea like bored kids, fidgeting over the rocket, feeling each other up under the table, watching the clock with schooldays desperation, longing for the time they could go home and climb into bed. Her friends, annoyed that she had been stolen from them, said it would never work; he was very pretty, and terribly sweet, but he lacked 'self-motivation' – the sex appeal of the nineties.

And as for upstairs – well, the bailiffs had been by.

No, he wasn't exactly what you'd call an intellectual, Maria conceded to herself. He was *intuitive*. She could remember the first time he'd seen her book-lined sitting room. 'Wow, I've never seen so many books! Have you read them all?'

'No,' she admitted. With Daniel you never had to pretend.

'Still, you must be very intellectual.' He laughed. 'I'm not. But you probably guessed that.'

He never read books, only comics; never watched the news, talked about the world, worried about money. But he had a gift for making things fun both vertically and horizontally. What more could a modern girl want from a man?

Her promotion meant they had less time together. She would often return from work as late as ten, exhausted, and want to go straight to sleep to be fresh for a meeting at nine the next morning. He wanted to play all night, as they used to. When she wouldn't, he'd sulk. In the mornings, he'd pretend to be sick, hoping she'd stay at home with him. But she wouldn't.

She began to notice that time, the great vandal, was starting to take more than a passing interest in Daniel. First off the starting block was the receding hairline, making his brow even more babyish. Then the lines started hanging out in gangs around his eyes. Spider legs of hair sprouted from his nose, and his stomach went from baby bulge to putative paunch without passing through adult flatness.

But as his body turned irrevocably towards middle-age, his mind broke ranks and sashayed off the other way. Working from home one day, Maria was appalled when she witnessed a typical day in the life of her nearest and dearest.

Arising at noon, he smoked a joint while watching the Disney Channel, and then began preparations for his 'early morning tub' – an operation which in terms of time, planning, manpower and mass movement reminded her rather of the Allied landing at Normandy. In went ghetto blaster, marijuana, comic books, portable TV, six-pack of cola, dish of M&Ms, ducks, submarines and Daniel – out came a lot of water.

'What, no kitchen sink?'

'Don't be silly. There's a sink in there *already*.'

That was the thing about Daniel – he inhabited a place beyond the reach of irony and sarcasm. But she couldn't quite work out whether this was a good thing or not any more.

Brunch consisted of Sugar Frosties soaked in chocolate milk. The afternoon was whiled away watching the tube, playing computer games and smoking dope.

She was shocked – repelled, almost. But he seemed so *happy*. What did she want him to do? – cut his hair and get a job in a bank? Too late, she realized she did.

It was Saturday morning at Sainsbury's, and it all came down. He'd been dragging his feet and whining as they trundled through the aisles. '*Maria. I'm tired.* Can we go home?'

'Just a minute.' She consulted her list, and put some Italian bread in the trolley. 'OK. It's a wrap.'

She turned to him. He was taking a marbled chocolate bunny, Mr Hop-It by name, from the shelves. 'Daniel, put it back,' she said wearily. 'We have so much chocolate at home. It's starting to bloom, some of it.'

'But we don't have a bunny,' he said in his baby voice.

'Not in public, for Christ's sake!' she hissed. 'Put it back!'

'*I want Mr Hop-It*,' he insisted, clutching the rabbit replica to his chest.

'PUT IT BACK!'

'NO!'

'YES! DANIEL, DO AS I SAY!'

And with that Daniel raised Mr Hop-It over his head and threw it on the floor. Then he jumped on the broken bunny and began to bounce, all the while screaming 'I WANT IT! I WANT IT!'

People gathered around to look – not gloating but curious. At first they seemed to think it was a joke, that Esther Rantzen or Jeremy Beadle would pop out from behind the beans and tell them to smile, they were on prime-time TV. Children stared in envious awe; adults smiled nervously and shook their heads.

A security guard touched Maria's shoulder. 'Is everything all right, miss?'

She was too shocked to speak.

'Well, at least I proved once and for all that I can act,' Daniel said as they walked through the car park.

'That was no act,' said Maria, not looking at him.

'And *that*,' he said, smirking, 'is the greatest compliment you can give an actor. Thank you.'

She looked at him, stunned.

He had been practising his act on her, all the time.

She was thankful for the week at the Frankfurt Book Fair – they both needed a break after the strange games of the past months. Touching down, she felt pleased at the idea of seeing him again.

She had been burgled.

The hallway looked as if a rubbish truck had hit it. Amongst the rotting food and broken plates that covered the floor, small pieces of her jewellery sparkled sadly. Her shoes, their heels sawn off, were scattered throughout.

She had been cut down to size, all right.

She followed a trail of excrement to the sitting room. Her books were on the floor, ripped and torn. Her furniture was turned over; her fish tank had been emptied over it, and her kissing fish lay dead in each other's fins.

She had heard of these invasions before. But of course, she had never dreamed it would happen to her. She had a *Filofax*. She was in *control*.

What sort of sick mind would get a kick out of doing this, she wondered?

In the bedroom she found the answer.

It was dark, and it stank. A body sprawled on the bed; a fat, naked bald man with a beard. The smell of urine was overwhelming.

It was her anger that made her stay; how dare this stranger do this to her? That he had dared to pass out from drink or drugs on her bed, as she had heard they sometimes did, was the final insult.

She picked up a heavy brass candlestick from the mantelpiece, and raised it above her head, taking careful aim. As she brought it down, the creature spoke one word before the crack rang out.

'MAMA!'

Mavis Cheek

Loosing the Shoe

She stood on the steps outside the Court and shivered as the wind wrapped itself coldly around her ankles. She wished she had had the courage to wear her boots after all. She squared her shoulders: not wearing comfortable footwear for the hearing was to be her last meek act as an apologetic, dependent woman. The smart black high heels winked up at her knowingly: you were too frightened to be yourself, they said. She thought of her scruffy suede boots cast aside in her bedroom. It wasn't even, the thought continued, as though the Judge could even *see* her feet from where he was sitting.

Freedom, she thought, and had a strong urge to kick off those shoes there and then and dance down the steps of the imposing building. Surely there was more to divorce than this? Where were the trumpets? The fanfares? The handshakes and congratulations? She had expected something. Maybe the skies to open, clouds to roll away, and a large patriarchal finger to come pointing awfully down in her direction. But no. All there was – apart from the sore foot – was a profound sense of jubilation. Ah well, she told herself, sooner or later this elation would pass. Sooner or later this sense of achievement, this sense of having finally salvaged herself from some terrible wreck and found an island paradise into the bargain, would vanish. He, her husband, her ex-husband now, had said as much. She had thought it, been convinced of it. It was only a matter of time before the joy left her and she would be sad, lonely, depressed – like the human residue of a Bergman film.

I must do something positive to celebrate, something tangible to remind me of this golden moment, this euphoric state, before the sense of failure overwhelms me. The world, she told herself, is my oyster. What shall I do with it?

She went into the basement of a large department store and bought a food processor. With attachments. He had always said they were overpriced and unnecessary. He talked about their design faults a lot. Meanwhile she had scraped away with a kitchen knife. Now she saw herself blending, mixing, shredding, slicing off into the sunset of her own convictions. She felt quite a thrill go down her spine when she wrote out the cheque and accepted the salesman's deferential Madam as her due. Other women buy hats, she told herself, I buy food processors. So be it. She contemplated taking the purchase back on the tube but decided it would cramp her style. Anyway it felt extremely grown up and very independent to have something delivered.

After this she wandered around the ground floor of the store fingering bright silk scarves and trying out as many perfume testers as she could find. Is your skin jaded? enquired a counter display. The model's face gleamed out at her: a seventeen-year-old face made up to look flawless and thirty. She poked a finger at it accusingly. I am thirty, she said, a real thirty, and these are my battle lines thank you very much.

When all the scents had finally mingled into one aromatic stench, redolent she mused, of a courtesan's armpit, she felt again the pinching of the shoes. Coffee and a sit down, she told herself, and made her way to the lift.

Several impeccably dressed, immaculately millinered ladies were already waiting there.

'At least,' said one, 'you can get a nice quiet cup of coffee here.'

'Yes,' said another, 'it must be one of the last respectable places left nowadays . . .'

The lift came, collected its passengers, and went.

She was still standing there. Decorous coffee rooms with decorous cream cakes struck her, suddenly, as priggishly decent. Knickers to that, she thought, and left the store.

The pub had only just opened for the morning. It smelt of polish, beer and gently frying sausages. He had always

Loosing the Shoe

drunk beer and found many a variation on the conversational theme of real ale. Wine had been the drink for her. She approached the bar and was astonished to hear her own voice say,

'A pint of bitter please.'

'Best or ordinary?' asked the barman, still polishing glasses, scarcely looking up.

'Best,' she said firmly.

He put the filled glass down in front of her. 'And . . .?' he said.

She was puzzled, then saw that he was looking over her shoulder, down into the depth of the almost empty pub. She understood.

'Nothing else, thank you. There is only me. How much?'

I will not sit in a dim corner, she thought, and chose a table in the middle of the room. Once seated she slipped off the shoe that pinched, wriggled her toes, and then took a deep draught of the beer. Instantly she regretted having bought it and wished she had chosen something else – possibly cider; but then, she was a pushover on cider – or had been – in the old days. All the girls were reputedly pushovers on cider then. She remembered how frantically the boys used to buy it for them. But really though, when it all came down to it, she had been the only true victim. All her friends had put on convincing acts of being squiffy but at the end of an evening they could still cross their legs and remove a wandering hand from their bra-elastic. But not her. Third year of university, home for Easter (all those bunnies and the sap rising) – cider with Dennis and bingo. Back to Hall for finals feeling sick and ill, and throwing up all over Modern American Poets. He said it was eighty per cent her fault – he was very exact about such things – and she agreed. Of course she should have been on the pill, wasn't every modern young woman? Well . . . actually . . . no. A hasty wedding, shivering in August – she had thought that was wrong: the thought compounded a fortnight later by a miscarriage.

She had been glad to move on to wine after that.

155

The beer became more palatable as she tackled it. She quite liked it but was constrained from total enjoyment by her continuing lack of misery: perhaps it had been countered by removing her shoe – for there is no pain quite like the pain of a pinched little toe. Yes, possibly it was relief from that which accounted for her astonishing mental harmony. She edged the foot back into the shoe and waited – but, no, the pain had really gone. Just to be safe she slipped her foot free again. No point in taking unnecessary risks.

She drew some circles around the wet rings of beer on the table. It would have been different if they had gone on to have another baby – she put two dots like eyes in one of the circles and drew a curving line for a smile. A spark of anger made a small inroad in her happiness. 'Fortuitous' was the word he had used, gently but firmly, sitting on her hospital bed with a bunch of grapes. And so it had proved. He had gone on to take a good degree, followed by an excellent M.Sc. and a very fine Ph.D. She had read a lot of novels, got a job in the local library and decided that one committed academic in the flat was enough. She pressed the idea of taking up a degree course as if it were a bruise but it caused her no discomfort. She liked the library, and he wouldn't be around any more to make her feel it was second rate.

She thought she had better have something to eat, remembering the two lots of burnt toast she had committed to the waste bin that morning. Better not risk all this new-found freedom on an empty stomach, she counselled herself, and stood up. As she did so her first thought was that the expected emotional reaction had set in at last; her second was that the beer must be much stronger than she had thought; her third, tinged with relief, was that the lack of equilibrium was caused only by the physical disadvantage of wearing only one shoe. She slipped on the other and immediately felt on an even keel again. A pity in a way, she thought, as she advanced towards the bar, because she was beginning to feel hard-bitten and unwomanly with all this continuing self-confidence. She really ought to have shed a few tears by now on such a day as this. Could all that crying she had done over the past few months be it? She looked down at her hands in hope – but no – they were rock steady. Worse, her stomach gave a terrific, unemotional growl. She really was inordinately hungry.

Everything looked disgustingly appetizing. The sausages in their wrinkled skins lay on a bed of transparent grease. She ordered three. And bread and butter. While she waited the voice of another customer cut into her hungry thoughts.

'Glad to get in out of that wind,' he said. 'Need this whisky.'

And she heard the sound of his hands rubbing together.

'Sausages eh?' he directed at her. 'They look good.'

She smiled at the lie as she watched the landlord fishing about in the greasy Pyrex. The sausages looked perfectly revolting really.

'Hope you're going to leave some for me . . .' went on the other customer in the same cheery tone.

She laughed politely and looked at him. He had a nice face, a little too bright and eager, but nice. Black, well-cut hair, greying slightly at the temples – smart grey suit to match. He looked very pleasant. She smiled again and picked up her plate.

'Mind if I join you?' he called as she walked back to her table.

Prepared for her usual politeness she astonished herself by calling back over her shoulder, 'I'd rather you didn't,' and resumed her seat without turning a hair. Well, well, she thought, and not even a newspaper or book to hide behind. In future, she promised herself, I shall sit open-faced in public places and not talk to anyone unless I choose to. That was even more grown-up than having a food processor delivered.

Later, coming out of the dim saloon into the bright lunch-time light she felt a glorious sense of freedom all over again. Her future, great and expansive, moved before her. It can't last, she advised herself, it really and truly can't last. She walked along to the tube station and forgot about looking at her own worrying reflection in the shop windows. At the entrance a news-stand announced: 'Quins born to Luton Woman.' She read the word 'Quins' over to herself, visualizing all those little fists and mouths, waiting for the sadness and regret to descend – but it did not. All she felt was a sense of relief that it wasn't her – either Luton or the Quins. Never for the former and not yet, anyway, for the latter.

She bought her ticket and gave the collector a warm smile as she passed through the barrier. I have turned to stone, she told herself, smiling at strangers on a day like this. Dennis would most certainly have thought so.

'I am sorry,' he had said, 'I know it will be hard and painful for you, but we must be divorced. I no longer feel that my future is with you . . .'

And just as he had predicted she had suffered, wept, felt remorse and guilt.

'It will get worse after the decree nisi,' he went on, 'and worse again after the absolute . . .'

She had nodded, wet-eyed then. Of course it would, he was always right.

And now? Now she was sitting, lulled by the District Line, thinking with pleasure of her food processor and the joys to come. This was, surely, impossible.

When she was fourteen she could fix her eyes on an object for long enough to make them prick and hurt so that the tears would begin to flow. This would be followed by sad thoughts so that she could really begin to cry. It worked when she was fourteen. It did not now. Instead of the poster exhorting passengers to have a good day out at the British Museum calling forth a watery mist of self-pity, she found herself becoming interested. She tried again with a brand of knitting wools but that, too, caused her less to mourn than to consider the benefits of a mohair cardigan.

The shoe began to pinch again. At least some part of her was capable of painful sensation. The train slid her into her station and, limping a little (and maybe exaggerating ever so slightly) she made her way home.

As a wife she had always responded to any anguish by losing her appetite, tossing fretfully through the night while he slept soundly beside her sending the occasional whiff of two helpings of supper across to her side. It was, therefore, doubly mortifying to find, as she limped the few remaining roads to the flat, that she felt hungry again. That really did mean she was beyond the pale. She dismissed all the sensible things that went through her mind – like lamb chops and cheese sandwiches – and made straight for the corner sweet shop.

The two-pound box of chocolates weighed wonderfully in her hands as she climbed the stairs and let herself in. She would eat all the nut whirls first, including the ones from the bottom layer, and she wouldn't have to offer anyone first choice. He had always liked those as well.

In her bedroom she took off all her clothes. She had forgotten to turn off the central heating but – well – there was no one now to hold a post mortem on the bills. She kicked off her shoes and rubbed the little toe that throbbed so redly and reproachfully. Never again, she told it soothingly, never, never again. And she picked up the scruffy suede boots and put them on – quite oblivious to the bizarre image she made, lying naked on a bed in the early afternoon with her boots on and a box of chocolates at her elbow.

The telephone rang. O God, it was him.

'Are you all right, Jennifer?'

'Yes.'

'You went.'

'Yes.'

'Everything go well?'

It was like an enquiry after dental treatment.

'Yes.'

'I'm sorry I didn't go but both solicitors advised against it.'

Transference of guilt – she suddenly saw it, naked as herself.

'That's all right. It was very quick. Painless,' she added, thinking of the dental analogy.

'Jennifer?'

'Yes?'

'I think you should know.'

'What?'

'I've met someone else.'

She paused, waiting for her heart to plunge. It did not.

'Poor girl' was actually her first thought.

'Good for you,' she said.

'Pardon?'

'I'm glad. For you . . .'

'You're all right aren't you? I mean – you're not going to do anything silly?'

'Well—' she said doubtfully, looking at the box of chocolates – for that had certainly not been a sensible thing for a generous size twelve to do.

'Nothing *very* silly,' she said finally.

'And you'll get in touch if you can't cope?'

Patronizing bugger, she thought.

Out loud she said, 'Oh – it'll be hard – but—' she riffled through the papers to the second layer of chocolates, selecting two nut whirls, 'but – in the circumstances . . .' she put them both into her mouth, 'I think I'm going to be all right.'

She wiggled her toes. Painless.

'Definitely,' she said through the chocolate, 'definitely going to be all right now.'

Judith Rossner

116th Street Jenny

Judith Rossner has written eight novels including Looking For Mr Goodbar, *which was turned into the controversial film starring Diane Keaton. Her latest novel,* His Little Women, *was published autumn 1990. Judith was born and raised in New York; twice married, she has two children and still lives in Manhattan with her partner Stanley. She hates leaving apart from brief excursions, and* 116th Street Jenny *was the result of one such recent trip to Venice. 'I was lying on my bed, looking on to the Canal, thinking I'd get bored if I didn't have something to write, when I suddenly remembered this incident of a friend who bought a painting, treasured it, and then was asked to relinquish it. That, combined with Venice, became this story.'*

At the beginning of the seventies my parents and my older sister and brother were all stable, married and teaching in universities, so that even if the sixties hadn't provided me with the rhetoric to explain dropping out or smoking dope, I might have felt the need to distinguish myself by doing both. In the middle of my sophomore year at Oberlin, I returned to Manhattan and with four friends moved into an apartment on the Lower East Side that was to be a sort of urban commune, a group disengaged from life's crude competitions and petty quarrels, unmoved by the need to plan for the future or take account of the past. Our arrangement lasted into the following autumn only because each of us was away for much of the time during the warm months.

In the early winter, I asked my parents if I could come home. They consented, on the condition that I return to college, Barnard or Columbia's School of General Studies. They both taught at Columbia (my mother, modern art, my father, twentieth-century European history) so that, aside from the school's other virtues, they would not have to pay tuition. Although I didn't yet know this, my parents had applied for joint grants that would take them to the Orient during the following academic year. They were concerned about renting to strangers or allowing the apartment to remain vacant and were delighted to find, once I'd moved back in, that I had calmed down, was not interested in sharing my living quarters with friends for more than an occasional night, and was willing to act, at least for a while, as though I valued a college degree.

I had grown up in that apartment, one of those huge Riverside Drive eyries built in the days when most large apartments had some provision for a maid, that is to say, for a person without the space and comfort requirements of the normal human being. There were four large bedrooms off a back hallway, then a tiny one next to the kitchen. Moving back, I suggested to my parents that since I'd been away and we'd all had more privacy, it might be just as well for me to sleep in the tiny room; the large bedroom that was still more or less mine could be a study and a second guest room. Of the rooms that had been my sister's and brother's, one had been furnished to suit the housekeepers they hired periodically then fired because they were inadequate as cooks.

My parents had an extremely strong interest in good food. Women hired in spite of their unfamiliarity with our favourites were given a certain length of time to learn them and were fired if they had not. From an early age I had exhibited a strong affinity for the domestic, a tendency to be in the kitchen while everyone else in the family was off at a desk. As I grew up I had become increasingly helpful in the matter of training new housekeeper-cooks, increasingly capable of making a good meal myself. It had been a puzzle to me when I was young, and remained a source of disgruntlement as I grew up, that my parents, for all their culinary obsessiveness, could not accept the notion of food drawing me more powerfully than academic subjects did.

That summer, while visiting their friends the painters Eleanora and Jason Stonepark at their home outside Florence (they'd become friendly when Eleanora was my mother's student), my parents had found and brought home with them a woman named Anna Cherubini. Anna's children were running the family's mom-and-pop style restaurant in Florence, for which Anna had been the chef until her husband died the year before. For reasons having to do with one of her sons' wives, Anna had begun to feel superfluous. After some deliberation she had consented to come to the States to work for my parents 'for a little while', tending the apartment and, of course, preparing her lovely meals.

In the course of learning from Anna how to cook her southern Italian cuisine, which included fresh pasta (still unknown in New York outside of the West Village, East Harlem and a couple of high-priced restaurants), and of helping her to translate the recipes for my parents' other favourites, I not only became a much better cook than I'd been, but also learned to speak decent Italian. Then, in the spring of 1973, Anna got a call from her family saying she was needed at the restaurant. *Rapido*. She went.

All this is by way of explaining how it came to be that on a weekday night when Eleanora and Jason (her maiden name was Stein, she'd married the person then named Jason Park, and in those days when the debate over keeping one's 'own' name, that is to say, one's father's name, hadn't even become familiar, both had legally changed their last names to Stonepark) were coming to dinner and both my parents had heavy teaching schedules, I cooked and served the meal. When Jason, learning it was my work, congratulated me in Italian and I answered in kind, we got into a conversation. Still in Italian, he asked whether I had spent time in Italy.

I liked Jason and did not attempt to impress him with the extent of the rebelliousness that had encouraged my parents to send me to camp instead of taking me on their travels, as they had my sister and brother. I was a change-of-life baby, born to a mother whose two real children had been civilized academics almost from birth. I told Jason I'd gone to camp with my friends.

He nodded. 'I can understand that. Do your friends share your interest in Italy?'

I grinned. 'Pizza's about it.'

I wasn't even certain it was legitimate for me to claim an affinity. I had become fluent in Italian because of my interest in food and the amount of time I spent with Anna. The food romance and the big-city romance had yet to marry and take New Yorkers on their honeymoon. Exotic, or even just plain foreign, foods were not available throughout Manhattan as they would be in another few years. Anna, during her first weeks in New York, had always been looking for ingredients which she did not, when they were located, deem satisfactory. My parents had initiated her to Zabar's, and Zabar's was all right for cheese and coffee beans (although she would not acknowledge that the *reggiano* bought there was identical to the one she'd grated in Italy), and she would make do with canned tomatoes when the real ones ('*pommadori nostrani*') went out of season. But it was I who had brought her to the Village and lower Second Avenue for sausages, fresh herbs and bread she judged good enough to eat, not to speak of vegetables like *fenocchio* and *broccoli du rape* that would remain unknown in non-Italian neighbourhood stores until the Koreans took them over. My Italian had come in the learning of the food even as I would become facile with Spanish, which I'd studied in school but never used outside it, when the Cuban-Chinese restaurants began to flourish along Broadway.

Jason asked if I knew that he and Eleanora had a home and vineyard in Gaiole that my parents occasionally visited. When I told him I remembered hearing about the place, which sounded wonderful, he said, 'Perhaps you'll come and visit us some time and see for yourself.' I smiled, dismissing the remark as a pleasantry, but as it turned out he had something quite specific in mind. The following week I accepted an invitation to Sunday lunch at his home. When I asked my father if he knew why they might have invited me, he shrugged and said that I had impressed Jason. When I pushed him to speculate, he said that one of the things he liked about Jason was that if the other man had something to discuss with me, he'd bring it up directly. I might bear in mind that my mother had a very high opinion of Eleanora Stonepark's talent. Eleanora was one of a minuscule number of students she'd ever chosen to see after graduation.

Thus did my father inform me (I would understand it this way only later) that I was on my own but in a place where I must not dishonour my family.

The Stoneparks lived in the building on Park Avenue in the sixties where Jason had been raised. The rooms were large and pleasant, the walls of most covered with paintings by Jason *or* Eleanora. That is to say, their paintings did not share rooms. Jason's huge oils, hung in the pleasant living room with its big, soft chairs and sofas in shades of teal and grey, were powerful and sombre abstracts in black, brown and grey, easier to describe than to look at, impossible to trace, at least with this viewer's brain, to the gentle soul who took an interest in other humans which his wife did not appear to share. On the other hand, it became apparent as I followed him from the living room, through a long hallway with hundreds of family photographs, into a large, bright room hung with Eleanora's paintings that was clearly the place where the family spent most of its time, that what *he* did not share with *her* was a talent for painting wonderful pictures.

The walls, the curtains and the chair upholstery were all a soft yellow that seemed to provide sunshine even on a day as grey as this one. The floor was covered by a sisal rug. Tall windows looked out on a terrace that ran around two sides of the room. Aside from those windows and their curtains, Eleanora's paintings and sketches were the only things at eye level or higher.

I'm not sure whether I actually gasped as I entered the room and saw them, or whether memory has me dramatizing a real reaction, but I found them beautiful and wonderful. Along with many watercolours (later, seeing Chianti country, my first thought was that the landscape was almost as beautiful as it had been in her paintings) were several oils and a few drawings of the (naked) female form, then a couple of portraits of (dressed) men. When I try now to remember specific pictures, I see one vast swirl of brilliant colour.

I was standing at the room's entrance, thunderstruck – artstruck, if you will – with Jason just ahead and slightly to one side of me, when I heard a child's voice mimicking an engine's sound, and at the same moment was knocked into Jason by that child as he barged past us into the room, thrusting before him the largest toy engine I'd ever seen.

Jason straightened us out and said, as we watched the boy (who was then eight) circling the room, still making his engine noises, 'Well, now you've met Evan, and I'm sure if you've survived at all, you're the better for it . . . You are all right, aren't you?'

'Mmm,' I said. 'I'm fine, thank you.'

My eyes returned to the nearest paintings while my brain wished for a few minutes alone with them before I was required to talk or to deal with Evan. It was not to be.

'Who're you?' the boy asked.

'My name is Carol,' I said.

'Are you my mother's friend or my father's?' he asked.

I replied with a straight face that actually *my* mother and father were friends of *his* mother and father.

'So how come you're the one who's here?' he asked.

Now I allowed myself to smile. 'They invited me.'

'They must want you to do something,' he said. 'Are you a good babysitter?'

Beside me Jason groaned good-naturedly and without serious concern.

'I don't know if I'm a good one or a bad one because I've never done it,' I replied.

'Oh, well,' Evan said. 'You will if you come to Italy with us.'

I turned to Jason and was about to tell him that I hoped his invitation wasn't about that because I'd promised my parents I'd go to summer school, when Eleanora Stonepark breezed into the room in a flowing black-velvet hostess gown of a sort I'd never seen before. Eleanora never wore anything but black, a phenomenon in those days in a way that it isn't now.

I find myself, as I try to describe the condition of my brain at this moment, going to a framed page of Eleanora's ink drawings I would see only later, as we sat at lunch. There was a tree in full leaf and flower. Next to it stood the same tree, recognizable but beginning to break into cubes and other less specific forms. And next to that a mad swirl, unrecognizable as the tree in any way you could specify, but that you understood to represent its soul.

Eleanora fixed on me one of her more dazzling smiles. (Later I would grade them as Earth and Sky Light Up;

Earth Only; the Neighbourhood; the Room. Her mouth made the same motions with each of them yet the range in effect was staggering.)

'So,' Eleanora said, 'are we thinking it all might work?'

I stared at her. I had the feeling gates had closed behind me.

'My dear,' Jason said, moving to her side, putting a protective arm around her although I was quite certain it was I who required protection, 'Carol has just arrived and I haven't told her about our idea.'

'Oh, God,' said Eleanora, a model of adorable dismay, 'I hope I haven't ruined things.'

'You have never in your entire life ruined anything,' Jason assured her. 'You have simply made it desirable for me to explain why we've invited Carol to lunch though we don't know her very well.' He turned to me. 'May I offer you a glass of wine? Lunch will be ready any moment.'

I nodded.

He pressed a buzzer on the wall and a maid appeared. She was asked to bring us some white wine. Eleanora had settled into an easy chair with a copy of *Vogue*, which she was flipping through as though some question had been answered and she could go back to thinking about whatever really concerned her. When the maid brought our wine, Evan said he wanted to have lunch with us and Eleanora, without looking up from her *Vogue*, said in Italian that this didn't seem like a good idea (I don't know if this is the time to mention that Eleanora was an upper-middle-class Jewish girl from Manhattan who was then thirty-four years old, to her husband's fifty), at which point Jason steered the protesting child into the kitchen.

'Let me tell you about the farmhouse in Gaiole,' he said when the three of us had settled at the table. Our first course, prosciutto and melon, was in front of us. 'It's an easy drive from Florence and we do it often. We spend as much time as we can at the house, we both have studios right there, and when Evan's on vacation, and so on, we're normally there. Our usual help, or at least those of our helps who've had the care of Evan, generally accompany us. But now, for a variety of reasons, we'd like to change that. Aside from any other consideration, he hasn't been learning Italian in the natural, you might say, manner we'd hoped he might. In the way you yourself did.'

Jason explained that it hadn't occurred to him to look for someone like me until the night of our dinner, when it had come to seem that each and every problem they had in Italy, beginning with the language matter, going on to the way they liked to eat (the female half of the live-in couple was 'a Sicilian with an exceedingly limited repertory', but transporting another cook to and home from the farm was a nuisance) and ending with the matter of having someone look after Evan whom he could actually enjoy, might be solved if I would come to Italy with them. This summer was particularly important because Eleanora was having her first major show the following winter and would be working even harder than she usually did.

'Now,' Jason said, 'you're not even to try to make a decision immediately. You are to think about the possibilities and enjoy your lunch.'

But the two were mutually exclusive; was I allowed to explain about my parents' insistence that I go to summer school to make up for lost time, or would I find out when I reached home that this had been a breach of faith?

In between the melon and prosciutto and our main course, a lovely fish salad I could barely choke down, Eleanor began sketching, using a piece of paper from a pile and a pencil from a mug filled with sharp ones that rested on top of it near her place at the table. A couple of times I could feel her glancing up at me and as we ate (she periodically put down her fork and sketched for a moment) I became convinced that I was her subject. My indecision about how to find out was made keener by the fact that there was very little conversation about anything, and no apparent sense, on anyone else's part, of something missing.

I had grown up at a table where four active academics reviewed aloud what they were doing, frequently with a sense of competition and/or urgency. Now, with my sister and brother gone, my parents discussed whatever concerned the two of them. I knew many details of their current grant proposals, geared to their eagerness to go together to Japan: my mother wanted to study the influence of Japanese art on Impressionism between the two World Wars; my father's proposal had to do with relations between Germany and Japan. Here, Eleanora's very presence made table chat superfluous, although Jason volunteered an occasional comment or offered me food.

I contained myself until I'd finished my fish salad but then I leaned over to see what was on her paper.

'You have a good face,' Eleanora said. 'I'd love to paint you some time.' She smiled winsomely, turning around the paper to show me a pencil sketch instantly recognizable as the Real Me.

I was dumbstruck.

'She's upset by my picture,' Eleanora said gravely to Jason.

'Oh, no,' I croaked, gasped, 'It's wonderful! I can't believe you just . . .'

She had *seen* me in some way that my parents, never mind my parents, *my best friends* did not. I was viewed by my friends as easy to get along with. It was my enjoyable peculiarity to be interested in what girls had once *thought* they were interested in – most particularly, of course, in cooking. My friends' mothers had gone to Barnard, Vassar and Radcliffe then married, learned to cook, read good books and joined the PTA. Their daughters, whether because they'd been galvanized by the new Women's Movement or because they had some specific interest, intelligence and/or drive, wanted to be lawyers (mostly), doctors (practising down South or serving in the Peace Corps) or, in the case of Theo, who was very tall and majestically beautiful and had a consciously political way of being in the world, to run for Congress. When we had group sleepovers, I cooked. If they apologized for putting me to work, I told them I didn't mind. But saying I didn't mind had nothing to do with being *agreeable*: it was the *truth*. I found the preparation of the food as compelling as the gossip, which I also enjoyed. Because the other girls did not share my pleasure in cooking, they attributed my willingness to virtue.

Eleanora Stonepark, in the most casual way imaginable, had seen my dark side. The face she'd drawn was of a quirky and difficult human being whose mouth had a distinctly sardonic turn – as my fleshly one did not. At the same time, the flaws in the person she had portrayed, perhaps because that person seemed intelligent and self-possessed, were tolerable to me in a way that the flaws in her model were not.

After lunch, Eleanor picked up the piece of paper with my soul on it and appeared to be about to leave the table.

'May I have it?' I asked, without debating whether it was acceptable to do this. My voice trembled and I was sure that I would cry if she said no, while I could not imagine why she would want to hold on to it.

'Of course you may,' Eleanora said graciously. 'But first . . . I want to play with it for a while, you know?'

I nodded, mesmerized.

'What I think,' she said, suddenly winsome, playful, 'is that by the time we've had our lovely summer, I'll be ready to part with it. For all I know, I'll have done a painting, by then.'

I was nearly dumbstruck.

'You don't understand,' I gasped. 'I'd *love* to go to Gaiole.' I probably would have wanted to go even without this cleverly mounted bait. Whether it was a judgement about her work or a reaction to her presence, or both, I had been conquered by Eleanora Stonepark, a person who could do something extraordinary and wonderful that no one else I knew could do. And then, of course, there was Jason, a moderate and easy person who would always be around if Eleanora's artistic temperament or my own somewhat anti-authoritarian bias, should pose any problems. 'I just *can't*. I promised my parents I'd go to summer school.'

'Are you telling us,' Eleanora asked gravely, 'that the only thing standing between you and a summer in Gaiole is your parents?'

I nodded.

Eleanora, who understood better than I her power over my parents, not to say over me and various others, smiled.

That evening my parents began the conversation that would end in my receiving permission to go to Gaiole by saying that they understood the only thing standing between me and the Stoneparks was their 'perhaps foolish' insistence that I push through six credits in school, and ended it by extracting a promise from me – as though I'd pleaded with them to go – to work harder than I otherwise would have during the term that followed.

This is not a story about my summer with the Stoneparks, which, if it wasn't always easy, was tolerable for a variety of reasons.

Gaiole was hot but very beautiful and there was a large pool on the land behind the house. (Most of the vineyard was on a hillside across a winding dirt road, the road that led to the *autostrada* on which we drove to Florence.) The household was run around Eleanora's preparation for her show. (It was understood that Jason was not under similar pressure, but unless I'm mistaken, there was always some reason for the house's being run around Eleanora.) It worked because most of her time was spent in the studio. My primary job was to keep Evan out of her way when he wasn't with his father. This became easier as Evan came actually to enjoy my company, forgetting that I was a hired hand.

My absorption in the physical matter of everyday life made it easier in a variety of ways for me to get along with Eleanora. When I was challenged about food (or almost anything else), I became intent upon solving the problem. This worked particularly well with Evan, who got hooked

173

into kitchen matters and began to learn Italian from me very much as I had learned it from Anna. Finally, I was fascinated by the operation of the vineyard, and my fascination led to a very agreeable affair with Angelo Ferrante, who managed that vineyard and several others owned by non-residents. (The Stoneparks' had its own beautiful label, designed by Eleanora. Framed in gold and printed in brilliant colours, its central image was a goblet of red wine resting on a rock in front of a green shrub.)

Angelo, a lively, homely man of thirty-one given to pronouncements like, 'all American girls are spoiled', always in Italian, of course, had been married for thirteen years, had five children, and was casually flirtatious, but became friendly when I spoke a non-touristy Italian he could readily understand. (He had English but wouldn't use it.) Our affair began less than two weeks after I'd arrived at the beginning of June, but our friendship began on the day I told him, in Italian of course, that he should not judge all American women by Eleanora Stonepark.

Angelo stopped in his tracks. We'd been walking between two rows of vines set on the big old tree branches that were his favourite stakes. He turned to me, hands on hips, and said something that translates as, 'Ah, finally! I thought there must be something wrong with you, that you never complain about the bitch!'

I felt more defensive than conspiratorial – yet, oddly, it was Eleanora, not myself, who I felt compelled to defend, with a little speech about how artists couldn't be held to the same standard as the rest of us. This infuriated Angelo, who said that artist or no artist, he'd kick the shit out of me if I ever acted like that.

I don't want to convey the impression that I really *liked* Eleanora, whose behaviour was very much that of the royal personage. But my sense of her as an artist whose work gave me great pleasure dominated my reactions, muted them when required. She was the way artists were *supposed* to be. And then of course there was my powerful desire, never voiced but with me every day of my life in Gaiole, to own the promised drawing – or, too much really to hope for – the painting she might choose to do.

Whether because veneration prevented me from getting angry at otherwise insufferable words and deeds, or because of the convenience Evan's attachment to me afforded, or because of my increasing skill at cooking fine French food, or because I didn't happen to have any of the habits that got under Eleanora's skin and turned her into a raving, screeching lunatic (talking a lot, saying *gezundheit* or God bless you when someone sneezed, and spending more than a few seconds gnawing the meat remaining on bones when most had been cut off, are crimes I remember offhand) Eleanora's behaviour towards me was very much the same when we reached the middle of August as it had been in June.

It had been understood when I took the job that I would leave Gaiole a week before the family did to register for my classes. As the time for my departure drew close, Angelo grew melancholy over the prospect of my disappearance, *la mia sparizione*. An early member of the first generation of females more scared of falling in love than of getting pregnant, I had assured myself, the first time I allowed him to show me the bedroom of an absent neighbour's villa, that it was OK because I wasn't going to fall in love with him. Now, as he pressed me to delay my leavetaking, I was finding that whether or not you called it love, if you liked it, you didn't want it to end.

Jason had taken Evan into town on some errand. Angelo and I were lying on a tarp at the far end of the vineyard. The sunset was particularly beautiful and the aroma of ripening grapes filled the air. I told him that I didn't actually have to be at school until the end of that week and he said he had business in Sicily, we could drive down the coast together. He would take me to the airport down there. Nobody (nobody was always Eleanora, whose name he was loath to pronounce) would even have to know. He would exchange my ticket, which Jason had already given me. I could tell the Stoneparks that he, Angelo, was taking me to the airport. He began immediately to plan for our trip to Palermo, where he had wine business. He'd always said that Sicily was *un altro mondo*, and it was a world I had to see.

I did not mention our trip in explaining to Jason that I wouldn't require transportation to the airport. Attempting to avoid a direct lie, I said something like, 'Angelo is going to drive me.' Jason simply nodded, but that evening, which was a week before the date I was scheduled to leave, Eleanora joined Jason, Evan and me for dinner for the first time in a while.

I had been wondering more and more whether she remembered about my picture, and if so, whether she would give it to me. I had a strong enough sense of her to know that I was best off not being the one to raise the issue; nothing riled Eleanora more than the suggestion of an act outside forces required her to perform. But I also knew that I was not going to leave without making a strong effort to get what I'd been promised. (I spent a great deal of time trying to decide which I'd prefer, the drawing or a watercolour. In one fantasy, she gave me both because she was so pleased with my summer's work. In another, she painted a marvellous portrait, parting with it reluctantly because she loved it – me – so much.)

Eleanora, a master of psychology when it might effect some improvement in her life, spent a lot of time praising the green soup I'd made the day before, yawning, and telling us that no matter how exhausted she was, she simply had to go back to work after dinner, she couldn't believe she had only two weeks left in Gaiole. Jason ate doggedly during this monologue but at some point he put down his soup spoon. He looked perturbed. He did not meet my eyes – or Eleanora's.

'I'm not sure which upsets me more,' Eleanora said, looking directly at me for the first time since she'd begun, 'my having to leave in two weeks or your leaving in one.'

Evan looked up from his soup. 'One? One? What do you mean, leaving in one?'

I smiled uncomfortably. 'I thought your parents must have told you already,' I said. 'I have to be in school the week before you do.'

'I am the guilty party,' Eleanor announced bravely as Evan looked from her to his father and back. 'It was too awful. I didn't even remind myself and I certainly never thought to tell anyone. Not that I've been able to think about anything except the paintings. I don't have three-quarters . . . No, that's not true . . . I'm lying to myself . . . I don't have *half* the number of pictures I promised Bruce and Leon. I really don't know what I'm going to do.' Her eyes brimmed with tears and her voice shook.

In what might have been the masterstroke of his entire childhood, Evan picked this moment not only to deliver a monologue that was at once a tribute to me and a threat about his behaviour when/if I left, but to do it *in Italian*, which he normally refused to employ when his parents were around, but saved for the time when we were alone. Weeks earlier I had given Jason permission to spy on us to determine that this was true. Not only was it true, but I was aware that Evan occasionally looked up words with the possession of which he'd later surprise me. He had developed a crush on me, and I had a more difficult day if he happened to see me talking to Angelo.

'I don't believe this is happening now,' he declaimed in patchy but adequate Italian. 'Tell me you're kidding around. Tell me the plans I've made don't have to be thrown away. All the things we wanted to do that we didn't have time for . . . All the . . . And I can't believe you didn't even *tell* me!'

'I thought you knew, love,' I responded, also in Italian. 'And I have to tell you, I'm impressed with your vocabulary, and I bet your folks are, too.'

'Impressed! Impressed!' Eleanora said dramatically. 'But what good will it do if you're not here to talk with him?'

This was classic Eleanora, unable to imagine a use for his Italian, now that he had it, beyond keeping him busy and

177

out of her way. I started to respond, if only for Evan's sake, saying I thought it would do a great deal of good because he enjoyed it, as witness the vocabulary he had, which meant he was – when Eleanora interrupted to ask me on which day I was actually required to register and Evan went around the table to sit on his father's lap.

I stopped dead in my verbal tracks, unable to answer because I hadn't thought out a lie and the truth would tell her I had an extra few days I could choose to remain.

'The truth is,' I lied, 'I don't exactly remember. I think it's the fourth but —'

'Would you like to call home and ask?' Eleanora interrupted.

'Uh, no, uh, not really,' I said. 'I mean, even if it's a couple of days later, I need some time to get myself organized, buy some clothes, that kind of thing.'

I looked at Jason, who was toying with his piece of bread, embarrassed, I believe, at what his wife was doing to me. Which didn't mean he was about to jump in on my side, a reality I was mulling over even as Eleanora began to speak.

'Well, I was just thinking . . . I have to admit I was thinking about it because Jason mentioned your leaving, and I was looking at that little sketch of you, you know, I have it on the bulletin board over my drafting table . . . Or maybe you don't . . . I don't know how recently you've been in the studio . . .' (I had been in the studio once at the beginning of the summer but had not been invited again.) 'Anyway, what I was thinking was about how I meant to do a little watercolour portrait, you were so pleased with the sketch, and now I wouldn't have time to do it.'

I thought – I might have imagined it because it's so perfect but I don't actually believe I did – I thought I saw Jason blush, although he didn't look up. Perhaps if he hadn't been a witness I would have caved in at that moment, promised to stay if Eleanora would do the watercolour. Evan was looking back and forth between us, not commenting on the transaction, which he already understood to be just that, and one in which his interests coincided with his mother's.

'How's Angelo?' she asked.

My breath was taken away. It was the first time she'd ever so much as mentioned Angelo, who dealt only with Jason.

'He seems to be fine,' I said stiffly.

'Is Angelo the reason you don't need us to take you to the airport?' she asked.

'Yes,' I said, trying to figure out what I would do if she asked any more questions.

She was smart enough not to. After a pause, she pushed away her plates, set both elbows on the table, her chin on her hands. 'OK. Here's the deal I have to offer. Stay till we go and I'll do the watercolour.'

I couldn't breathe, much less cry, though I had a strong desire to do both. Something prevented me from caving in right away. I turned to Evan and told him that no matter what I decided, I cared about him and would stay in touch when we were all in New York. Eleanora's words were repeating themselves in my head, and when I had delivered this message to him, I turned back to his mother.

'You said you'd do it,' I pointed out. 'You didn't say it would be mine.'

She smiled. 'My goodness, love, you've gotten so suspicious. Of course it will be yours. I'm only doing it for you.'

Note the tense; if I did not assume she would have her way, Eleanora already did. And of course she'd forgotten her original notion that my face was too fascinating *not* to paint.

The stumbling block was Angelo. While I wanted the painting even more than I wanted to drive south with him, I'd not only looked forward to the trip but was terrified of his reaction when I told him I couldn't go. With Jason's permission, I called my parents, who would be leaving for Japan in between the time I'd been supposed to arrive and the time when I would if I stayed, to ask if one of them would register for me if I remained in Gaiole until the Stoneparks left. It is fair to say they were happier to do it for this reason than they would have been for another. Then I told Eleanora that I would remain if she would give me the picture before that extra week arrived. Until then, I would hold on to the ticket Jason had already given me, for the earlier flight out of Florence.

'Trusting little soul, aren't you,' Eleanora commented, at once pleased by her work's importance to me and irritated by the doubt that was implicit in my condition.

'I trust,' I said calmly (I'd been preparing the line from the moment I awakened that morning) that your work is the most important thing to you and that you'll do whatever you have to do to keep it going.'

She let out a hearty laugh, and slammed a hand down on the table.

'Is that the one you had waiting?' she asked. 'Is that why Jason got Evan out of here?'

In fact, Evan was angry with me, which was why he had chosen to go to the tennis court with Jason. I'd explained to him about school and about how the whole arrangement had been made before I even really *knew* him and had nothing to do with anything but preparing for school, but my explanation hadn't altered his feelings. That evening, when Eleanora had capitulated, telling me that if I wasn't 'too busy' I should visit her studio in the evening, I told Evan I hoped to be able to remain with him in Gaiole until the end, after all. He became provisionally friendly without displaying any interest in how or why this had been arranged. Informed that we were all set, he became affectionate again.

Angelo was even less easily mollified, my explanation of why I could not go down the Coast being greeted by an extraordinary diatribe in Italian (he refused to speak English during our remaining time together) punctuated by curses I hadn't learned yet but could identify as such. It was only when he expressed incredulity that I should care about anything done by that *puttana* and I told him maybe *I* was the whore because her paintings were worth big money in the States (a lie I didn't yet know would turn into the truth), that his rage diminished and he became interested in the matter of what her work was worth.

At nine o'clock, when Evan had gone to his room with his father, I walked around the grounds for a few minutes then went into the house and upstairs to the back, which faced north and held Eleanora's studio. (Jason's faced south. He was said not to mind the summer heat or to need the northern light preferred by painters.) I knocked twice and waited for what seemed like a very long time until she called to me to enter. I did so.

It was a breathtaking room, even at night, when the glass wall at its far end was no longer letting in the entire countryside and all the (indirect) light in the world. Eleanora's unfinished paintings were propped against the otherwise bare walls, giving the lie to her suggestion that she worked on only one at a time. Finished works stood in racks against one wall. Her easel and worktable were near the window. She sat at the former, facing it and nearly invisible to me. 'Sit down,' she ordered. 'I'll be with you in a minute.'

Was she going to make a great show, I wondered, of rushing to finish the painting she really *should* be working on in order to deal with my selfish demands? I decided I couldn't anticipate all the possibilities and simply had to remain firm. My terms were my terms. I relaxed somewhat into this posture and spent my remaining waiting time admiring the unfinished pictures, surreptitiously watching her work, wondering what she was painting. It's probably easy to imagine how I felt when after perhaps fifteen or twenty minutes, her left hand came around the easel to beckon to me, and I walked, nearly on tiptoe, to the easel, and she brought me around to stand beside her, and there, on the easel, was a delicate and still damp watercolour that had obviously begun with the pencil sketch of me, which was nowhere to be seen.

I gasped.

There I was. My straight brown hair, my murky brown-green eyes, the blue turtleneck sweater I'd worn to their house for lunch months earlier and hadn't worn since but which she'd apparently remembered as she apparently remembered every visual detail once taken in, and, most importantly, the sense of her subject's power that had first captivated me, perhaps even more emphatic than it had been in the drawing.

I couldn't have minded less. That is to say, if she had been looking for a little revenge upon the youngster who was extracting a price, she failed to find it. In any event, I doubt she could have made me look bad enough to anger me and I don't believe she'd actually tried. Her artistic conscience, surely the strongest of any of the kinds of conscience she might have possessed, would not have allowed her to turn me into anyone substantially more monstrous than I was. I prepared to have her hand me the painting and wave me out of the room but if I was already more than satisfied with the work, she was not. I sat for more than an hour as she painted and fussed and finally, when she'd announced that she was finished and I, with tears in my eyes, had told her it was wonderful, promised to look in the attic the next morning for a frame that fitted. I could have it in the evening.

I did.

I had it and I treasured it. Even if the summer had been far more difficult, possessing my picture would have made it worthwhile. When we all went to Florence that weekend for our farewell visit to Evan's favourite restaurant, I picked up a large, touristy satchel whose sole virtue was that it would safely hold the painting (between two pieces of corrugated board) during the trip home. On the plane I sat stiffly with the bag behind me, the corrugated board cushioned in turn by laundry on both sides. I was unwilling to put it under the seat in front lest it slide away. Reaching home (my parents had left two days earlier), I decided to return to the big bedroom that had once been mine and use the maid's room for my guests. The apparent reason was that with my parents gone, most of the apartment was unoccupied. The real reason was that fond as I was of the little room, it had no wall that could do justice to my painting.

I hung it so that it faced me as I lay in my bed in the big room. Had it been feasible, I would have removed not simply all other decoration but the two narrow bookcases standing against that wall. I did set them as far as possible from one another. The portrait of the interesting human being perceived by Eleanora Stonepark hung solitary, nearly regal, between them. It would not be exaggerating to say that although I didn't think about her all the time, the world scared me less when she was with me than it did when I was alone. She was my promise that somewhere inside me there was a real person who might some day do something of interest.

I'd returned to school the previous year because it was my side of an agreement, not because the world of knowledge had come to seem more inviting. I felt alienated from the younger students by what I'd learned out in the real world but I lacked the desire to pass on reality's wisdom (dope or no dope there were dishes to be washed, and so on). With all the time I'd spent congratulating himself on not thinking that I was in love with Angelo, I was dismayed to find, as I walked around the campus looking at scraggly-haired Jewish suburbanites and Midwestern blondes who rolled reefers with the same ease as they'd once caught pop flies, that I missed him more than I'd dreamed I might while I was exchanging my painting for his company.

Not that I ever regretted that exchange. It was, after all, my future self, as revealed to me by Eleanora's painting, who assured me of being a real person with interests I would develop, if only I were allowed to do so. In fact, at some point during the autumn it occurred to me that it was no coincidence that the person who had portrayed me as an interesting human being was also a person who seriously appreciated my cooking.

I began to daydream about attending the Culinary Institute in upstate New York, a fantasy that seemed a little more realistic than the notion of getting my parents to pay my tuition at one of the great cooking schools in France. Then the very possession of a daydream about something I wanted to do diminished my sense of being empty and uninteresting enough to allow me to make a few friends.

Perhaps it's simplest for me to quote the letter from the Root-Pierson Gallery, dated November 21st of that year, in its entirety.

Dear Miss Kaplan:
As you probably know, the Root-Pierson Gallery is planning an exhibition of the paintings of Eleanora Stonepark to open in New York on January 1st of next year, and after three weeks here to tour six major cities.

We understand from Mrs Stonepark that you own one of her few watercolour portraits, *116th Street Jenny*, which we would like to include in the exhibition. We would need to have it in the gallery by December 20th. We would, of course, take care of all transportation and insurance costs.

We very much look forward to hearing from you, at which time we will send the Gallery's formal loan agreement. And of course we hope you will attend the opening. Eleanora Stonepark will be present. We will be sending you the announcement and invitation at a later date.
    Sincerely,
    Bruce Pierson

It took me very little time to frame my response:

Dear Mr Pierson:
I have your letter asking me to lend you my picture.
I am sorry that I cannot do this.
    Sincerely,
    Carol Kaplan

There was no question of my being willing to risk the kind of damage that might be done to my precious picture. I hesitated only over the matter of explaining my need to live with the person I did not and never would think of as 116th Street Jenny. But the phrases that came to my mind when I considered such an explanation were at once so precise and so melodramatic ('I'm sorry, I can't live without her, she is my promise of a future') that I decided to forgo an explanation.

At the beginning of the school term Evan had called, wanting me to spend that Saturday afternoon with him. I'd been unable to do this. When I'd called him a couple of Saturdays later because I had some time, Jason had told me Evan was visiting a friend. He went on to say they thought of me often and felt the summer had been very good for Evan. I'd not talked to either father or son since then, but now I had a call from Jason. The matter of lending the painting had left my mind completely once my letter was mailed, and when I heard his voice, I assumed he was calling because I had failed to do so.

'Hi,' I said. 'I want you to know, it's not that I haven't been thinking about him, but I'm so busy, and when you said he was getting along, I guess I just . . .'

'I wasn't actually calling about Evan,' Jason said. 'I was calling about the business of lending the painting.'

'Oh, yes,' I said quickly, still far from understanding the nature of the ground I was treading upon. 'I can understand why they want it, but . . . if anyone knew how much I love it, how important it is to me . . .'

'Yes, of course,' Jason said. 'That was why Eleanora gave it to you. She could see how you felt about the work.'

I did not awaken to the gravity of the matter. Nor did it occur to me to point out that her reasons had been somewhat more complex and selfish than he was suggesting.

'Mmm,' I said. 'By the work in general, I mean, I love all her stuff, but then there's the business of . . . I mean, she *saw* me, you know? I never felt as though anyone knew who I was, I didn't know *myself*, and then Eleanora *saw* me.'

'Ah, yes,' Jason said after a moment. 'Well, what she's seeing at the moment is a young woman who won't lend her back her own work when she needs it desperately for a show.'

Now I heard him. It did not cross my mind that I should part with my portrait, but I realized, finally, that my refusal was not a simple matter.

'I don't,' I began after a while, 'I don't . . .' My voice cracked. I had no way to finish the sentence. For the first time since they'd gone overseas, I wished desperately that my parents were home. Maybe they'd have come to my aid. Explained to Jason what a delinquent I'd been, and how the painting . . . I began to cry, covering the receiver so Jason would not hear me.

'Carol?' he said after a moment. 'Are you there?'

'Yes,' I said, sobbing.

'Can you tell me . . . Are you afraid you won't get it back at the end of the show?'

I was afraid of not surviving its absence, but I knew this was crazy and I mustn't say it.

'What I really . . . It's the only thing on the wall. The wall will be . . . I mean, I look at it all the time. She's *with* me. I can't imagine . . . I mean, it's a very long time, Jason.' Until then the difference between three days and three months had seemed unimportant. Without realizing it, I had begun to bargain. 'You know, I only took the job because I loved her work so much.'

'Well,' Jason said after a long pause, 'what if we gave you one of Eleanora's sketches to keep on the wall while we had the painting?'

'Gave me?' I repeated moronically. 'Sketches?'

He misunderstood, thought me in better command than I was of the conversation's content and bargaining for a better offer.

'I'd offer you another watercolour, but the whole problem is that there are only a few watercolours Eleanora feels are good enough for the show, and there's no other portrait, and she hasn't been working in watercolour, and she usually works very slowly, that painting was a freak, in a sense, and she's particularly fond of it. She didn't want to let go of it when she finished, but she never would have dreamed of failing to honour her part of your bargain.'

Particularly when I had yet to honour mine.

The thought passed through my brain once again but made no effort to drop into my mouth. In fact, I was silent as I tried to absorb what he was saying and understand what it meant to me and my portrait. Jason, a sophisticated slave to the Empress Eleanora, waited for me to grasp the magnitude of what she had done for me, the ignominious nature of my response.

'I'm sorry,' I finally said, not apologizing but expressing regret at the difficulty of our situation.

'Well,' Jason said, 'I accept your apology, but of course you haven't accepted my solution to our problem.'

My problem was his telephone call, which I wanted desperately to be finished with.

'I have an idea,' Jason said in a different, perhaps artificially hearty voice. 'I think you and I should go to Eleanora's studio, where you'll be able to look at her sketches and the paintings that won't be in the show and find one you'd like to put in Jenny's place. How does that sound?'

'OK,' I managed to say after a very long time in which my brain hadn't accepted the notion, but had come to understand I had to do it.

'All right, then,' Jason said. 'There's someone waiting for me and I have to go now, but I'll be in touch in a day or two. Bye.'

I said goodbye and hung up, then returned to my room, stretched out on the bed, looked at my picture, and gradually allowed my saner self to come into control of my brain. Loving the picture didn't mean I had to see it every day of my life. I loved people I didn't see for years at a time and then, there they were again, and it was just as it had been before. If I missed my girl (her name was not and never would be Jenny, dammit, much less the demeaning 116th Street Jenny) terribly, I could visit the gallery . . . at least the one in New York. And it wasn't as though

I would miss her because of a space on the wall. Someone – or something – would be there, keeping her place for her and for me. I could almost feel good about Jason's solution. Certainly I could wish it had come more easily. In any event, it would be exciting, to visit Eleanora's studio. I could almost look forward to hearing from Jason.

But two days later there was another letter from Bruce Pierson that made me regret having opened myself to the whole idea.

Dear Miss Kaplan:
This is to confirm your telephone conversation with Jason Stonepark in which you agreed that you would go to Mrs Stonepark's studio to select a substitute for the watercolour you will lend to the Root-Pierson Gallery's exhibition of her work, January 1st through March 31st.

We have enclosed a loan form which we ask you to return to us as soon as possible so the pick-up can be arranged. Thanks so much for your cooperation in this matter.
Sincerely,
Bruce Pierson

I was as angry as though I'd never agreed to the substitution plan. Did they really believe I was going to turn over my painting and then sit around waiting for a phone call? What kind of an idiot did they think I was? Even if Eleanora Stonepark hadn't been a difficult and duplicitous human being, Jason a subservient one who would say anything to appease her, I would have been a fool to consent to such an arrangement. I sat down and fired off a letter to Pierson that I can't bear to quote here, but which began with the suggestion that they were treating me not only like a child, but a dumb one, and ended by saying there were no circumstances under which I would now permit my painting to leave my room and I didn't want to hear from any of them again.

I did not.

*

Eleanora's show opened to great acclaim, remained open for a month in New York, closed. I paid little attention. I was determined to do enough schoolwork so my parents wouldn't claim I'd failed to keep my side of our bargain, and I had a reasonable social life by this time. When my summer money had run out, I'd taken a four-nights-a-week babysitting job with a neighbourhood mother, Jackie, a working divorcee who was attending night school. I got along with Jackie as well as with her children (she couldn't get over the fact that I happily cooked meals and baked bread and cookies with the children), and in the spring she told me she and some friends had rented a house on Fire Island for the summer and needed a responsible housekeeper-babysitter. I explained that I would be in summer school but could make a weekend – perhaps even a three-or-four-day weekend arrangement. Jackie found someone who would take the other days until the week in August when I would be finished with school. That week coincided with my parents' return from Japan. I did not see them, although we spoke on the phone, until we all returned to New York after Labor Day.

They were pleased with the way I'd kept the apartment, satisfied with what I told them of school, and glad I'd found a job that did not interfere with my schoolwork. (I would return to part-time babysitting for Jackie.) I judged them unready for a conversation about cooking school, nor did I have any reason to rush. I had applied to the Culinary Institute of America but knew there were far more applications than there were places and I had no assurance that I would get in. They admired Eleanora's painting and exclaimed over her generosity in having given it to me. I told them I'd made a deal with her, but the story of the deal, briefly told, appeared not to alter their vision of her virtue, and I could not make myself tell them what had happened. My natural reluctance combined with their obligations accumulated during their year in the Orient to delay the day of reckoning.

Then, on a Sunday evening in late autumn, when my

father and I were reading *The Times* in the living room, my mother entered with a funny expression on her face and, leaning against the wall next to the entrance, asked, 'What happened with the Stoneparks?'

Startled, terribly anxious, I tried to remember what I'd decided to say when this question arose. All I could think of was my father's telling me, a zillion years ago, what a high opinion my mother had of Eleanora.

'The Stoneparks,' I repeated.

My father looked up.

'What happened . . . basically . . . is . . . they wanted my painting.'

'*Your* painting?' my mother said. 'You mean *her* painting that she was so extraordinarily generous as to give you?'

'She wasn't exactly being generous,' I said, feeling the muddy water come up around my eyes. 'We made a deal where she would give it to me if —'

'Did you or did you not refuse to let her borrow her own painting for her own show?'

I nodded. This was going to be even worse than I'd feared. My mother's eyes were closed and her body – could it be my imagination? – sagged against the wall. After a moment she felt her way along the wall to the nearest chair, a stiff-backed uncomfortable job she occasionally piled magazines on but that none of us ever sat in. My father had put down his newspaper.

'I didn't exactly refuse,' I sid. 'At least I wasn't *going* to. I mean, I was, then I wasn't, and then I got this awful letter.' They were staring at me in horror. I had begun to plead. 'You don't know what went on with that painting. You don't know what I went through to get it. It was the only reason I took the job in the first place, she sort of promised it, and then when I finally got it, I mean, I had to stay an extra week and not take a trip I wanted to take and then I only —'

'Maybe,' my father said, 'you had better bring us the letter.'

'Letters,' I corrected automatically.

'Letters,' he said.

My mother's eyes were still closed. Her mouth trembled. I went to my room, finding the correspondence easily since it wasn't with all the stuff I kept on the top of my desk because I might need to look at it again. Now I could see that was wishful thinking. I was going to have to make clear the extent of the picture's importance to me; it wasn't just the idea of the promise, I cared about the *picture*. If they didn't understand that, they'd never forgive me for angering their friends. They'd kick me out of the house before I ever mentioned the Culinary Institute!

I returned to the living room. They were sitting together on the sofa, my father's arm around my mother. They looked as though they'd come from a funeral.

'There's something I want to explain before I give you the letters,' I said.

'You can explain later,' my father said.

I handed them over. He did not look at me, nor did my mother. I turned to leave the room and was ordered, in a voice I'd seldom heard, to sit down. I sat in the chair my mother had used earlier and waited, trying, with only limited success, to breathe.

'Oh, my God,' was the only thing my mother said – so quickly that I thought there must be some mistake.

When they had finished, they looked up at me. They appeared to be considerably more astonished than John Hinckley's parents would be, some years later, upon learning of their son's attempt to kill Ronald Reagan.

'What on earth possessed you?' my mother asked, her voice breaking. 'How could you possibly . . .' But she trailed off, failing to find the words to describe so heinous a crime.

'That's what I was trying to explain,' I said. 'I couldn't imagine doing without it. I hardly had it on the wall when they wanted it back and I couldn't . . .' My voice broke as I pleaded for understanding. 'I love her. It. I couldn't imagine parting with her. She was my company when I was alone here. I —'

'Of *course* you love it,' my mother broke in. 'Of *course* you

. . .' But she was still unable to cope with the enormity of my crime and once again, her words trailed off.

'The issue is not whether you love the painting,' my father said. 'The issue is whether you have the right to refuse an artist the chance to show her own work.'

I was silenced. In truth, my brain hadn't framed it that way at any point. It didn't change the way I felt about Eleanora or the painting but it gave me something to think about. In truth, I hadn't thought of it as hers but as my own. What my father was saying was that even if it was *my* painting, it was *her* work. It had become mine without ever ceasing to be hers.

'Well,' he finally said, 'while we're having this painful conversation, you might as well tell us your version of the story so we can figure out what we can possibly say to Eleanora.'

With some difficulty, I told them about the summer, reminding them of that first Sunday, when I'd come home dazzled by the sketch she'd promised me. I said that dealing with Eleanora had been the most difficult part of my job but I hadn't minded because of my respect for her as an artist. I told them about the friend I'd made in Gaiole who was going to show me southern Italy and how, as I planned to leave exactly when I'd said before I consented to take the job that I had to leave, she had bribed me to stay with the picture.

'But you didn't have to leave,' my mother interrupted. 'You said you were going to take a trip with your friend.'

'That's not the issue,' my father said wearily. 'Let's stay with the issue.'

I was no longer certain what the issue was, but I proceeded with the stuff I'd been sure of before this matter of who owned a painting had arisen, my tale of the imperious Eleanora and the servant who wanted to please because she valued the reward.

'All right,' my father finally said. 'So, you made your bargain and you got your picture. Eleanora kept her side of your bargain.'

'I got the picture first, I was afraid —'

'Yes, yes.' He waved a hand in the air. 'You told us about all that. You hung your picture. And then you got the letter from Bruce Pierson. You did not understand, I gather, that it is overriding custom to give an artist back her own work whenever she wants to show it. I've not previously heard of anyone's refusing such a request.'

I hung my head in shame. Tears rolled down my cheeks and dropped on to my cotton T-shirt.

'So, you wrote your unacceptable letter, saying you could not do this, at which point Pierson spoke to Jason, who called you and made the extraordinarily generous offer to let you have something else while this was in the show.'

'I accepted!' I pointed out eagerly. 'I was going to do it. Jason said he'd bring me to the studio, and I could choose something to stay in its place, something she didn't need for the show, and I was still miserable about parting with my picture, but I was going to do it!'

'And then?'

'And then I got the letter.'

'This one.' My father held up Pierson's letter saying that after I'd signed the form, my painting would be picked up.

I nodded.

'And?'

'Look at it!' I pleaded. 'I promise to give them my picture as soon as they want it and all they promise is that at some later date I'll receive a call and go to the studio! They could have taken the picture the next day and let me replace it a week before the show got back! I could have had a bare wall for months! I wasn't sure I'd ever get it back!'

My father was looking at the correspondence again. My mother was staring at me as though trying to figure out how she'd managed, for all these years, not to notice the degree of monstrousness of the creature to whom she'd given birth.

'The loan agreement,' my father said, 'specifies a pick-up/delivery date of November 22nd or 23rd, that is, a week before the show opens, and a return date of two or three days after it returns to New York. Why should you think for a moment that they wouldn't honour it?'

I stared at him, thunderstruck. Whatever he was reading was utterly foreign to me. It wasn't that I'd forgotten. I'd never seen it! Was it possible I'd never even looked at the agreement that came with the letter? Yes, I had to admit, not only was it possible, but I could almost remember slamming down the letter and the papers stapled to it without a glance at anything past the first page.

'Why do you look so surprised?' my father asked. Beside him, my mother, her arms wrapped around herself, keened like a captain's wife upon hearing that the ship has gone down. 'Is it possible that you never even bothered to look at the agreement?'

'Bothered isn't right,' I cried out – before crying in. 'It wasn't about *bothering*.' I hadn't even looked at the contract but had been relieved to have an excuse . . . an arbitrariness to the letter . . . to go back on my promise to Jason. 'It's that I freaked when I thought about it, and when I read the letter, I just . . . It was as though . . . I couldn't let someone like that have me. I mean, the picture of me!'

My mother, unable to tolerate this babble, stood up and walked out of the living room. My father sat, shaking his head, looking down at the papers in his hand and then back at me as though some new indictment of my behaviour had presented itself and he needed only to find a way to frame it. Finally he stood, walked over to me holding the papers in his hand like a hangman's noose and handed them to me.

'I can only hope' he said, 'that you have a somewhat better understanding of the trust involved in holding an artist's work than you did before. Not that I have reason to believe it will help. Our friendship with Eleanora is probably lost, and it would be difficult to exaggerate how painful that will be for us if it turns out to be true. You might want to try writing her a letter, now that you have a slightly better understanding of what was expected of you. If you decide to write, you'd better show me the letter before you send it.'

Who could tell what I, a monster of no sensibility, might say to further offend the Lady Eleanora? There was no danger, in any event, of my writing to her. If I'd been told I would have to leave home if I failed to write, I think I would have returned to my room and packed my bags instead of locking the door, throwing myself down on the bed and crying, as I did, until I fell asleep. I don't know what I dreamed but I remember quite precisely the moment when, having slowly awakened and gradually pulled myself together just enough to get up and head for the bathroom, I realized that I had walked past my picture – *the* picture – without once looking in its direction. That is to say, I had looked at the floor to make sure I would *not* look at it.

Gradually, over a period of months, she ceased to cause me pain when I glanced her way. But I could not recapture the pleasure of looking. Where once I'd played games with her – peeking, for example, to see if her eyes followed me when I walked across the room, as the Mona Lisa's eyes were said to do – now she was just there, like a lot of other people. 116th Street Jenny. If she was the person I would become, it was ridiculous to have assumed that I would like that person. I would live with her the way one lived with, or at least dealt with, a lot of people one wasn't crazy about.

Life went on. Gradually my parents became civil, then casual, and finally friendly enough so that I didn't skitter into my bedroom at every free moment instead of hanging around for some conversation or a meal. The process was assisted immeasurably when my mother published a monograph from a lecture on women artists she had given at Columbia. In it she offered the opinion that there was no painter on the American scene more talented than Eleanora Stonepark. I could not swear that it was only after the monograph's publication in *Art News* that the two couples became friendly again. I simply know that it was then that the name Stonepark (as in Dinner 8 – Stoneparks) began to appear on the calendar hanging on the refrigerator door.

I broached to my parents the notion that cooking school, not a university, was where I belonged, and they told me that, while they were not unsympathetic, university, not cooking school, was what they would support. I resisted pointing out that they didn't *have* to support Columbia. I tried arguing with them on the grounds that they, with their active devotion to good food, should find it not simply reasonable but utterly delightful that I wanted to become a chef. They said that as far as they could see, I was already a chef and could improve my skills as much as I needed to at home. Home was for cooking and school was for learning the subjects that would enrich my mental life and provide me with a profession suitable to a young woman from an academic family. When I asked if that wasn't a snobbish argument, serving some notion of who I was supposed to be rather than who I was, my father smiled complacently and said, 'Guilty,' thus putting an end to the discussion.

The issue was not joined again until a spring evening when we were at dinner. Over the weekend I'd babysat with Jackie's children while she went to Westhampton to investigate sharing a house in a new location. When I returned on Sunday evening, they were eating in the kitchen. My mail, which included a notice of acceptance from the Culinary Institute, was at my place. I flushed when I saw the envelope. When I had opened and read it I smiled sadly, put it back in its envelope without speaking and helped myself to some of the cold leftovers on the table.

'Do I gather,' my father asked after a while, 'that you have applied for admission to this . . . uh . . .'

'School,' I said, expressionless. 'It's a very good school for cooking. It's called the Culinary Institute of America.'

'Indeed,' he said. 'And have you been accepted?'

'Yes,' I said. 'I have been accepted. But I can't afford it.'

I had been trying to figure out a way, a set of ways, that I could raise the money to attend, but the fee was daunting to someone who had managed to put aside a negligible amount of money. If I'd felt that pleading could get me someplace I surely would have done it, but I had no hope at all.

'Your mother and I have been talking,' my father said to me the following evening. 'You know our feelings about paying for —'

'You've told me,' I broke in.

'Yes,' he said. 'Well, we still feel the same way, but it occurred to us . . .'

I looked up, hearing the opening for the first time.

' . . . that there was room for negotiation on the matter.'

'Where?' I asked. 'What? What do I have to do?'

'Well,' he said slowly, 'what occurred to us is that while we have the money but don't want to spend it that way, there is another way that we might spend it, without, you might say, compromising our principles. That is, we might spend it to buy something we wanted.'

I stared at him uncomprehendingly. He waited. *Something they wanted*. When I understood that he was talking about my painting, it was only because there was no other possibility.

He smiled. My mother smiled. They had not been so wrapped up in their work and their social-artistic life as to fail to notice that I was unhappy. Now they were pleased to have found a way to let me do what I wanted to do without compromising their academic principles and while obtaining a painting they would love to own. I was, after all, the only member of the family who possessed an Eleanora Stonepark. They knew from the place in my room to which Jenny had long since been moved that I did not want to look at her.

I could not smile back because my mind, long before it had a reasonable explanation for doing so, refused even to consider letting them have her.

Their smiles faded. I doubt they believed that I would give up the Culinary Institute before I would part with my picture. But it was occurring to them for the first time that I might not jump at their offer. When I told them days later that even if it meant giving up the Institute, I could not accept, they smiled at each other in sad confirmation: I had always been contrary.

Surely I needed to find a way to be my own person rather than theirs – or, as they would have it, to be contrary. But I don't think contrariness made me cling to my painting. I was beginning to suspect that I would not remain in my parents' home long enough to get a degree. I had no clear idea of what I would do when I left, that is to say, of how close it would be to what I *wanted* to do. I didn't know which of the friends I'd made at school I would keep or whether I would make new ones, nor did I have any assurance that my parents, the fixed point in my life whether I was being my own person or theirs or trying to find some reasonable combination of the two, would remain friendly as I floundered around, looking for a life. But the young woman in my picture was my assurance that I would find one, and whether I liked her or not, whether or not she made me happy, I needed to keep with me the difficult young woman another difficult woman had named 116th Street Jenny.

Sarah Harrison

Mike's

Sarah Harrison grew up scribbling: she wrote spicy adventures during her years abroad as an army child, and romance at boarding school in England. A few years into work, her stories started to sell, and she went full-time. Two novels followed that were universally rejected before Flowers of the Field *became a bestseller. Also known for her children's books and comic novels* (Hot Breath, Cold Feet), *Sarah's fiction focuses on that interesting battlefront where domestic realities conflict with public bluffing. Married with three children, Sarah's new story* Mike's *stems from her own position as not quite omniscient mother: 'Now my daughter's growing up, I realized how arrogant it would be for either of us to assume that we knew the other inside out . . .'*

Julia

I think my mother must have sprung from the womb as a worldly woman. I say this because while I, at thirty, am single, and a solicitor, with several what one might loosely term affairs to my credit, my mother was married at nineteen, had me when she was twenty, was widowed at forty and has led a life of blameless widowhood ever since. And yet – here's the problem – she makes me feel like a bumbling adolescent. Not on purpose you understand. She just seems to have a natural grasp of what my father (who was much older than her) used to call 'the womanly arts'. I'm devoted to her, but sometimes I could choke her for the ease and grace with which she handles men. After all, fifty is just out of the egg these days as Joan and Jane demonstrate, and there are occasions when I feel I'm uncomfortably close to lapping her.

She teaches Craft in one of those amazingly privileged little mixed prep schools, all scarlet blazers and Suzuki violin. Give her a tea chest full of old household rubbish and within minutes she will have turned it into a model of Buckingham Palace by moonlight, with the Queen gazing out of an upstairs window. I'm quite sure the children worship her. And there have been several discreet escorts over the past ten years, always kept rather in the background for my sake. It's difficult when you feel that you are being given all the space you need, but aren't filling it very excitingly.

But we do get on awfully well.

Susan

I worry about Julia, because she's like her father – a hopeless romantic. I look at her in her business suit and sensible low-heeled courts and I know it's just protective colouring.

There's only been one man of any consequence in her life, and that was Paul – he's still hovering on the sidelines actually, a possible contender for the title. He's all right, I suppose. Nice looking, smart, dependable, on the up and up. Gets off on money, not sex, and I'm not necessarily saying that's a bad thing. It means his small store of human affection would all be Julia's. He wants a wife, to whom he would almost certainly be faithful, and whom he would support in her career, or in domestic comfort, whichever was appropriate. Julia gave him the elbow about a year ago, and there hasn't been anyone serious since, but as I say he's still there in the background. Full marks for tenacity, especially as he is by no means one of your safe, dull, also rans.

Be that as it may, I still worry. It goes with the territory. No matter how many articles I read which tell me that young women are leaving everything later these days, I'd like to feel that Julia was a fixture in someone's life. She isn't one of nature's freewheelers, whatever she may think about herself. I remember even when she was little, how earnest she was. She'd ride her bike round and round the back garden, at a steady pace, as if she was counting the laps, with this grim scowl of concentration on her face.

She works incredibly hard. She needs – I know I shouldn't say this – she needs looking after. And not by me.

Julia

It was a notably inauspicious meeting. I turned up at the tube station having cut things a bit fine anyway, to discover that there was a delay on our line. I hailed a taxi, but when it drew up this man obviously thought *he'd* hailed it and we more or less jammed in the doorway.

'I'm sorry, but I believe this was mine,' he said.

'I don't agree,' I replied.

Just to prove that chivalry is moribund the driver weighed in on his side. 'I saw this gentleman first.'

'This what?'

'Come on, love, give in gracefully.'

I was so cross I couldn't think of a smart retort.

'Excuse me,' said my rival, and climbed aboard.

'Well, where are you going?' I asked.

'Great Portland Street.'

'That'll do, let's split the fare.'

'Fine.'

The way he said this implied that it was anything but fine, but I really did feel I was being perfectly reasonable.

In the very best romantic tradition I had taken an instant dislike to him. Not only had he been boorish to begin with, but he was insufferably pleased with himself. I don't like vain men. He was dressed in an Armani-ish mint-green suit with a white T-shirt underneath and white moccasins. Advertising, for sure, I thought. Heaven help us.

His attitude seemed to be: 'She invited herself in, who says I have to make conversation with her?' so I decided to show that I at least had some manners.

'Are you a regular on this line?' I asked.

'Happily not,' he said.

'It's generally very reliable.'

'Wonderful.'

I do know it's pointless to take issue with complete strangers, but on this occasion I was sufficiently annoyed to do so.

'Since we're sharing this cab,' I said, 'to our mutual advantage, couldn't you at least manage to be polite?'

For the first time he, looked at me as though he was seeing me, and I felt as though several hundred volts had been pumped into me via his eyeballs.

'You're quite right,' he said. 'I'm so sorry.'

That did it, of course. I'd been expecting cold steel and had been given a bouquet of roses. In that instant I noticed his eyes were the colour of treacle toffee . . . that his hair was thick, black and curly . . . that the smile now on offer was a little lopsided, and put a deep crease in his left cheek . . . that without the designer suiting he would not have looked out of place at the Appleby Horse Fair.

'Oh, that's all right,' I said feebly, 'these delays are pretty trying.'

'Still, it's an ill wind' – he held out his hand – 'since I now find myself in a small enclosed space with a beautiful woman.'

Beautiful woman! Such extravagance. Especially as by any objective standard it's completely untrue. I know when I'm being flannelled, but it's a real pleasure to be flannelled by an expert.

By the time we'd chugged to Great Portland Street through the rush-hour traffic, I had warmed to Michael Murphy. He owned two clubs, one in Birmingham and one in London, both called Mike's. This, he explained, was why he had been so unpardonably brusque. He wasn't used to being up and about at this hour. My social life revolves around drinks parties, dinner parties, the theatre, and tennis. Theatre and tennis are my two absolute things. I'm a Friend of the RSC and the National, a regular at the ENO, and actually went on one of those tennis-ranch holidays in Portugal with Paul a couple of years ago which totally altered my service grip . . . But clubs. It was another world.

'Why don't you let me atone for my rudeness over a cocktail?' he asked.

I heard a little voice say that would be lovely. He didn't discuss dates and times, but simply pressed a card on me and said: 'Friday, eight-thirty.'

Susan

There is somebody new in her life, and I must say she looks well on it. Hair, skin, eyes – it's true what they say about love (sex) being better than a tonic. She'll never be pretty, but on her day she can be beautiful. She hasn't said much about him, which is unusual. She's not a secretive person, and is generally very free with those sort of details. I of course am being painfully discreet.

Julia

It's ridiculous, of course. We have absolutely nothing in common. He's like a creature from another planet, and I'm just a curiosity. But we are attracted – physically. I never really believed in the chemistry theory of relationships, but I am now a convert. My other men were friends who became something more – a sort of natural progression. That was especially true of Paul. But we're just two complete strangers who can't keep our hands off one another. Even thinking about it makes me go hot. What on earth is happening to me? I confided in Sophie, with whom I share a house, and her attitude was typically unhelpful – what was I complaining about, did I want him taken off my hands, that kind of thing. Sophie is a Sloane's Sloane, both hard boiled and prim, a peculiarly rebarbative combination.

He's never free in the evenings because of the club. I go along there and perch on a bar stool and sometimes he draws alongside and we have some time together; more often than not he's talking to other punters as he calls them, or business contacts, or the staff, who are all young and beautiful. To be frank I feel a complete fish out of water sitting there with my spritzer, in my Austin Reed Options silk shirtwaister (well I truly don't go to clubs as a rule), and trying to look vivacious and cool at the same time. Sometimes I long to be having a quiet curry with Paul at the Bombay Bra, or to be wallowing in Peter Grimes at the ENO . . . But then along he comes, and drags me on to the dance floor and I'm totally, utterly lost. He is the most wonderful dancer – or at least I enjoy dancing with him, which I appreciate isn't quite the same thing. By the way, I am talking about proper, old-fashioned dancing here – we have no truck with Dire Straits, Prince or Smiley Culture. We clasp, sway and undulate rhythmically, cheek to cheek, his arm right round me so that my waist feels small (it isn't) and my hand held against his chest in the region of his heart.

If my heart weren't making such a racket I'd say it had gone AWOL.

Susan

I met him! Julia and Sophie had one of those Sunday fork lunches of which Sophie is so fond, and they very politely invited the aged parent. Sophie's people live in Dorset, as you might imagine. I like to think Julia only goes along with these occasions to keep Sophie sweet, since it's Daddy who forks out for the house in Bellingham Mews. It's quite extraordinary, there I was surrounded by young men and maidens in their Sunday best, all presumably eyeing, if not touching, each other up – and all I wanted to do was yell 'Great balls of fire!' or something equally inappropriate and do the bump and grind on top of the baby grand. They are dismayingly bloodless, these thrusting young professionals. I mean Paul was there, helping to pour drinks and hand round crudités, and I thought: 'How can he bear it?' I kept expecting to see blood seeping through Turnbull and Asser's fine lawn shirtfront. But no.

And then he arrived. There was no mistaking who it was; Julia lit up like a Belisha beacon at his approach, and I was introduced forthwith, though very casually. She was obviously hoping to pass him off as just another of her and Sophie's batch of well-heeled rent-a-squires. There was no chance of that. If Julia's transformation hadn't given him away, then the black-and-white striped suit and black singlet would have done. A zebra crossing to go with the Belisha beacon. A slightly over-long handshake, wonderfully bright, attentive eyes, and the winning charm that comes from always having been cock of the walk. I estimate either the only boy in a family of girls, or an only child. Age uncertain. Utterly delightful, completely untrustworthy. I have never fussed over my daughter, but at that moment I wanted to take her in my arms and beg her to be careful. But she was so proud, so thrilled, so *turned on* – I saw for the first time the exact force of the expression – to do so would have spoiled everything for her. I could see Sophie torn miserably between well-bred distaste (my dear, that suit!) and gut-corroding jealousy. That was rather gratifying, I must say, I could take quite a lot of that . . . But then there was poor Paul, so manfully staunching and concealing the flow of his heart's blood (at least I hope he was). It's unfair that for some people getting love is as easy as breathing, and for others it's like scaling the Old Man of Hoy. The rules of the game don't change, even if attitudes do. Julia's only a part of Mr Murphy's life, but at the moment he is the sun, moon, stars and oxygen of hers.

'You're not in the least what I expected,' he said, offering me a cigarette. Partners in crime. I'm willing to bet she never tells him it's a disgusting habit.

'I can't imagine you've given it much thought,' I replied. I'm not usually tart, it must be the maternal tigress coming out. 'I haven't,' he agreed disarmingly. 'But now I see you, you are unexpected.'

Sophie hove in view to tell us the buffet was in the other room, adding: 'But don't go through till you've finished those beastly things – house rules.'

He gave her a crocodile grin, wide and threatening. 'Don't you worry about us, sweetheart.'

Julia came over. 'Are you both all right? Would you like me to bring you some food?'

I was about to say no, of course not, we wouldn't be a minute, but he just said 'You're an angel of mercy,' and off she trotted. Don't ask me what we talked about. But he was amusing.

Julia

They got on brilliantly. I know I don't need my mother's approval for anything I do, but I value her opinion on such things. Not that I expect her to sidle up to me and say 'He's delightful, darling', that wouldn't be her style. I just need to know that I haven't gone completely mad. While I was dishing up their Coronation Chicken, saffron rice and salad, Paul appeared. He was being terribly nice and useful.

'How are you keeping, Julia?' he asked. 'It's been ages.' I said I was absolutely fine, and then he said: 'Lovely party. And nice to see your mother again. She is such a good egg.' He uses those sort of expressions. It's positively the last phrase I should choose to describe my mother.

He hovered a bit, and then added: 'She seems to be getting on like a house on fire with your stripy gent.' 'Yes,' I said. 'I must take this to them, excuse me.'

Susan

I left the party as early as I decently could, which is the proper thing for representatives of an older generation to do. A curious reversal of stereotypes – Paul was a bit drunk and sitting on the back of the sofa in his shirtsleeves holding forth; Michael was in the kitchen with one of those gorilla aprons over his suit, washing up plates. There were far more people in the kitchen than in the sitting room. As I said goodbye to Julia, and thanked her, she gave me a most unJulia-ish hug, warm and prolonged as if she were thanking me for something. I have to remind myself that she's thirty years old and spends her days conveyancing and drawing up wills and grappling with people's life or death problems. She does not need a mother's advice. Correction: she does not want it.

Julia

We went to Amsterdam for the weekend. I've been before and simply loathed it, but this was different. I submitted with a good grace to being dragged round the red-light district and tried to be sporting about all those extravagantly appointed women in their pink-lit lairs. In exchange he came to look at paintings and was exactly the right companion, of course, full of fresh insights, and not one of those who stand dutifully for forty-five seconds in front of every single picture as if under an ultra-violet lamp.

On the way back he had to go to the Birmingham club, and I went along for the ride. The club there is newer and bigger than the one in London – pretty frightful if I'm honest, but I stuck it out. Mike had business to do, so someone called Spiro was assigned to look after me. The poor chap, I felt sure he likes his women hot, sweet and preferably in black satin. I think he was mystified by me and my connection with the boss. However, we drank margaritas (disgusting) and were quite chummy by the end of a couple of hours.

Sometimes I don't recognize myself these days. I wouldn't use the phrase lightly – but I think I must be in love.

Susan

I'm not being flippant. I think it's love. On her side of course, not his. He wouldn't recognize an altruistic feeling if it blacked his eye. I don't ask, but from what she said on the phone the other evening she's trailing round after him like a Red Indian squaw. I suppose it's a case of whatever makes her happy, but let's not be mealy-mouthed about it – the happiness won't last. I mean, I'm my daughter's greatest fan, but I'm at a loss to know why he's stuck around this long.

Julia

The sensible thing would be to get out of this while I'm ahead. I'm not so green that I can't see it'll probably end in tears. But he makes me so happy. He may be neglectful in some ways, but he can always make it up to me in bed. I didn't know what sex was before this. I know I look good on it – my mother commented on my appearance the other day saying how bright-eyed, bushy-tailed and generally sprauncy I looked. Sophie disapproves. An excellent reason for carrying on.

I'm dragging him off to *Don Giovanni* on Saturday. Why should he have it all his own way? I told him he was getting like Basil Fawlty, always breathing down the customers' necks. He looked blank. Sophie is away doing whatever she does in the shires for a couple of nights, so we shall have the place to ourselves.

Susan

She looks absolutely shattered – exhausted. And the weight loss has gone too far. A healthy sex life is one thing, but from what I can make out they never get together until about two in the morning; and it's all very well testing bedsprings all night if you can then lie in till midday (which of course he does), but Julia has to get up and go to work.

Julia

The weekend was a disaster. On Sunday as I was making cooked breakfast and he lay in bed with the *Sunday Correspondent*, nattering to Spiro on the cellular phone, I experienced my very own Road to Damascus. The scales fell from my eyes. I didn't need this.

I didn't say anything. I just turned the grill off and went out for a walk in the park. One thing Michael has taught me: you can do whatever you like in life.

I got back feeling wonderful. He was grouchy. Where had I been and whatever happened to breakfast? I climbed back into bed and everything was right as rain. Afterwards I told him I'd got a lot to thank him for, but this was it. He acted up a bit, as though he felt it was expected of him, and then he was as sunny as you like, which confirmed me in my opinion that I'd done the right thing.

I never knew I had it in me.

I feel a new woman.

Susan

He came round! You could have knocked me down with a feather. I was listening to the Vivaldi on Radio 3, with a whisky and water. He said he knew it was a bit out of order, but he'd got my address out of Julia's Filofax, and just wanted to know if I had any idea why he'd been given the bum's rush.

I said I was sorry, I didn't even know that he had.

'Oh,' he replied, 'only I got the impression that you and she were close.'

'We are, reasonably,' I said. 'When was this?'

'This afternoon. Right out of the blue. I'm gutted, I don't mind telling you. Totally gutted.'

Actually he did seem upset. He looked tired, he hadn't shaved, and he was uncharacteristically subdued.

'Will you have a drink?' I asked.

'Thanks.'

'She was so different,' he said, 'I really needed her.'

I suddenly realized that was probably true. Poor Michael.

'You must be so proud of your daughter,' he said. And then his voice broke. There were tears in his eyes.

'I am, of course,' I said. 'And I am so sorry – truly – that it's ended like this.'

I went to hand him his drink and he put his arms round my waist and pressed his face into me.

It's funny, I wasn't surprised. It seemed the most natural thing in the world to stroke his hair and shoulders and try to comfort him.

Perhaps we're two of a kind. At any rate, I felt I understood him.

Julia

Sophie got back and observed, in a tone of poisonous well-bred restraint, that the place was a mess: there were still two rashers of smoked back and a couple of Cumberland bangers under the grill, in a rather congealed state. I dealt with them. And meanwhile Sophie embarked on a lengthy telephone de-briefing session. I packed my stuff and took a taxi round to Paul's flat in Prince of Wales Road.

'Can I come and stay for a bit?' I asked.

He just opened the door and stood aside. I thought it was the most dashing gesture he'd ever made.

Susan

Of course it's awkward. It would be ghastly if Julia found out even if she is no longer interested. The whole thing is completely bizarre and undignified, but Cupid is a knavish lad and so forth.

I just try to be here for him. It's a high pressure life he leads, and it's nice to have someone to cook for again. The unsocial hours are a bit stressful, especially during Consultation Week and when we were doing the *Water Babies* (I was wardrobe mistress), but at least they assist the necessary secrecy.

He is something special. I just wish I wasn't so tired!

Julia

I'm enjoying my work, which I haven't done for ages. I've got this great sense of the future stretching out before me, and all its possibilities. I want to make plans. When Paul suggested marriage the other evening (something he was wont to do with monotonous regularity), it didn't seem quite such a ludicrous idea. We went to bed together to think it over.

'Holy Cow,' said Paul. 'Forget marriage, Julia, you'd make some lucky fellow a wonderful mistress.'

We decided it was time to get to know each other better.

Susan

Last time I saw Julia she looked absolutely wonderful. When I said as much she said she wished she could say the same for me, and that she'd be a lot happier if I'd go and have a complete MOT at the doctor's.

It was one of those remarks that put ten years on you at a stroke. But when I mentioned it, jokingly, to Mike, he said not to worry, he fancied me just the way I am.

I shall take that as a compliment. I'm sure he meant it as one.

Felicity Wood

The Moses Basket

Felicity Wood was runner-up in the New Woman, New Fiction Competition 1990. Her atmospheric entry was prompted by several accounts she had heard of adopting babies from El Salvador; her story looks at it from the mother's point of view and is based strongly on the imagination. Felicity, married with one daughter, regularly goes on residential writing courses and swears by them as an aid to new writers: 'They don't teach people to write, but they help to bring out of people what they want to say.'

Yesterday Jesus looked down at Violeta with a pitying glance as she prayed. He had watched her with the same expression the day after the Englishwoman took Tomaso away. These days she saw little but reproof in the way he raised his arm towards her, porcelain finger pointed towards the cupola above them both. She felt sometimes that he would never forgive her for what she had done.

But yesterday had been different in so many ways that it came as no surprise that even Christ pitied her. In the morning the fighting in her district had been fiercer than anyone expected. And for once she stayed indoors, heeding the urgent tone of the government warnings on the radio. Watching the comings and goings of rebel soldiers on the narrow street below, she had feared for them. Their machine-gun fire, shuddering through the afternoon stillness while she rested, always heralded their approach. When first roused by the sound she had hurried to the window, just in time to see two young boys, their khaki uniforms barely disguising their youth. They pressed their bodies flat against the double doors of the lock-up garage opposite as they slithered past like frightened chameleons, their cotton shirts clinging to their backs in patches of sweat. Reaching the corner of an alleyway on the other side they disappeared into its darkness. Echoing footsteps died away through the open treads of the steel fire escape as a group of army soldiers came into sight under Violeta's window.

If she had gone to work – as she normally did on lazy Saturdays when newspaper men and taxi drivers drank away their wages in the bar where she worked – she would not have witnessed those scared boys on the run. But the night before she had simply told the owner Guillermo that she needed the day free for unfinished chores in the flat. He leered as she spoke. Violeta flicked her tea-towel angrily along the shiny counter to stop herself from saying something she might regret. No dramas or arguments in front of customers – his first instruction to her when she had taken the job three years before. And so she never gave him any, biting her lip or disturbing the dust with her cloth. But she refused to tell him why she needed a day's holiday. Not even her lover Pablo knew that.

He would not remember Tomaso's birthday. He had kept his distance in those days, knowing that the father could still be seen skulking in the bars on the other side of town. But he did come to the flat yesterday to look for her. When he asked why she was not at work, Violeta mumbled her feeble excuse, avoiding his glance. But as she cleared away an empty beer can from the kitchen table in front of him her hand slid deliberately across its surface, gathering up in her palm the only photograph she possessed of her son. Even Pablo must not see it.

Somewhere at the back of the church a woman was murmuring a prayer to herself, the words rolling hurriedly over her breath. The cloying smell of candle wax soaked the warm air. Here at least there was peace from the sirens of ambulances and gunfire. Some said you could distinguish the sound of government bullets from the rebels'. But Violeta could find no difference in the hiccuping sound ripping away the silence from the district. As she listened a lizard scuttled across the slabs of tile in front of the altar. She had caught one in her hand the day after her return from Guatamala two years ago. Gripping the creature loosely between her fingers, she had opened her palm to find nothing but the muddy stump of its tail. As the events of those days passed through her thoughts she felt the courage which had brought her to the church seeping, and fading, through her memories.

She had not wanted the baby at first. Disgust at her own bloated stomach made her surly as she wandered each afternoon to the bar through the war-scarred streets, bullet sores like ulcers strewn along sandstone walls. Rats eyed her through torn doorways while the prospect of years tied to the creature inside her drove the fury up through her thoughts like a whirlwind.

Worry about money kept her silent. Tips were scarce in the bar. Funds were low at the church. Father Abbas would not help her. She saw no point in asking him. She even hid her sickness from Guillermo at first, afraid of his sniggering sympathy. Yet his genuine concern took her by surprise, comforting her with his gravity, his questions. But still she did not want it. He slid the name of a lawyer, scrawled across the inside flap of a book of matches, along the sugar-grained counter to her. She closed her hands over it, mumbling her thanks.

News of her pregnancy drove away the father – gradually, so gradually that at first she had hardly noticed how the number of days between his visits increased. He muttered his excuses, sliding his glances away so that she would not see the lie in his face. When eventually she challenged him, saying she knew that he spent his free time in other bars, he twisted his shoulders away from her, and refused to explain. He did not come again.

He did not see how the child swelled her breasts or how her anger at its being grew less with the months. The city had been quiet then, its uneasy peace canopied across the shanty huts in the foothills. The sound of cicadas had soothed her as the child kicked out. And she found herself hating it less each time it did so – wanting, almost, to keep it. She would murmur saints' days to herself, searching for a name, as she climbed the dusty stairs to her room at night after Guillermo had locked up the bar. Those journeys home became longer with the months. Her breath grew shorter. Her limbs ached like the months stretching ahead. Lying across the bed, night heat made her drowsy, pressing down on her thoughts as she counted away the weeks before the child's birth in time to the dripping tap in the corner basin. And in that time between waking and sleeping she wondered to herself if its father would have stayed if she had promised to keep the child.

No one warned her about after the birth.

The foster-mother came to take away her son two days after he was born. Violeta barred the door, shouting at her through its flaking painted panels to leave them alone. Somewhere, flies gnawed at the peace in the room as the woman returned down the stairs one by one, sandal-straps flicking the bare steps as she went. And Tomaso snuffled and fretted as he lay in the cradle Violeta had made for him in the bottom drawer of the wooden chest.

Violeta had gone to the lawyer's office herself, Tomaso strapped across her front, to find the address of the hotel where the couple were staying. When she asked him Señor Garcia shook his head, sweat slipping down one side of his face. Violeta would fly to Guatamala to hand over her child. It was safer that way, he explained – for everyone. A faint smell of garlic caught in his wake as he turned to open a drawer in the filing cabinet.

As he stood with his back to her, for one precious moment she thought she had the courage to tell him. I want to keep my son, she would have said, I don't want to let him go. But her throat went dry and the foolishness of her wish overwhelmed her, making her clumsy with the pen he gave her to make her cross on the paper. Señor Lopez talked of doctors' check-ups and certificates. She scarcely heard his instructions, so full were her thoughts of her need to keep Tomaso. He's mine, she thought to herself over and over, just mine. Her heart ached at these words, weighing heavily against her efforts to show nothing to this bulbous-faced man with his pile of notes. She looked at him as she handed back the pen, his false and eager smile mocking her.

She met the couple at the airport. The soles of her shoes had stuck to the hot tarmac, their weight increasing with every step as she walked from the bus to the terminus. While she sat waiting in the lounge, a prim, reproving voice announced over the tannoy the departure of their flight. Trolley wheels squealed in protest at the heaps of luggage being transported home by a group of Americans meandering across to Passport Control.

Just when Violeta had allowed herself the hope that the couple had already gone a young woman, her hair the colour of corn cob, came through the automatic doors. She paused, looking around her while she tapped her chin impatiently with a photograph. Violeta made no sign that she recognized her from the photograph the lawyer had shown her. She hoped that with her stillness she could stifle and suffocate the moments lying ahead in waiting. At first the woman drifted a glance over them as though she had not seen Tomaso bundled in the sling across Violeta's front. Perhaps, Violeta wondered afterwards, the way she turned instinctively away from the woman had drawn her attention to them. For one moment, she wanted to protect them both from the woman's intention, to turn her back on it. But as she swung round, one arm across Tomaso's body to hide him, a whisper of recognition passed across the woman's face. Excitement swept through her movements as she hurried towards them. Certainty quickened her pace so obviously that Violeta knew there was no going back.

The woman stood gabbling over them, sweet foreign perfume flurried the air behind her. Violeta stared at her, stunned, confused. Until that moment she had not believed they would come for Tomaso. She had shut the prospect away. But as the stranger bent over to take a look at him her urgent manner and bothering fussiness drove away the empty hope.

She thought she may have smiled as the woman held up the photograph of Tomaso. One of Señor Garcia's secretaries had taken the picture at the flat the day after the foster-mother visited. Violeta held her hand out towards it. But the woman flinched, drawing it back to her chest as she looked anxiously at Tomaso. She seemed to be waiting for something. Then she looked again, first at the picture, then at the child. And at last Violeta understood. There was to be an exchange. Tomaso for the photograph.

Reluctantly she untied the canvas fasteners of the sling, holding Tomaso close to her while she released its hold. He stirred, throwing his short arms up in the air as though startled. As she put him down on the seat with its slippery plastic covering he began to scream, a long, angry cry that filled the terminus with its helpless protest, its need for her warmth.

Violeta remembered little of the journey to Guatamala. The husband had arrived at the terminus just as the woman was unwrapping the woven shawl Violeta had made. She covered it round him loosely again, not in the neat, tight way Violeta knew to cocoon him from flies and dust, and then returned the child to Violeta for the last part of the journey. She carried her son through Passport Control to the plane as Señor Garcia had instructed her. In a daze she watched the mountains pass under them, green pines carpeting the slopes like thousands of erect spears. The muffled voice of an air hostess announced their approach to Guatamala. Then, somewhere in a strange airport lounge, while American music played from a jukebox, its hollow, cheery jingle echoing across Formica-topped tables and plastic-cushioned stools, Violeta handed over Tomaso for the last time.

Standing at her window yesterday she had thought again of those last few moments before the English couple hurried away with him to catch the plane to Los Angeles. He had slept when she put him in the basket they had brought for him. She willed him to wake, needing some small gesture to take away with her. But he gave her none as the couple walked away. The girl glanced back every now and then as though afraid Violeta might snatch away the basket.

She had seen one just like it yesterday, wicker sides bent inward to protect its whimpering contents as a woman scuffled forward from the building opposite. Fear showed on her broad-boned Indian face as an army soldier nudged her with the butt of his rifle. He had not seen the alleyway running down the side of the building, presuming instead that the rebels had sought their refuge inside it. The fretting child cried louder. Its mother crouched down against the wall, shielding the basket with her body while the youth snarled something at her. The woman shook her head miserably, frantic in her denial of the crime. '*No se, no se.*' Desperation gave truth to her words. The soldier shouted at her uncontrollably. He was asking again where the rebels were hiding. As he did so the child raised his cries in helpless confusion of fear and hunger.

A mindless act, the papers had called it this morning – spreading the ghastly news with their cheap print.

Journalists skulked round the ambulance, eager for a sight of the bodies. For the rest of the day they prowled the district, gleaning handfuls of useless information about the dead woman and her baby. By nightfall the street was empty. Somewhere a radio droned the news again and again.

Father Abbas gripped the end of Violeta's pew with one hand as he knelt before the altar. It was several moments before Violeta realized that she had been staring at him. Mass had ended three quarters of an hour before. But he still hovered in case any of his remaining congregation needed confession. Violeta had waited in the hope that no one would see her approach him. Her greatest sin, she knew without anyone telling her, was her pride. But it was not this weakness which had brought her to church this morning. As she knelt there, the felt covering of the pew cushion digging into her knees, she remembered the sound of the dead child's cries. They drowned the sirens and embarrassed fidgeting noises behind her. She had lain awake last night, listening to its echo across the alleyways and streets outside.

She had sold her son. It seemed so dreadful when she contemplated the deed that for two years she had not allowed herself to think of it at all. She had told Guillermo and the others that fever had killed him in the week after his birth. How easily the lies had slipped from her as she twisted cotton cloth round glasses to dry them. They still believed her now. They trusted her just as Tomaso had done when she laid him in the basket the English couple had brought for him. Wicker creaked as she leant forward to take one last look at him. She had promised herself then that no one would ever know what she had done. Not even Father Abbas.

The reasons why she let him go did not count any more. The act itself showed something about her, some chink, a seam unfinished or rucked, chafing any reassurance that she could be an ordinary mother. When Pablo asked her yesterday to marry him she shook her head violently. '*No niños, comprende?*' No children, you understand? After Tomaso there could be no more children. And without children there could be no marriage.

He ignored her words, meaning to have her as his wife, to win her over with his sweet talk. The pressure snapped inside his beer can as he pulled on the ring tag. She had her back to him, still watching the ambulance men in their white overalls darting like moths around the corpses. If she stood there long enough, with her face hidden from him, he might not question her. She caught a trace of the bitter scent of beer as spray threw out a foamy trail across the lino floor. And as he drank his first mouthful she felt the question slipping from his thoughts.

Her sort always gave away their babies. She could see the belief in the brusqueness of Señor Lopez, the locks of his briefcase springing back like alligators' teeth when he opened it to look for documents for her to verify. She sensed it in the disapproval of his secretary, in the way she moved round the bed, searching for the best angle from which to take the photograph. She smelt it in the antiseptic air of the doctor's surgery while he checked over her son and signed the health certificate. Her kind had no right to a baby. Give him away then, sell him to those who deserve him, she decided as the bus whined along the highway to the airport. A bad girl then, a bad, bad girl.

She had glanced out of the window again as she moved around the flat, tidying ashtrays, straightening bed linen. The attendant lingered round the open doors at the back of the ambulance as the wicker basket disappeared inside. A ripe, gold sun threw its four-o'clock light across the sandy street. There was always a peace in that rich afternoon light, when the glaring heat had spent its worst across the city and only drowsy warmth, honey-bright, remained. Someone in the flat opposite raised up a mourning cry as the ambulance began to move slowly towards the end of the street.

Violeta watched it crawl to a junction, growing smaller in the distance. The sound of weeping cut through the silence. Listening while she stood there, she realized that she was still clutching the photograph of Tomaso in her hand, still holding it close to her. She looked down at the narrow, sleeping face and remembered the white cotton counterpane across his basket with its cleanness, its smell of safety, bothering the breeze as they walked towards Passport Control.

She was still kneeling, hands clasped together, when she heard the fulsome sound of Father Abbas' cassock skirt brushing the ground as he walked slowly up the side-aisle beside her. Her son was safe. No longer hers, perhaps, but safe at least.

A musty smell rose from Father Abbas' clothes as he passed by. Pablo wanted to take her to see his family this afternoon – still refused to listen when she turned down his wish to marry her. He had grown angry when she would not explain her reasons for rejecting him. And she knew that if she could do this one thing there would no longer be a reason to deny him. The priest hesitated beside a flower stand, fingering the thick varnished surface of clay pot as though he sensed in her stillness the need to speak to him. Her blood felt like water as she pulled herself up slowly on to the pew behind. Father Abbas turned suddenly towards the front of the central aisle as though some pressing duty had recalled itself. He began to stride towards the altar. Violeta's throat went dry as she stood up, her cheeks reddening with confusion. She stretched out one arm in place of words and, her body wooden with awkwardness, looked at the priest.

He turned his head, clearly startled by her movement.

'Please, Father, I need confession.'

She looked at him, her breath shallow with fear that he might refuse her. And as he nodded, somewhere outside the sound of an ambulance siren played out its thin, familiar tune.

Patrick Gale

Dislocation

At 28 Patrick Gale is one of the youngest, most prolific and talented of Britain's writers. He has produced six novels, including Facing the Tank, Little Bits of Baby *and his newest,* The Cat Sanctuary, *published autumn 1990. His darkly comic, very English style has been likened to Iris Murdoch on pep pills. Patrick also writes articles and reviews for the* Daily Telegraph, *the* Washington Post, Harpers & Queen *and* Marie Claire. *He lives in North Cornwall with architectural designer Patrick Pender. 'I wrote* Dislocation *for a girlfriend whose man had just dumped her,' says Patrick, 'to show her that everything was much easier to view if you made fun of it in a story . . .'*

Rose slipped out of the lotus position with a cracking sound, which she ignored. Sitting on her heels she splayed her fingers across each knee. Leaning forwards, she opened her eyes and mouth as wide as they would go. Breathing out with a thick sigh, she tried to lick her own chin. She relaxed her face and sat back on her heels as she breathed in once more, then she repeated the gesture. The yoga manual lay on the carpet beside her, flattened open at the right page with the corner of an armchair. She glanced at the next position offered.

'Drawing air in across the tongue in this manner may feel unnatural at first,' she read. 'Persevere. Not only does it suppress the appetite but it is said to render one next only to the Gods in beauty.'

Obediently Rose placed the tip of her tongue behind her upper canines and sucked for all she was worth. Something flew into her mouth. Fluff from the carpet perhaps. She stopped to feel for it, wrinkling her nose, and drew out a blond hair, some four inches long. It was one of his. Disgusted, she abandoned her yoga to fetch the vacuum cleaner with which she tried to rid the room of his presence for the third time that week.

When the doorbell rang she was still soaking in the bath. She ran dripping to the intercom, shouted 'Hi!', then unlocked the door and ran, shivering, back to the water. A few minutes later there were childish, stamping footsteps through the flat and Fred appeared, panting, in the bathroom doorway. He examined her for a few seconds, pulling off his mittens, then yelled over his shoulder,

'She's still in the bath!'

'Hallo, Fred,' said Rose, and sank a little lower. Tracey appeared behind her son, cheeks pink from the cold. She leant against the door jamb to stare with him.

'You *are* in a bad way,' she said, and grinned.

'Hallo, Tracey,' said Rose. 'How are you?'

'Fine. Cold. In a hurry.'

'I'm sorry. I started hoovering and didn't realize how late it was.'

'Hoovering? That's *bad*.' Tracey shook her head and began unbuttoning her petrol-blue overcoat. 'I've got some news that will make you feel worse.'

'What?'

'Or it might make things better. I'm not sure.'

'*What*?'

'I've found out who she is.'

'No! Tell me.'

Tracey crouched to take off Fred's coat.

'Get out of that tub and come to the kitchen. I'll tell you over a coffee. I've only got forty minutes to get to the clinic.'

'Here I come.'

Tracey walked back through the flat to switch the kettle on. Watched by Fred, Rose stood to pull out the plug, dried herself and treated her body with deodorant and baby powder. Then she padded through to the bedroom where she found clean underwear and recycled yesterday's shirt. Even this child looked bored at the sight of her body. Her jeans had just been washed and Fred smiled as she strained to button their fly.

'Stop being paranoid,' Rose told herself as she brushed her hair. 'Stop being grotesque. He's too young to know better.'

'Caffeine's ready!' Tracey called.

'Coming,' Rose called back. 'Come on Fred.' She patted the back of his head to send him ahead of her. He had inherited Benedict's black curls and Tracey's almond-shaped, violet-grey eyes. Rose's hair was mouse and her eyes were brown and mismatched. Fortune was rarely fair but sometimes she was an out-and-out bitch.

'So tell,' she said, sitting at the kitchen table.

'Have you got anything to go with this?' Tracey asked, opening cupboard doors. 'Like a biscuit or something? It's not for me, you understand, it's for my child.'

'I baked some brownies yesterday. Coffee and walnut ones. They're in the tin on the left-hand side.'

Tracey turned, cake tin in hand, eyes wide with disbelief.

'You started *baking*? Sister, this is serious. I'm not sure I should tell you anything at all. Let's just all have ourselves a brownie and we can talk about frocks or something. Brownie, sweetheart?' She offered one to Fred who took one, meticulously thanking Rose for it. 'Rose?' Rose shook her head. Tracey helped herself then sat across the table from Rose, stirring a low-calorie sweetener into her coffee. As he chewed, Fred was peering from one woman to the other waiting for them to begin.

'Tell me,' said Rose. 'Tracey, you've got to. I'd tell you if ever Benedict was . . .' She remembered Fred. 'Fred?'

'Mmh?'

'If you look on the sofa you'll find a bag and in that bag there's a new game for you to play with.' Fred slipped off his chair.

Tracey waited, head cocked for the sound of tearing paper, then faced Rose across her coffee cup.

'She's an earth mother,' she said.

'*What*?'

'She's called Naomi French. She's in her late forties with two children and a house on Primrose Hill. She wears kaftans and Indian cottons with no perceptible irony and, wait for it, she works in the small mammals department at the zoo.'

'Wait. Wait!' Rose stilled her, tensely drinking in every detail. 'Naomi French. Naomi. Where on earth did he meet her?'

'How should I know?'

'You seem to know everything else.'

'Look, I've no idea. Someone brought her to a party probably. He used to go to parties without you occasionally.'

'Frequently. He'd keep quiet about them until he was sure I'd made other arrangements. He did it so that I would feel I was letting him down. Jesus! The small mammals department. So is she a vet, or what?'

'I really have no idea and I don't think you should try to find out. Just accept.'

'How did you find out?'

'Three guesses. Make it two.'

'Benedict?'

'Benedict may have been speaking to him at work but if he has he hasn't dared tell me yet. But you're close. Try again.'

Rose took a mental flick through her ex's address book, which she had done often enough when he lived with her. Her finger stopped at a queeny bachelor, lethal at twelve paces, who worked on the arts pages with him.

'Dan Quilty?' she asked.

'Right first time. I met Benedict for a drink after work and Miss Quilty had tagged along with him. Seems he lives a few doors down from her and saw Lover Boy moving in.'

'He moved in?'

'Oh. Yes. Sorry. I was going to break that one to you slowly. He moved in on Saturday. Dan said it looked as though he'd been living out of the car – doing his unreconstructed, pre-feminist caveman bit, I've no doubt.'

'She took pity on him.'

'Yeah,' Tracey said doubtfully, 'he drove her home from the party then doorstepped her for a few days. Warming as she does to all defenceless mammals, large or small, she finally cracked and asked him in for a coffee. When did he come back here for his things?'

'He didn't have anything. Nothing he couldn't take with him first time; two boxes of books, the guitar, his records, his clothes. He didn't own any of the furniture, thank God.'

'Just that creepy painting that used to hang in your hall. I notice he took that.'

'Oh. Didn't you like that?'

'I always *hated* it. So Summer of Love. Naomi New-Age will be thrilled. She'll probably hang it over their bed. Oh. Sorry.'

'You're going to be late.'

'Am I? Tracey shot a glance at the clock. 'So I am.' She jumped up. 'It is sweet of you taking Fred for the day. Are you sure you don't mind? The sooner Benedict forks out for a nanny the better.' She kissed Rose, who had risen too, and they walked out to the hall. 'Look, I'll pick him up at four – if the old trouts have booked in any late patients for me I'll just tell them to piss off – then we can have tea and you can tell me the latest news about the book.'

'There isn't any. My agents are still waiting for a reaction.'

'Oh God. Well. We'll have tea anyway. Fred I'm going. Watch your language in front of Rose, she's in a bad way.' She crouched to kiss her son then swooped out of the flat, shutting the door with a bang. Rose turned to Fred who was holding what looked like a death-ray gun. He had made it from the construction game she had bought to keep him quiet.

'Well, Fred,' she said, 'we're all alone till Mummy comes back at four. How about a trip to the zoo?'

So far Fred had enjoyed the Reptile House best. He crowed with delight at a pair of lizards locked in inscrutable coitus and disgraced himself by unzipping his miniature jeans to have a surreptitious pee in the gutter outside a tank draped with pythons. Rose was enjoying herself too. In a way. She had not been to the zoo since her childhood and although the enclosures were smaller, crueller than she remembered, she gained an adult pleasure from communing with the gloomier or unkindly endowed creatures. A lizard called the stub-tailed skink had particularly caught her fancy as had a perfectly hideous bald crane. The Reptile House was deliciously warm, fugged up with the gases of fear and she would have liked to linger to watch the restless swinging of an elegant emerald snake called a boomslang. Fred was showing too much interest in a disgusting display of photographs illustrating the effects of cobra venom, however, and she feared it might haunt his dreams.

'Come on, Fred,' she said, taking his hand again. 'What do you want to see next?'

'Monkeys!' He shouted, enjoying the corridor's acoustics. 'Monkeys fucking!'

The day being wintry, the zoo had few visitors but most of them seemed to have chosen that moment to come into the institution's warmest building. Disapproving glances stung Rose through the gloom.

'Come along, then,' she said. 'Monkeys it is.'

Fred was growing increasingly overexcited. He bounced along beside her, swinging his mittens on their strings and imitating a chimpanzee. She had often wondered whether he might not be hyperactive. Tracey let him eat anything that took his fancy – the more processed the better – claiming that her own mother had instilled in her offspring chronic food anxieties through too aggressive a control of their childhood diet. Benedict claimed his son was a mercilessly early riser, and Rose had noticed that whenever she took care of Fred he went through the entire day without the usual sleepy spell. As they entered the primate section, walking past the gorilla colony and a clutch of peaceably flea-picking baboons, she glanced at her watch and saw with relief that it would soon be time for him to go home. His company had been a welcome distraction from self-torment but now she was tired, and her head felt stuffed with the slightly bossy platitudes of which conversation with children seemed to consist.

They reached a large cage in which colobus monkeys were swinging and chattering from metal branches, their breath steaming on the cool autumn air. At last Fred fell silent. He stared at them, breathing heavily.

'Do you like those, Fred?' she asked, and he nodded. Then he took a few steps back. There was a thick metal fence placed to spare visitors the temptation of thrusting fat fingers within range of a monkey's bite. Rose assumed that Fred was standing back so as to have a clearer view over it. He was several feet away from her and she was taken entirely by surprise when he ran forward and sprang, with unnatural agility, on to the fence's top. As startled as she was, the monkeys leapt about with renewed energy.

'Fred!' Rose shouted as one of them whipped down on to the mesh nearest Fred and cackled furiously at him. 'Fred don't!' Rose ran forward just as Fred reached out to poke at his new playmate. He lost his balance just as she caught his arm. She swung him clear and, enraged by her own irresponsibility, smacked him smartly on the hand.

Fred's shout in the Reptile House had been loud but now he shrieked. As if his legs had turned to rubber, he fell to the ground and writhed, his face a scarlet mask of impotent fury.

'Fred, stop it,' said Rose. 'Stop it at once. That was very silly of you and you could have had your hand bitten off. If I hadn't stopped you, you'd have fallen into that nasty, muddy ditch and we'd have had to call a keeper to get you out.' A woman passing by, trailed by her own toddler, smiled in sympathy.

'First it's Terrible Twos,' she laughed. 'You get a year off and then it's Fearsome Fours!'

Rose leered back at her then returned her attention to Fred who was still yelling, tears running into his hair. She tried cajoling him.

'Come on, Freddie. It's not the end of the world. Look! The chimpanzees are waiting to say hallo and then we can go home and have tea with Mummy. You can have another brownie,' she added, thinking 'How low can you go?'

Then Fred stopped shrieking and said with terrible clarity and Benedict's voice,

'I think you've broken my arm.'

'Oh God!' Rose whispered. Crouching she stilled his writhing and touched his arm. This produced another shriek. 'Oh God!' she said again. 'Fred I didn't mean to. Can you try to stand up? No? Here. Put your good arm round my neck and I'll carry you.'

Whimpering now, Fred did as he was told and Rose began stumbling in search of help: the St John's Ambulance Brigade, perhaps, or a first-aid room. She assumed there must be such a place. All thoughts went from her mind but an appalling sense of guilt.

'Can I help you?' a woman's voice asked from behind her. She turned. The offer came from a short female of indeterminate middle age, shaped like a pepper pot but with an extraordinarily kind face. Her silver-flecked blond hair hung in a faintly grotesque braid on her back. She had on a white cotton coat like a doctor's and was carrying a file. Her voice was so warm, her appearance so reassuring that Rose nearly began to whimper too.

'It was so silly,' she said. 'He suddenly jumped up on to the fence back there and I grabbed him by the arm to stop him trying to touch the monkey and, well, Oh God! I think I may have broken it.'

'Was there a crack?' the woman asked her.

'No. I don't think so. He started crying almost at once so I couldn't be sure.'

'Come with me,' she said and tapped Fred on the nose. 'Soon be right as rain,' she said, 'you'll see.'

She led the way back past the gorillas, around the side of a red brick building and through a door marked PRIVATE.

'In here,' she said. Opening another door she waved them into a small room with glass-fronted cupboards around the walls and a small operating table in its centre. The woman closed the door then unfurled a paper sheet from a roll and spread it across the table. 'OK,' she said, 'Let's get your little coat off first then we'll lie you down here. That's it!'

Rose stood Fred on the edge of the table while the woman slipped off his coat as carefully as if it had been made of gold leaf, then she laid him down and touched a soothing hand to his forehead.

'Are you a doctor?' Rose asked.

'Not exactly. I'm a vet. Our training is rather longer. Now young man look out of the window for me.' Still whimpering,

Fred looked out of the window as the woman slowly reached for his bad arm. 'Now,' she said, 'I want you to count the number of branches on that little tree for me. Out loud.'

'One,' Fred whispered, 'two, three, four,' he said more loudly. 'Five, six, seven, eight, OW!' He yelled then stopped and turned to the woman, who was still grasping his arm, and gave her a smile straight from heaven. 'How did you do that?' he asked.

'Secret,' said the woman.

'I . . . I don't know what to say,' Rose stammered. 'It wasn't broken?'

'I thought it might have been a greenstick fracture if he'd fallen on it, but when you told me how you caught his arm and he started hollering I knew it was simpler.' She crouched to pat Fred's knees as he swung his legs from the table's edge. 'Mummy dislocated your elbow for you,' she told him.

'God!' Rose exclaimed.

'Commonest accident mistaken for child abuse,' the woman chuckled. 'You catch their arm to stop them doing something silly and the next minute they're screaming blue murder.' She winked at Fred.

'How can I thank you?'

'You can let me get home for my tea.'

'God! Yes. We're late too! Come on Fred. Thank you so much, er . . . thank you.'

'Not at all,' said the woman and Rose caught a whiff of Irish brogue. 'Can you find your way to the exit all right?'

'I think so.'

'I'll see you a bit of the way. I need to lock the outside door in any case.'

She let them out of the room then led them along the corridor and out of the building. She bade them good afternoon and locked the door behind them. Rose suddenly realized that she had never asked her name. She turned back, meaning to rap on the window to catch her attention. The woman was walking back down the corridor, taking off her white coat as she went. She had on an unseasonal Indian cotton frock, the kind with little bells threaded on braids that swung from around the bodice. Rose's knuckles froze in mid-gesture and she pretended to Fred, who was too short to see in, that she had been seen and was waving. She led him towards the exit sign.

'I didn't tell her you aren't my mummy,' he said. 'Do you mind?'

'No,' said Rose. 'Not really.'

Rachel Billington

The Butterfly

Rachel Billington was educated at a Catholic school in London, read English at university, then escaped her huge, charismatic family by going to New York to work in television research. There, she met her husband, Kevin, and got the inspiration for her first novel, All Things Nice. *They moved to England in 1967 and have lived with their four children in London and Dorset ever since. Dorset was the setting for her latest novel,* Theo and Matilda, *a witty and surprising epic of two people in love across the centuries. Rachel's new story,* The Butterfly, *contrasts idyllic dreams of family life with a much more intriguing reality. 'I'm very interested in the relationship between mothers and daughters,' says Rachel. 'It can be wonderfully protective, but can also become dangerous. . .'*

It was the sort of day when flowers open under your eyes. The air was so mild, so sweet, so fresh and light. 'Dulcet,' said Lydia out loud, although there was no one to hear. 'This garden feels dulcet.' I am happy, she added, although this time under her breath because you must not tempt the gods too far.

Lydia sat on a wooden bench at the end of her mother's garden and could not imagine a better place to be. Above her head a blackbird began to warn her off but not very aggressively, as if he too was pacified by this early spring. 'I am going to have a baby.' Again Lydia whispered the words to the garden, as if she were offering her credentials to belong to this bright new world, this brave fertility. 'In a month I will be a mother.'

'Lydia! Lydia, darling. Ly-ydi-aaa!'

Lydia smiled. They had moved to this house when she was eight and as long as she could remember, her mother had called for her with exactly the same intonation. She had always responded at once, 'Co-ming, Mu-ummy, coming!' The other children, her younger brother and sister, sometimes didn't answer or ran away and hid, but she always came at once. How else could she reply to the enormous love her mother had poured out to her?

Already walking along the narrow paved path, Lydia paused for a moment and frowned. Carey thought she took too much notice of her mother. 'Lydia! Are you coming?'

'Coming, Mummy, I'm coming!' Carey was not coming down till that evening in order, as he had said, to give her more time with her mother.

'Darling. There you are!' The moment Lydia saw her, so lovely, poised by an azalea bush, her anxiety (small as it had been) vanished in joyous affection.

'I was sitting on a bench in the sun,' she explained,

wanting to share the experience.

'There you are,' repeated her mother, taking her arm. 'I wanted to show you the first butterfly.'

'It's far too early for butterflies,' exclaimed Lydia, delightedly.

'I know. It's ridiculous. Anyway it flew away in the direction of the cabbage plants.'

'Oh, Mummy. How do you manage to make everything so lovely here!'

'Silly thing.' Lydia's mother, whose name was Dorothy, smiled in a pleased way. She was small and neat and with such a good complexion that it hardly crinkled more than her daughter's when she smiled. 'If you were a lady of leisure instead of a thrusting executive, and lived in the country instead of a London flat, and had a husband who enjoyed digging instead of a busy young doctor, then you too could have a garden like this.' She paused for effect. 'As long as you employed me.'

They both giggled. It was an old joke. Lydia could make nothing grow. She only had to look at a plant for it to turn up its toes.

'Lunch time, now. Daddy's off to golf at two o'clock.'

Lydia had not realized her father was at home but they all had lunch together agreeably enough. The long windows were open and Lydia's father sat at the head of the table, his chair rather pushed back as if he was only temporarily present. It had always been like this and Lydia hardly talked to him because she hardly noticed his presence.

Dorothy, on the other hand, smiled readily in his direction and made certain that he paid proper attention to her quips. 'Your mother, as you can see, is in the pink,' said Ronny as he rose to go. He was a big man, still handsome, and he had to bend his prow-like face right over to kiss first his daughter and then his wife.

Lydia repressed a flash of irritation but had to admit that her mother did look 'in the pink', with her cheeks flushed by a glass of sherry and her silvery hair curling round her blue eyes.

'See you for cake and tea, dear.' Dorothy waved off her husband with her usual good humour, then she and Lydia settled in for a whole afternoon together.

'Let's look at the baby clothes.' They had been promising themselves that treat ever since Lydia had become pregnant.

The sun dappled the bedroom Lydia had used as a child, now turned into a storeroom. The baby clothes, wrapped in tissue, still seemed to smell sweetly of lux and talcum powder.

'Of course Hattie used them after you.' Dorothy held up a tiny nightdress with a duck embroidered on the front. 'So they're not as fresh as they were.'

Lydia frowned. She liked to feel that the clothes had come directly from her mother to her and from her to her baby. Mention of her sister Hattie was a slightly tactless diversion, she felt. Not that she disliked Hattie, who she looked forward to seeing for lunch the next day. But she was not very important.

Soon there was a pile of little garments on the bed and the sun had sunk below the window sill. Lydia remembered how she used to lie for hours on this same bed reading until it became too dark to see the print.

'Yes and I must finish my weeding,' Dorothy thrust the clothes towards her daughter. 'And then see about supper.'

Lydia watched her hurry to the door. 'I'll stay here a moment.'

Carey found her there two hours later. She had fallen asleep, clutching one of her old matinée jackets. Instead of admiring such a touching sight, the dark curly head, the round body in its floral smock, he woke her abruptly.

'I've arrived.' Carey had a loud voice and, although not tall or large, the sort of personality which filled a room very quickly.

'It was so peaceful,' Linda murmured placatingly.

'You haven't even unpacked your case.'

This was a feeble accusation so Lydia sat up and gave him a kiss. 'Was the drive terrible?'

'Do you mean is that why I am cross?'

'No,' Lydia stood up and smiled sweetly. 'You're always cross when we come here.'

There was nothing more to say on that subject so Carey put his arm round his wife and they moved towards their bedroom.

Downstairs, Dorothy shook a pan of mange-touts with one hand and smoothed her hair with the other. It wasn't her fault, she thought vaguely, that she enjoyed her life so much. She had always tried to make the children feel the same. Tomorrow she would make their favourite bouillabaisse which might help to soften the blow. It was a good idea, she felt convinced, to tell them the news all together. But then Dorothy, who lived her life for others, usually thought her ideas were good.

Lydia decided to change for supper. 'It's such a luxury not to cook,' Lydia sighed contentedly. Carey stroked her arm. 'Your mother spoils you.'

'Don't let's talk about her,' Lydia turned to Carey and looked him in the eye. 'I had a lovely day. Thank you.'

Carey thought this looking him in the eye was one of her mother's mannerisms. In London she smiled and ducked and weaved and was exhausted. In London she always needed him.

'Let's go down.'

Candles were already alight in the dining room. 'Ronny, we're going to eat!' Dorothy called as soon as she saw her daughter and son-in-law, and Ronny came obediently from the television.

'It all looks very pretty,' said Carey politely and slightly guiltily as they took their usual places. More often than not, he and Lydia grabbed a sandwich. He saw her now smiling broadly at him.

Perhaps I am still a child, wondered Lydia. But then she thought about her job and how competently she took quite difficult meetings and decided that anyone, child or adult, deserved being looked after now and again. Who better to do it than a mother?

'How much longer are you working, darling?' enquired Dorothy.

'This soup is delicious,' replied Lydia as if it were more important, before adding, 'Next week is my last week. Executives simply can't afford to waddle.'

'I can't imagine you ever waddling,' Dorothy looked at her daughter with admiration. 'You've always had perfect posture.'

Putting down his soup spoon, Carey realized that he never paid his wife such fulsome compliments.

Ronny stood up to collect the soup bowls. When he reached Carey, he whispered in what was supposed to be a cockney accent, 'Are we lucky or are we lucky?'

Dorothy and Lydia began to talk about Lydia's job and the generosity of her company in allowing three months' paid maternity leave. Carey waited for Lydia to explain her night fears about someone taking over her job while she was away. When she continued to paint a picture of joy and light he interrupted, 'Lydia's extremely concerned her stand-in will pinch the job.' His voice boomed through the billings and cooings.

Ronny who was carving the chicken lifted the knife in the air like a baton.

'I'm sure there will always be a place for Lydia.' Dorothy spoke sweetly but firmly. Home was not a place to bring problems. Ronny lowered his baton again.

Carey followed his will o' the wisp of rebellion. 'We need the money now that I've decided to specialize.'

Mother and daughter gave him the same blank stare. Money, too, did not enter their paradise.

'Breast?' offered Ronny. 'Or leg?'

'Carey will want leg, dear,' Dorothy smiled cosily.

Lydia who knew her husband preferred breast and indeed positively disliked leg, said nothing.

That night as Lydia prepared for bed, she remembered the awkwardness at supper and her contentment was ruffled.

'I'm afraid I've got indigestion,' she appealed to Carey who was already sitting in bed.

'It can't be your mother's cooking.' Carey peered over the top of his newspaper.

'Of course it's not my mother's cooking. I am pregnant, after all.'

'And very nice too.' Carey put out his hand to stroke her tummy but she moved away.

Lydia sat in bed stiffly upright and thought how happy, how perfectly utterly happy she'd been that morning. She thought of the beautiful early butterfly (she forgot she'd never actually seen it) and how her mother had been so intimate. 'I love my mother,' she cried, 'and I don't know why you make such a fuss about it!'

'I only said her cooking can't be the cause of your indigestion.' Carey was reading about the cricket in the West Indies and felt remarkably relaxed. 'She just sometimes strikes me as quite unreal.' He even smiled.

'I'm going to sleep,' Lydia humped herself away from her husband.

'Good idea.' Something occurred to Carey. 'Have you discovered why the whole family's gathering for lunch tomorrow?'

'Daddy's birthday?' suggested Lydia sleepily. She had decided that Carey was jealous of her mother so she wasn't too upset either.

'Even I know your father's birthday isn't tomorrow.' Carey rattled his newspaper disapprovingly.

'Uhm,' murmured Lydia, taking no more notice.

It was another lovely morning. The sun spattered through the flowery curtains. Lydia knew these curtains from her childhood. She could have painted them by heart, the yellow marigolds, green fern background, the occasional sprig of forget-me-not.

'How did you sleep?' Carey always asked her that.

'Well. How did you?' When she was a child she used to

wake to the sound of the radio in the kitchen and her mother making breakfast.

'Turn over so I can hold you.' Lydia turned over but as she lay cradled in her husband's arms, she thought of her mother.

Sunday morning used to include church in the past but this morning everybody felt lazy. Besides, Hattie and Nick were expected between eleven and twelve. 'They're sure to be late,' Dorothy told Lydia. Hattie and Nick were the younger children, to be patronized a little and indulged.

'Shall we go and search for your butterfly?' suggested Lydia who had now remembered she had not seen it.

'What a lovely idea!' Dorothy agreed at once, although her mind was really on her bouillabaisse. 'You go on and I'll follow you in a moment.'

So Lydia wandered out into the charming garden and the air was as balmy as the day before. But for some reason she didn't feel as absolutely contented. It was not just that her mother did not follow her – she knew she was busy. Nor was it the uncomfortable squeezing going on in her tummy, as if her ribs were being forced apart. Nor was it the sight of her husband and father laughing heartily together through the sitting-room window – after all, why should that disturb her? But there was something unsettling in the atmosphere, something about the way her mother avoided her eyes.

Hattie and Nick beeped the car horn cheerfully as they drove into the neat little driveway. Hattie drove fast and when she stopped gravel swished up round her tyres. Lydia watched this from the garden and saw her brother and sister jump out of the car arguing amicably. They had always been a pair, born four years after her, but only a year apart from each other.

'Hattie! Nick!' She waved at them so that they came straight to the garden.

'You are enormous!' cried Hattie. 'I am jealous.'

'Perhaps that's why we've been summoned to lunch,' said Nick, 'to watch you giving birth.'

'It's not due for months yet,' protested Lydia.

'But why this family lunch?' Hattie flicked her hair about as if to air it. 'We've been arguing about it all the way down.'

'I've no idea,' Lydia admitted.

Now Dorothy was hurrying down the garden path, arms wide and welcoming. 'Darlings! Sneaking down here without saying hallo to me. What rotters!'

Lydia bent down and picked a primrose. Then two or three more and a couple of leaves. They would look pretty on her dressing-table in London. Behind her Nick was complimenting his mother on her looks and saying he would have brought his current girlfriend except that he had a feeling this lunch was especially family.

'No feelings please,' Dorothy was a little coy. 'Feelings will have to wait for the bouillabaisse.'

'Bouillabaisse!' shrieked Hattie. 'Then it must be an important announcement.'

Lydia followed them back to the house. Nick had his arm round his mother and Hattie was entertaining her with stories of her latest job as bicycle courier. 'I am the only woman in the team, mother, the only one.'

'Darling, you're so brave!'

Lydia's feet dragged and she sniffed the primroses rather desperately.

Ronny and Carey had laid the dining-room table. They had decorated each plate with a large cracker. 'We forgot them at Christmas,' explained Ronny, 'so it seemed a good idea to use them up.' He caught his wife's eye and returned her frown with a wink.

Lydia was not at all hungry. The smell of the fish made her feel queasy. She sipped from her wine and wondered why everyone else seemed in such particularly good spirits.

After the plates had been cleared away, Ronny tapped his glass with a knife and exclaimed with quite untypical dominance, 'Now is the time!'

Lydia felt her baby do a backwards shove and bile rose in her mouth. 'I'm sorry. I think I . . .' She half stood.

'It won't take a minute, darling.' Dorothy gave the sort of commanding smile that made Lydia sit down at once.

'To cut a long story short,' Ronny peered about him like a conjuror and Lydia raised her hand to her mouth. 'To cut a long story short,' he began again, 'your mother and I have decided to sell this house and move to Spain.' Since no one spoke, he continued, 'We had an extraordinarily good offer quite out of the blue. Too good to refuse, we thought. And then, as you know, we've always loved the sun. So now that you're all grown-up . . .'

Lydia thought she was going to be sick. And then knew she was going to be sick. She dashed from the dining room and just made the downstairs lavatory in time.

Carey found her there, no longer heaving but tears running down her cheeks. He put his hand on her shoulder and then reached for a piece of lavatory paper to stem the flow.

'How could she? Now. How could she leave me?'

Carey thought it a good thing she could speak and patted her shoulder kindly. 'I know. I know. I can't say I think much of the timing. But I suppose they had no choice if there was this terrific offer.'

'But now! Her first grandchild.' Images of the pretty baby clothes they had sorted through the afternoon before made Lydia start to cry again. 'How could she not have given me the tiniest clue? Prepared me a little.'

'Perhaps she felt guilty.'

'Lydia, where are you?' Dorothy came across the hall, calling. 'Lydia, darling, are you all right?'

'She knows how much she's hurt me,' whispered Lydia fiercely. 'I don't want to see her.'

'Sshh.' Carey went out and shut the door. Lydia stood up and looked at herself in the mirror. She had always appeared pink and healthy in that mirror since a child but now she seemed so pale as to be green.

'It was the fish,' she heard Carey explaining. 'Nothing serious. I'll take her upstairs to lie down. You go back and finish lunch.'

Lydia lay on her bed and stared at the ceiling. Carey sat on a chair by the bed and held her hand. 'You've still got me and the baby,' he said with a minimum of irony.

'It's the shock.' Lydia was trying very hard not to cry.

'It's not as if over the last years you've spent all that much time in her company.'

'But she's always been there.'

'She'll still be there. In Spain. Probably Carey did not mean to be cruel. 'Doubtless she can come over for the baby's birth. Or perhaps they won't even have gone by then.'

'It will never be the same.'

Carey stood up and walked over to the window. He was not hard hearted. It pained him to see Lydia suffering. For he knew it was genuine suffering.

'She still loves you.' He looked out at the sunlight streaking the grass.

'She doesn't love me. Not in the way I thought she loved me. If she loved me, she would never ever sell our home and live in Spain.'

'Perhaps Ronny wants to move.'

Lydia didn't bother to answer this. She turned on her side and closed her eyes.

Carey continued to stand by the window. Soon his attention was caught by a fluttering sound and he saw a butterfly had become trapped between the two panes of glass where the upper pane was pulled down. There was just room for him to ease his fingers into the space and encourage the butterfly upwards. As it was about to fly away, he cupped his hands.

Lydia couldn't imagine she would ever want to move again. She felt as if her whole life had been based on a false premise. The word 'traitor' sounded over and over in her head.

'Open your eyes.' She could sense Carey standing over her. 'Open them!'

Reluctantly Lydia raised her lids and as she did so a flash of brilliant colour circled round her head.

'That's how I feel about you.' Carey watched the butterfly too. 'About you and our baby and our future together. You are the first butterfly of the year.'

Lydia sat up. For a moment it struck her as unbearably sad that Carey should have found her mother's butterfly and brought it to her. And then she saw his face and, understanding what he was offering, she took a deep breath and stretched up her arms.

Shirley Lowe
and Angela Ince

Glasnost

Shirley Lowe and Angela Ince met each other early on in their working lives and kept in touch through job changes and raising families. Then, in 1985, they wrote a comic novel together, Losing Control, and went on to write Swapping and Taking Over. Funny, sophisticated and very clever, their writing presents a gleeful kaleidoscope of life; just when the characters think they know it all, they get all shaken up and the picture changes. That's exactly what happens in Glasnost. Shirley and Angela both live in London: 'Near enough to get in touch when the plot thickens,' they say, 'but far enough apart to stay on speaking terms.'

They first became aware of Dean and Thelma at Samarkand airport.

'There,' Edward said smugly to Joy, 'are a couple of American tourists who could have come straight from Central Casting.'

The Richardsons were very good at looking at tourists and despising them; they themselves, of course, were travellers.

Other people in Gerrards Cross went to the Bahamas, Corfu and (of all places) the South of France. Package tours, that sort of thing. At early autumn dinner parties, when friends produced photographs of 'me outside the Uffizi with that nice woman from Edinburgh whose wallet was stolen,' the Richardsons retaliated with portraits of gnarled old men with slanting eyes leaning against mules: 'Han Toi, our guide over the foothills. Such a character when you got to know him.'

Home videos of children learning water-skiing at Frejus were effortlessly trumped by two hours of Joy and Edward travelling by elephant up one side of Thailand and down the other. 'You don't want to go to Bangkok, of course; everybody goes there.'

As Joy and Edward never tired of explaining, you get a totally new perspective when you are accepted into an alien culture. Other people went abroad for the sun and the food; the Richardsons went abroad for the people.

This year it was to be Samarkand. 'After all,' as Edward had said on the 8.19 to Waterloo to a largely unresponsive audience, 'we've all seen the Hermitage and Red Square. Joy and I thought we'd break entirely new ground.'

They were slightly put out when they discovered that they would be staying at the same hotel as Thelma and

Dean; neither of them looked remotely like a trail-breaker.

Thelma first spoke to Joy in the ladies' cloakroom, not an auspicious beginning to any relationship, since they were both heaving at the time.

Joy, an enthusiastic and adventurous traveller, had one weak spot: other countries' lavatories. She always packed twice the number of rolls of good old Andrex that were recommended in guide books, and caught herself wondering, when watching a documentary about Lady Hester Stanhope, how she had Managed.

'I have some toilet tissues in my purse, dear,' said Thelma. 'It's something you learn when you've travelled as much as Dean and I have.'

'Thank you, I have some of my own,' said Joy, turning on a hot tap out of which nothing came. 'Are you staying in Samarkand long?' she added, rather hoping that Thelma would say, 'no, we're going to Bokhara tomorrow.'

'Three days, and we have taken the precaution of hiring a personal guide . . . say, I have actually found a tap which functions, you'd better get over here before it changes its mind.'

When Joy got back to the Intourist waiting room, slightly pink about the eyes, Edward looked at her sympathetically. 'How was it?' he said.

'Unspeakable. A hole in the ground with a foothold either side. I say, Ted, those Americans from Central Casting, I met the wife in the loo. She said we should join up.'

And indeed, Dean, shepherded by Thelma, was already forging his way towards them.

While Joy didn't mind Thelma, Edward took an instant and sustained dislike to Dean, who spoke disparagingly about his camera; it was not, apparently, in the same technologically advanced class as Dean's Hasselblad. Edward took this badly, since he prided himself on his really excellent photographs. It was a pity that not many people seemed to want to look at them.

As they waited, interminably, for the taxi that had been

promised 'in five minutes', Joy had the uneasy feeling they were being watched.

'That man over there,' she whispered to Edward, 'the attractive one in the black leather jacket and the sable hat, he's looking at us.'

'KGB, probably,' said Edward. 'I say, hadn't we better do something about the taxi?'

'Leave it to me,' said Dean. He went over to the desk and palmed a packet of Marlboroughs across it. 'I'd be very grateful,' he said to the Intourist girl, 'if you could hurry things up.'

She put down her lipstick and make-up mirror, dimpled charmingly, and slid the cigarettes into a drawer already crammed with packets of Marlborough. 'Of course. Please sit down. It will be here in five minutes.' She picked up her lipstick again.

'Excuse me,' the man in the sable hat was at Edward's side, 'I happen to know that the Intourist taxi has broken down. I saw Mikhail pushing it into the garage on my way here.'

'Why didn't that girl tell us?' said Edward.

'They are trained to say nothing, that is the backbone of the Communist system,' said the man quite loudly.

Edward looked round nervously. Last time they were in Russia armed soldiers manned the airports, and nobody made jokes about Communism, or anything else.

'My name is Dima Rashidov,' said the man, bowing politely. 'I am going back into Samarkand now. Perhaps I might take you in my car?'

Dean looked wary. Thelma picked up her vanity case and put it on her knee.

Edward flicked an eye towards Joy, who flicked back an almost imperceptible nod. In her view, a man who looked like Jack Lemmon in *The Apartment* had to be trustworthy.

'How very kind of you. I'm Edward Richardson, and this is my wife, Joy.'

Dima picked up Joy's suitcase.

'Getting into the car of a total stranger?' hissed Dean.

'Boy, are you asking for trouble.'

The two couples met up again in the hotel bar after dinner. Joy and Edward had been assigned a waiter who spoke English. This meant, they found, that he could say 'beef'; so they had cold beef with cream and mushrooms for the first course, and hot beef with cream and mushrooms for the second.

'We certainly didn't think we'd see you again,' said Dean.

'Oh, we had a wonderful time,' said Joy. 'Dima took us to see a working mosque on the way here. And he's going to show us a collective farm tomorrow.'

'We were advised to hire an official guide,' said Dean. 'You can't be too careful.'

'Nonsense,' said Edward, 'Dima is a professor of English at the University. He told us so.'

'And he's just been to America on a lecture tour,' said Joy.

'Oh, really?' said Dean. 'Did he tell you that, too?'

Perhaps Dean was right, Joy thought, as she and Edward climbed into Dima's Lada next morning. He was accompanied by a burly, unshaven man he introduced as, 'Alexander, my older brother.' Alexander spoke no English, but smiled a lot, revealing a mouthful of neglected teeth.

'Alexander says it is a privilege to meet my English friends,' said Dima, crashing into gear and casually pulling out in front of a dishevelled lorry which hooted angrily. Alexander laughed loudly.

They did the old city of Samarkand in the morning. The mosques and mausoleums in Registan Square and the Street of Tombs were as breathtaking as the guide books promised, but Joy, jostled by biblical crowds, felt an intruder in her sensible Jaeger coat. In the teeming market old men in quilted jackets and turbans gazed at them with fierce disinterest, gypsy children clutched avidly at the hem of Joy's coat, and traders beseeched them to buy.

'Do look,' said Joy, 'saffron. And only 30 kopeks a jar. That's three pence in our money, what brilliant presents.' She bought ten jars and gave the spice seller three roubles. 'I say, Dima, do tell him how expensive it is in our country.'

Dima looked appalled and spoke sternly to the spice seller, who shrugged his shoulders and threw in another five jars. Alexander slapped Edward on the shoulder, and laughed loudly.

'Why do they have all that raw meat hanging up at the side of the road?' said Joy.

They had left Samarkand and were driving up into the foothills of the Chupan-Ata.

She wished she hadn't asked; Dima, who was driving slowly in the middle of the road, turned right round to tell her. Alexander turned right round, too, and laughed, which meant that the only people with their eyes on the road were Edward and Joy.

'It is the new private enterprise,' said Dima proudly. 'Now, people who work on the land are allowed their own patch of ground, to grow and sell their own produce. We Uzbeks are never short of good food. Not like Moscow. If those Russians had their way, they would bleed us dry.' He muttered to Alexander who answered at length. 'Alexander says that soon we will have our own international airport, big hotels, business conferences, independence.' Alexander spoke again. 'He says we will get much money from the West,' said Dima.

So when they stopped for lunch – piles of delicious grilled chicken and no cutlery – Edward felt he should insist on paying.

Dima wouldn't hear of it. Alexander laughed and shook his head. 'It is a pleasure for me to talk to English people,' said Dima. 'In summer I even take my students into the streets and request tourists to have conversations with them.'

'In that case,' said Edward, 'we must insist on taking you out to dinner this evening. You really have been so kind.'

Dima wouldn't hear of that, either. 'In Uzbekistan we say that your guest is even more important than your father. It would be an insult to me if you did not come to my home. My wife, Natasha, would never forgive me.'

The Rashidovs' house was in an ill-lit, seedy street; Joy wondered, as they drew up outside, what Dean would have made of it.

Dima ushered them through the door. 'Take off your shoes when you come in, please.' He handed them decrepit carpet slippers, and they shuffled past a tiny bathroom, through a kitchen not much bigger, into a sitting room decorated with rampantly floral carpets and wallpaper. It didn't look like a professor's house to Joy. The room was dwarfed by a giant television set and a heavy, dark, wood room divider, on which sat the family treasures and an aggressively new ghetto blaster. Behind it, Joy glimpsed a double bed with a satin quilt and a flounced dressing table.

'All this space is a luxury in our country,' Dima said, 'one of the advantages of being a professor. Ah, here is my wife.' He looked with great love at the plain woman coming through the door, unbuttoning her tight cloth coat. 'Natasha, I have brought you visitors.' He spoke as though he was presenting her with a bunch of rare orchids, rather than unexpected dinner guests.

'Dima,' said Joy, 'please tell Natasha we don't want to be a nuisance . . .'

Natasha smiled. 'I teach English at the school, but I do not speak so good as my husband.' She shook their hands formally. 'Guests are never a nuisance in Uzbekistan. Where is my apron, Dima?'

An hour later they were sitting around the kitchen table, now laden with a selection of salads, meats, fish and pickled vegetables, chunks of bread and bottles of vodka.

'Two years ago we could not have done this,' said Dima. 'If I had invited you into my home I would have had a visit from the KGB; who are they, why did they come to your house, what did you say to them? And so on and so forth . . . *Glasnost*!' He raised his glass.

'*Glasnost*!' said Joy and Ted, clinking their glasses against his. It was the first of many toasts that evening.

'What a delicious meal,' said Joy, wondering if she would have room for coffee.

'If only I had known you were coming I could have prepared a proper dinner,' said Natasha. She opened the oven, lifted out a steaming bowl of white cabbage and minced meat, and ladled it generously on to their plates with a large wooden spoon.

'What a lovely spoon,' said Joy. The cabbage smelt absolutely delicious, but she didn't feel up to talking about food for the moment.

Dima leapt up eagerly and made for the door. 'How splendid. I carved that spoon in my workroom, and I have another just like it for you.'

'Oh, I couldn't really . . . ' Joy protested.

'You've done so much for us already,' said Edward.

Dima returned with the spoon and presented it to Joy. 'For the beautiful English lady. Natasha, is it not time for you to make the pilau?'

'Our national dish,' said Natasha, putting on her apron again. It will only take me half an hour.' She began chopping onions and meat.

Dima opened another bottle of vodka. 'To the English, who will always be our friends.'

'To the Uzbeks, the most generous friends in the world,' said Edward, who was beginning to see the point of all this toasting.

They heard the front door crash open. 'It will be my son, Slava,' said Dima. A small boy with tear-stained cheeks ran in and flung himself into his mother's arms, sobbing as he spoke.

'Disaster!' said Dima. 'Slava's bicycle has been stolen.' He picked up the boy and hugged him. 'It was a birthday present, a prized possession. He was the only boy in his class to own one.'

'I say, what rotten luck,' said Edward. 'Will he get it back, do you think?'

Dima shook his head. 'Most unlikely. The bicycle cost ninety roubles, a fortune. I told him he must always padlock it carefully.' He kissed Slava, and put him down. 'But enough of sadness. We must enjoy our pilau.'

It was past midnight when the evening ended. 'How can we ever thank you enough?' said Joy, putting on her shoes. 'Oh, Natasha, what a beautiful rug.'

Dima looked fondly at the small square red rug which lit up the drab hallway. 'It is a Bokhara, and has been in my family for generations,' he said.

'Quite splendid,' said Edward. 'Now Dima, Natasha . . . I hope you are free for dinner tomorrow night?'

'Tomorrow night,' said Dima, 'Alexander has invited you to his house.'

Dean and Thelma joined the Richardsons for breakfast and told them more than they wanted to know about the Observatory of Ulag-Beg.

'We had a wonderful day, too,' said Joy. 'Dima took us to the market and up into the mountains, and then his wife cooked us an amazing dinner.'

'And they gave Joy a hand-carved spoon,' said Edward.

'Wonder what they're after?' said Dean.

'The Uzbeks are famed for their hospitality, actually,' said Joy. 'Everybody knows that.'

'I bet they're planning a visit to England,' said Thelma.

'We've invited them, of course,' said Joy, 'but heaven knows if they'll ever get a visa.'

'I wish there was some way we could repay them,' said Edward.

'I'm sure they'll think of something,' said Dean.

'I did have an idea,' said Joy, 'poor Slava's bicycle . . . '
She turned to Thelma, 'Their son's bicycle was stolen
yesterday. He was so upset.'

'And I bet they just happened to mention how much it
cost,' said Dean. 'Talk about innocents abroad. Come along,
Thelma, our guide will be waiting.'

'How sad to be so cynical,' said Joy, 'what a lot of pleasure
they must miss.'

'Wasn't there a bicycle shop on the way to the market?'
said Edward, 'with the new rate of exchange ninety roubles
can't be much.'

Joy hugged him. 'Darling, I do love you. Let's get it
now.'

When Dima arrived to take them to Alexander's house, they
were standing on the hotel steps with the bicycle between
them.

'Oh, Dima,' said Joy. 'I do hope it's the right size for
Slava.'

'For Slava? But why?'

'A small thing in return for so much kindness,' said
Edward.

'Slava will, of course, be altogether over the moon.' Dima
looked at the bicycle sorrowfully, 'but it was not necessary.
Your friendship was enough.'

The night before they were due to leave Samarkand, Dima
turned up at their hotel with a badly wrapped bundle under
his arm.

'It is yours,' he said to Joy.

'Oh, Dima, thank you! What is it?' She unwrapped the
parcel.

'Your Bokhara rug! Oh, no, Dima.'

'You admired it,' said Dima.

'But we couldn't, could we, Ted? It belongs to your
family.'

'Terribly kind of you, Dima,' said Edward, 'but honestly
. . . it's too much.'

'Slava is so pleased with his bicycle,' said Dima.

'But that's quite different,' said Joy.

'Please. Now you will remember your friends in Uzbekistan when you are back in England.' He wrapped his arms
round both of them. 'I will brook no more argument on the
subject. And I will be back tomorrow morning to take you
to the airport.'

When they boarded the plane back to Moscow, Edward had
the little rug rolled up under his arm as hand baggage. There
had been no convenient way of packing it, and anyway, Joy
didn't want to let it out of her sight.

'Did you manage it, about the vodka?' Joy said.

Edward looked pleased with himself. 'Left a box of a
dozen bottles in the boot. Dima didn't suspect a thing.'

As soon as the plane was up and they were out of their
seatbelts, Edward unrolled the rug and laid it across their
laps. It seemed to Joy to glow with the generous impulse of
their Uzbek friends.

'I see you've been to the bazaar, too,' said a passing air
hostess. 'We have six of those rugs on the flight, today.'

'The bazaar?' said Joy, 'Oh, no, this is . . . '

Dean, who was sitting across the aisle from them, with
Thelma clutching his arm (she only really trusted PanAm
and TWA), leant over and turned up a corner of the rug.
'If this was a genuine Bokhara, it'd set you back, oh, three
thousand dollars. But these modern Afghan copies, I sure
hope you didn't pay more than a few roubles for it, it's
pretty well worn.'

'But it *is* an old Bokhara,' said Joy, 'look at it, it's
beautiful.'

'Joy, dear,' said Thelma, 'Dean is in floor furnishings,
back home. What he doesn't know about carpets . . . '

And now that Joy looked at it again, the rug that had
gleamed and shimmered in the Rashidov's hallway seemed
flatter and diminished, as if it felt the weight of their
disparaging glances. The subtle colour, Joy now saw, was
harsh and chemical, and the tiny flaws she had assumed were

mistakes made by peasant hands many years ago, were, in reality, errors missed by some bored factory inspector.

Edward rolled up the rug and put it on the baggage shelf.

'Oh, well,' Joy whispered to him, 'never mind, Ted, we had a lot of fun. We'll put the bicycle and the vodka down to experience.'

Edward fidgeted and looked out of the window. There was something he hadn't told Joy. He had wrapped up his treasured Nikon and hidden it beneath the vodka bottles, with a note saying, 'To the best of new friends. Until we meet again in England.'

The letter from the Rashidovs arrived just after Christmas. They could not wait, it said, to put pen to paper and tell their dear friends of their wonderful news. They had visas! It was all arranged; Alexander and his wife would look after Slava, Dima and Natasha had obtained leave of absence; now all that was necessary was to arrange details. They planned to come in April; a beautiful month, they understood, in the southern district of Britain. Lake Windermere, Marks and Spencer, the Changing of the Guard, there were so many things they wished to see in the company of their dear friends.

'They've got their nerve,' said Edward shortly. He had convinced himself, over the months, that he had been cold-bloodedly conned out of a child's bicycle, a dozen bottles of vodka and a very expensive Nikon.

It took Joy three days to answer the letter. Though the message was quite simple – the Richardsons were very sorry, but they would be out of England in April – it was an awkward letter to write. And when Dima wrote back, saying they could delay their visit until May, Joy thankfully decided that the kindest thing, really, would be not to answer it at all.

Anyway, they had more important things to think about. Emily, their only child, had met the Real Thing, and was bringing him home to meet them. He was, apparently, amazing:

'So kind, and so funny and so nice. He's an auctioneer. Terribly clever. Oh, Mum, wait till you see him.'

Jake came to dinner, and turned out to be perfectly pleasant.

'I think he likes you,' Emily said, in a congratulatory manner when Jake left the room after dinner. 'Dad, you won't talk about golf, will you? Sssh, he's coming back.'

Jake walked into the room with the Rashidov Bokhara cradled across his arms.

'I say, I know it's none of my business, but you had this in your downstairs loo. You really shouldn't let people walk on it, you know . . . '

'Oh that old thing,' said Joy, 'we picked it up in Samarkand.'

'I'm told it's a modern Afghan copy,' said Edward.

'Whoever told you that?' said Jake, laying the rug on the floor and gazing at it with reverence. 'I don't know how much you've got it insured for, but . . . '

'Insured?' said Edward. 'Why on earth should I insure it? Kind of you to take an interest, but to a knowledgeable eye . . . '

'Dad,' said Emily. 'For heaven's sake, Jake works at Sotheby's. He's their expert in Oriental carpets.'

The Richardsons are going to the South of France (of all places) this summer. For the sun and the food.

Bel Mooney

Over the Road

Bel Mooney, a Liverpudlian by birth, made her name as a newspaper columnist before concentrating on novels for adults and children. Her most recent was The Fourth of July, *a thought-provoking examination of the world of soft-core pornography. Bel is also an accomplished television and radio interviewer: currently she has a series on Radio 4 and is planning a major series for Channel 4. The inspiration for* Over the Road *came in Paris. 'I saw a young married couple who were very much in love . . . and very plain. It made me think how beautiful people who have no inkling of real love can be very arrogant about those who do . . .'*

They moved in quite early one morning. Simon had gone so I was pulling off the bedlinen when I heard the van changing gear, then the piercing chatter of its reversing, just opposite my flat.

The furniture the men were carrying was predictable. Sofa and two armchairs in a chintzy print, reproduction dining suite in rosewood, a few antique tables and, last of all, the double bed – a large, deep divan, with a padded headboard in pale blue fabric. King-size, I thought, so they've plenty of room to escape from each other. I never wanted to be married.

At that moment the phone rang. It was Simon. 'I just want to tell you I love you,' he said.

'Oh – yes. Thanks,' I said. One of my nails was splitting.

'What about tonight?' he asked.

'No, darling, I've got to stay in. My mother's going to ring, and you know what she gets like when I'm never in,' I said.

'Why not ring her?'

I yawned. 'She's ringing me. It's arranged.'

'Look, Caro . . . ' Simon was beginning, with that note of annoyed supplication I detest.

'Sweetie, I *have* to go . . . ' I said, and put the phone down.

You can tell people by their furniture. I go to value houses for sale, and play a game before I enter, guessing from the curtains what the people will look like, what sort of colours they will have chosen, how the selection of Formica or pine or black ash in a kitchen is a sure indication of the human heart. Of course, knowing the agent is coming, some of them tidy up – another indicator. If underwear is still strewn on the bedroom chair, and there is a coffee cup from the night before on the glass table, you know you are with the confident upper classes. The rest are afraid. They want to impress, even though they may never meet you again.

I knew, even before I saw them, that the people over the road would never leave underwear on the bedroom floor. Just before I left for work I saw them come out together, and stand briefly on the step, arm in arm. 'Mr and Mrs Dormouse,' I thought, and smiled. He was tall, she was short, but both were bespectacled, in identical baggy jeans and navy sweaters. Mrs Dormouse had a neat, straight brown bob, and Mr Dormouse's hair was curly, giving him the air of a rumpled schoolboy. He was certainly the more attractive of the two, although that was giving a hamster the edge on a mouse.

The next day was Saturday. I woke early, and leaned on one elbow, looking at Johnny as he lay asleep. He was certainly marvellously good-looking, but I sighed. My clothes lay all about the floor, mingled with his. Easing myself off the futon I picked them up, leaving his where they lay, and threw them all into the linen basket. Then I went to shower.

After a few moments he put his hands playfully round the curtain, seeking me. 'Can I come in?' he whispered, in that voice which flattered me over restaurant tables, and excited me before bed. 'No,' I snapped, 'Look, Johnny, you've got to go. I can't even give you breakfast, because my mother's arriving in half an hour.'

'Can't I meet her?' he asked.

'Don't be ridiculous,' I said.

When he had gone, looking slightly sulky and begging me to see him soon, I made coffee, put on a record and stretched out on the kelim, looking at the ceiling. I love to be alone in my flat, amongst my cushions, low chairs, good rugs and paintings (I buy something each year, taking advice). With no one to talk to me or come up behind to hug me or ask me for something I simply can't give, I feel myself again.

Of course my mother wasn't coming. I see her as little as possible, which makes me guilty, of course, but there is nothing to be done.

About forty minutes after Johnny left I heard my buzzer. 'I'm sorry to disturb you,' said the crackly female voice on the intercom, 'I'm from over the road. Just moved in . . . '

She stood on the doorstep, looking pink and shy. Today she wore a longish gathered skirt in a tweedy material, and a plain grey sweater, and looked dumpier than at first. Her glasses were round. Her unattractiveness made me shiver with relief. To look at that face in the mirror, to be imprisoned within that form. . . .

'I pressed the three bells,' she said, 'but you're the only person in.'

I explained that the other two flats, one beneath me, one above, belonged to businessmen who travel a good deal.

'Yes, it must be the same with the houses each side of us,' she sighed, 'because I can't get a reply. Well, anyway, I only really came to introduce myself. I'm Jane Renshaw, and my husband's name is Paul. We thought, as we're neighbours now . . . '

'Oh . . . yes . . . It's nice to meet you,' I said, feeling at a loss. Nobody ever does that in this street.

Jane Renshaw was looking disappointed. 'We've come from a little village near Basingstoke, and everybody knew each other. But Paul got this wonderful chance of a partnership – he's a solicitor, you see – and we thought it would be an experience, until we want to start a family. Then we'll move out again, I expect.' She went slightly pink, and looked momentarily confused, as if already she sensed that people don't tell each other things like that.

'What do you do?' she asked, after a pause.

'I work with Barrett and Brown – you know them? They're the Estate Agents just down the road.'

'I'm a teacher – Primary – so it was easy for me to find a job.'

Just then her husband appeared at their front door, immediately opposite. 'I've made coffee,' he called. 'Come over – both of you.'

I suppose that was the beginning. Ten minutes later I was sitting at the small, varnished pine table in their white kitchen, drinking coffee from a pottery mug and telling them amusing stories about my job. I glittered at them, even in the ordinary morning light, dressed in my velour leggings and the baggy matching top which kept slipping off one shoulder – I couldn't help it.

'You've got a good-sized kitchen,' I said, in a pause, guessing correctly that Jane Renshaw liked to cook, and would leap up immediately, pulling open cupboards with pride.

During that moment Paul Renshaw and I were alone at the table, and I leaned forward, deliberately letting my bare shoulder show. It had nothing to do with *him*, this need to dazzle a mousy solicitor with rather thick gold-rimmed glasses, wearing ill-fitting cord jeans and a chain-store sweater.

Anyway, it was then I felt my first tremor of disquiet. Because as my hair swept forward over my face, and I tossed it back lazily, with one hand, knowing it would slide forward again and I could glance up at him through its curtain – as I did that, Paul was looking fixedly at his wife's behind, bunched up as it was in her saggy, unfashionable skirt, as she bent over the oven to display its size. He actually *stared* at her with an avidity that was almost indecent. I could have been a hundred miles away.

Then, when she returned to the table to refill our cups, she leaned against him briefly, and seemed to meet an answering pressure from his body. That was all. But there was something in that slight movement, the small moment of melding, which left me feeling uncomfortable.

I didn't see much of the Renshaws in the following weeks. My life was full: work each day, then out most evenings, eating in restaurants with Simon or Johnny or David or William, and then occasionally with Alexander Brown, my boss's son. Alexander was newly married which gave his hurried visits to my flat an added piquancy. Sometimes, pulling the curtains at one in the morning, I would forget, in a terrifying moment of amnesia, which man lay on my futon, waiting. Then I would glance across to the Renshaws' darkened house feeling a savage pleasure that my life was not like theirs.

About five weeks after the Renshaws had arrived, I treated myself to an evening in, to put a pale-auburn rinse on my hair, and generally recover from too much champagne and too much sex.

It was October; at nine-thirty the street was dark – the gauzy purple of autumn which always makes me restless. I stood by my window, just behind the curtain, gazing absent-mindedly into the road, when my eyes were drawn to the Renshaws' house. Their sitting-room light went out, and a few minutes later the bedroom window blazed – exactly opposite where I stood. As I watched, a figure crossed the room, perfectly visible through the filmy nets. It was Mrs Dormouse.

Entertained, I thought how typical that she would go to bed so early, wearing a flowery nightie, no doubt, and curled up with a good book. She went as if to pull the heavy curtains, but then turned suddenly towards the figure who came behind her, curving her body into his arms with a movement that was almost desperate. 'Aha, a lover!' I thought with amazement, not really believing the notion. Then, a second later I recognized the man. It was, of course, Paul Renshaw.

As I watched they swayed together, almost *cramming* each with each, until at last they broke apart. Then, very slowly and deliberately, with a movement of indescribable tenderness and sensuality, Mr Dormouse raised his wife's arms above her head, and peeled off her sweater. Suddenly they realized the curtains were open, and he turned quickly to jerk them shut. I was left staring at the warmth of light through fabric, reminded suddenly of walking up the garden path at home when I was a child, knowing that the fire would be lit and the tea on the table – that everything wholly comforting lay behind the curtained sitting-room window, to be possessed by me, in a matter of minutes.

But not now. I stood there alone, imagining (I couldn't help it) what was going on in that room. The bed had been large and soft-looking . . . And now, there they were, Mr and Mrs Dormouse, Paul and Jane Renshaw, making love. I had seen the beginning, seen their folding together in passion, and now pictured the consummation, in the warmth of that king-size bed – whilst I stood alone at the window, before walking through to lie stiffly on my futon, staring up at nothing.

It is hard to explain why this shocked me as much as it did. They were a married couple of five years' standing; naturally they went to bed together. But I found myself thinking of little else all the next day.

The next evening I stayed in again and at nine-thirty I lingered near the window to see if they would go upstairs early once more. They did. But this time Jane Renshaw went straight to close the curtains, so I could not see them embrace. Yet in my mind I did. I saw it clearly.

The pattern of my evenings changed. Cancelling date after date, I would find myself drawn to the window, fascinated, to spy on the Renshaws.

The light would stay on for a long, long time; no fumbling in the dark for these two, no hasty coupling under the bedclothes before immediate sleep. I pictured their spectacles resting side by side on the bedside table, and Mr and Mrs Dormouse fuzzily reaching for each other, not able to see properly – which was just as well, considering how unglamorous they both were . . . But such attempts to ridicule my neighbours worked no longer. No – I understood that what went on in that room was grave and deliberate as much as it was joyous; each night they returned to celebrate each other's bodies. It was something I had never known.

Occasionally they would be so absorbed in each other that they would forget to draw the curtains at all; then I would witness their kisses, through the nets, the movement of their bodies like an achingly erotic ballet, before the gradual withdrawal into the depths of the room, so that I could see nothing. As the days passed, and I went through this performance most evenings, I realized with horror what I was becoming.

From time to time Jane would wave cheerfully to me, and once she shouted, 'We must get together.' Indeed, I became consumed with the desire to meet them again, to talk to them as if such contact would give me access to . . . but what?

So I wrote a note and put it through their letterbox, inviting them to supper the coming Saturday. Pink with pleasure, she appeared on my doorstep to accept. When the day came I went to a great deal of trouble: smoked salmon with herb mousse, lemon chicken accompanied by basmati rice and salad, dolcelatte torte with seeded bread, and some excellent grapes. There was mineral water and Chablis – plenty of that. To begin, I opened a bottle of Moët, leaving the Renshaws' Bulgarian Cabernet on the kitchen table.

Why was I taking all this trouble? It was hard to explain to myself. Clearly the Renshaws had expected me to invite a man; they glanced questioningly at the table set for three. It occurred to me suddenly that they might be disappointed, might have wanted to meet 'people'. But how could I introduce them to those I knew? Simon or Johnny or Tricia at work would have taken one look at this meek, matching couple and yawned. Besides, they were mine.

Jane exclaimed over the meal, whilst Paul ate in silent concentration. I could not avoid staring at him; there was a rumpled, vulnerable professorial look about him so much at odds with the lean, naked figure I had glimpsed briefly through the nets, it made me dizzy with curiosity.

I let my knee brush his leg beneath the table, as delicately as my perfume tinged the air about his head. When I crossed my legs the purple silk of my trousers made a tiny slithering, sensuous sound I knew he must have heard. Mrs Dormouse was wearing a navy-blue dress my mother would have described as 'shirtwaister'. For that matter, my mother might have worn it. No make-up sullied her pleasant round face, and her hair was brushed smooth like a cap.

Jane was talking about the local church they had found, with evangelical tendencies of which they approved. They went every Sunday, she said, and it was rather like the atmosphere in their church back in Basingstoke. This was too much. Repelled, confused, I realized suddenly that I *knew* nothing any more; felt out of my depth in a conversation which stumbled on. She told anecdotes about school, and Paul watched her tenderly. 'She gets very tired,' he said to me.

Was that a hint? I wondered.

'Please, if you want to go . . . ' I began, biting off the phrase, ' . . . to bed early,' not wanting to put the idea in his head. 'I mean, if *you* want to slip home, Jane . . . '

'We're not late-night people,' said Paul.

At eleven, as if by a prearranged signal, they both yawned. 'Well, it's been lovely, but . . . ' she said.

'Past our bedtime,' he finished.

'Yes,' I said drily, already feeling the emptiness of the flat close around me once more.

That night I noticed with satisfaction that their bedroom light went off immediately. Too tired, tonight, I thought, feeling a spasm of satisfaction that *I* was the cause of that exhaustion.

A few days later I saw Paul in the market, wandering from stall to stall, buying vegetables with slow deliberation. I watched him for a while, noticing the ease of his movements, the laconic hunch of his shoulders as he frowned with concentration over a tumble of avocados, reaching to touch one – assessing ripeness. His fingers were long.

Turning, he saw me, and I felt myself colour, like a schoolgirl following a boy she has a crush on. And was that it? I wondered, with amazement, only to reject the thought at once. I knew I did not *love* this man from over the road. I simply wanted to know what it would be like to have him turn to me, as he turned to her; I needed to experience that mystery I had spied through curtains.

He was talking about the price of food, and I kept my eyes fixed on his all the while, as if fascinated by the subject of tomatoes. Then he said, 'Anyway, I'll be cooking for myself for a couple of days.'

'Why?'

'Jane's father's ill. It's not easy for her to take time off school, but the headmistress understands. He's really bad. She's going to see them.'

'Oh – I'm sorry,' I said, feeling exultant. 'But you could come and have a meal with me, if you like.'

'That's kind,' he said, 'but I'm snowed under at work. Some really complicated cases. I told Jane it'll be a good opportunity for me to catch up. It's peaceful working at home late at night.'

'Ah, burning the old midnight oil,' I said, foolishly.

I saw her leave, clutching a small, battered brown holdall. They hugged each other on the doorstep for a long time; when she turned to the taxi I thought I saw tears, but it might have been the low sun on her thick lenses. That evening I glanced from the window from time to time; their front room light was on until well after midnight. Mr Dormouse really was working. I wondered if the insistent throbbing of my loud Ravel might carry across the street.

All through the next day I brooded, wondering what to do. Then something Simon or Johnny had said slipped unbidden into my head: 'If you want something, all you have to do is ask.' Now it seemed a profound truth.

I was home by 5.45, and watched for Paul Renshaw. At 6.30 he was standing on his doorstep, fumbling for his keys. I allowed half an hour, and then I telephoned.

'Paul – it's Caro, from over the road. Look, I don't want to be a nuisance, but I've got a problem, and I wondered . . .'

'Oh? What sort of problem?' he asked.

'Well, it's a sort of legal matter. To do with my mother. You see, she's made a will, and I'm not sure if we're doing the right thing . . . Oh, I'd much rather explain properly, if you can spare me half an hour. I wouldn't impose, but she gets easily upset because she's been feeling ill just lately, and if I don't phone her tomorrow . . . ' I allowed myself a sharp little intake of breath, and heard the answering concern in his voice.

'Look, of course. I understand. Shall I pop over?'

'No,' I said, 'I'll come over to you. In about an hour?' When I put the phone down I glanced across at the Renshaws' dark bedroom window. *There*, not here. That was what I wanted.

I bathed, then stood naked by my wardrobe, wondering what would be suitable. I chose soft black leggings, and a huge sweater in scarlet angora, decorated with small black beads around the neck and shoulders. The soft wool tickled slightly; I wore no bra. Flat velvet shoes with gold and red embroidery on the toes – and I was ready. The outfit was simple but interesting, I thought, with not enough sophistication to frighten Mr Dormouse. But then I stood, staring at my own image in the glass, thinking that nothing could intimidate the man whose body enfolded his wife's with the confidence, the sensuality I had witnessed so many times.

Paul had changed too; his black corduroy jeans and fine black polo-necked sweater made him look like a philosophy student. He suggested coffee, but I hesitated for just the right amount of time, so that he offered wine instead, suggesting we sat in the kitchen.

'Wouldn't we be more comfortable . . . ' I murmured, thinking that a chintz sofa was infinitely preferable to the spirit of Mrs Dormouse amongst the pots and pans.

The sitting room was conventional – boring, I would have said. In one corner was a tapestry on a wooden frame; Paul saw me glance at it and smiled broadly. 'Jane's new hobby,' he said, and picked up a finished cushion from the sofa, waiting for admiration.

I spent fifteen minutes asking him about the informal home-made will my mother had made, and he explained the legal situation I knew already. He suggested that I should bring her into his office to regularize matters . . . and I sipped my wine, faster and faster, until the glass was empty. There was a moment's silence. Then he noticed, coughed, said, 'Oh well . . . ', and drained his own glass, refilling them both to the brim.

'Oh, isn't this *nice*,' I said, snuggling back into the sofa, conscious that the light must be falling very prettily on my red-gold hair.

'Yes, it is. To tell you the truth, I didn't much feel like working tonight,' he said, stretching out his long legs.

'Well, I should think you do enough in the daytime. In my book, the evenings are for enjoying yourself. Especially at this time of year,' I said.

'Why?'

'Well, you know, there's not much to do, you don't want to go out . . . isn't that why lots and lots of babies are born in the summer? It's these chilly autumn evenings.' I giggled and shivered prettily, cuddling the scarlet angora around my breasts.

The truth was, I felt nervous. This silly chatter was not my normal style, but then normally I would never find myself in this position of . . . of . . . but what *was* I? The word *supplicant* came unbidden to my mind.

Paul Renshaw laughed. 'Oh yes, I hadn't thought of that,' he said, smiling at me. I was getting somewhere, I knew it. He poured some more wine, and I smiled back at him over the rim of my glass, feeling a part of myself dissolve slowly as the wine worked (I had eaten nothing that day), the room grew warmer, and I could feel both of us relax. We talked a little of work, and ways of easing tension; the conversation was going along the lines I wanted.

I was sitting in the chair by the fireplace, whilst Paul was on the sofa. So I crossed the room to look at one of the watercolours on the wall above him, leaning forward to praise the muddy little landscape – so that my sweater brushed his arm, and I was was sure he must realize I wore nothing beneath it. Then I eased down next to him, leaning forward in the same movement to reach for the bottle. 'Oh, no,' he said, 'this wine's going to my head. I've had no supper.'

I wanted the wine to go to his head. I wanted my perfume to go to his head. I wanted. And Simon or Johnny had said all you have to do is ask.

We were silent for a few minutes. I could hear Paul breathing. I knew that he must find me desirable – imagined how shy he was feeling, wondering how to make the first move. So I put my glass down on the table, and turned towards him, swivelling my body so that my knee pressed against his.

'Can I ask you something, Paul?'

'Of course. What is it?'

'Go on, try to guess,' I wheedled, tossing my hair back.

'Oh, I know,' he said ruefully, 'it's the sort of thing women always want to know. Can I cope on my own, or am I one of those men who goes to pieces when his wife is away?' I sat back. 'Well, the truth is, Caroline, I'm *not* very good on my own. Jane and I *hate* being apart. I'm pretty hopeless when she's not here. I bet that's what you expected me to say.'

'Mm, no,' I mumbled, 'I thought you'd be more .... um . . . independent.'

'Oh no, not me,' said Mr Dormouse, seriously. 'The thing is, Jane and I haven't really been apart since we got married. I had to go to a conference once, and it was murder. Couldn't bear it – came home a day early, in fact.'

I knew I had to change the subject; this was not what I had planned at all. So teasingly I said, 'Actually, Paul, that *wasn't* what I wanted to ask you.'

'No?'

'No. I wanted to ask you something really silly . . . like . . . do you think I'm attractive?'

He flinched as if stung, and stared at me with embarrassment. 'Of course I do,' he said, 'I mean to say, I can't imagine anybody *not* finding you attractive. You're a . . . a . . . very pretty woman.'

'Well, will you go to bed with me?' I asked, taking hold of his hand.

He gazed at me with growing horror. The silence lengthened and deepened as he stared first at me, then down at our hands, then back at me. Widening my eyes, I held his gaze, then slowly smiled – a wide, knowing smile that spoke of a thousand successful seductions. I had won, I knew it. I could tell from the tingle beneath my fingers, and the crimson that spread up from his neck. I saw him swallow hard.

Then, very gently, as if he was handling a tiny fragile creature, he rested his other hand on mine, slowly pulled my hand free from his, then folded his own hands in his lap.

'I'm afraid . . . ' he said.

'Don't be,' I replied.

'No, I don't mean that. I mean – I'm afraid there's been a *terrible* mistake,' he blurted.

I felt a pain in my stomach. 'No mistake,' I said, then leaned against him, rubbing my head against his shoulder, like a cat. 'Oh, come on, Paul. You said you find me attractive, and I'm alone tonight, and you're alone, so why don't we try to make each other happy? What's the problem?'

I wanted to shout at him, 'For God's sake, I've been watching you. It'll soon be nine-thirty – so come on, Mr Dormouse, let me show you something beautiful, for a change. Let me make you forget that little frump you live with. Let me *try* . . . I know you, Mr Dormouse. You must want it. You must want *me*.' But all the time I went on silently caressing his shoulder gently with my hair.

I heard him cry out, as if impatient. He pulled away, and sprang to his feet (so that I was in danger of overbalancing) then quickly crossed the room to stand by the fireplace, putting the table between us. I half expected him to pick up a chair and level its legs at me.

'What's the problem, Paul?' I whispered, 'Don't worry, it'll all be all right, I promise you . . . '

He looked at me sadly and shook his head. 'You don't understand, Caroline,' he said.

'Understand what?'

'You see – *I love my wife*.'

'Of course you do,' I said, in a soothing voice, 'That's all right. I don't expect . . . '

'No – you don't understand. You can't possibly. You just think . . . Oh no, that's cruel.'

I stood up, and faced him. 'What's cruel? Say what you were going to say.'

'No – but I've met women like you before. You think that because you're beautiful . . . it's so *crass*. You simply don't understand – I *love* my wife, *really love her*. You don't know about that. It's like something warm in my stomach, there inside me, all the time, growing. It's the most wonderful feeling, and it means I could no more touch someone else than I could fly. Oh Lord, this is terribly embarrassing.'

'Yes, it is,' I said flatly, 'I'd better leave.'

'Look Caroline, I understand you. You didn't mean . . . You're just lonely. Jane and I, we've talked about you a lot, about your life. You seemed to have lots of boyfriends, we noticed them at first, er, different ones – but not lately. So something's gone wrong, and I know that Jane would be happy to talk . . . er . . . *woman-to-woman*. You know, sort it out. Don't be lonely over there in your flat. And if you feel you need *real* help you could come to church with us one Sunday. We have a woman lay preacher who's really . . . '

I was fleeing into the hall. He followed me in silence. On the doorstep he said, 'I'm sorry if I've spoken out of turn.'

'It's me who should be sorry,' I said. 'Look, let's not mention this again, OK?'

As I crossed the road he said, 'Don't forget, if you need us, just phone. We're always here.'

That night I could not get warm. Sleepless, I rose and stared for a long time at the house over the road, my eyes dry and hard. Everything was utterly silent. Over there, Paul Renshaw was lying alone, reaching out into the space normally occupied by his wife, to find nothing. And he would turn over in his sleep, I knew, and pull a pillow to his hollows like a child, wanting her, missing her, needing her. *I love my wife* . . . In that second I saw my own life stretch out ahead, growing older, marrying Simon or Johnny as I was bound to do, decorating our dinner parties with my presence, and going to sleep quickly at night, never knowing what Mr and Mrs Dormouse knew in their funny little nest. . . . *Really love her*.

Lying down again, I felt that pain again. At last I fell asleep, and did not wake until late. I looked at my watch in a panic, saw it was ten, sat up, then realized it was Saturday. Remembering the night before I groaned aloud, curled up into a ball, and ground my fists into my eyes, in rage. I cursed Paul Renshaw and his hideous little wife, and wished them back in Basingstoke, where they could have rows of bespectacled little children just like themselves. How *dare* he offer help?

My buzzer was sounding. Assuming it must be the postman, I pulled on my dressing-gown, and padded downstairs. But someone else was standing on the doorstep, brandishing a small bunch of freesias. I looked at the flowers, then up at my mother.

'Hallo, Caro dear, these were on the step,' she said.

'But Mummy, what are you doing here?' I asked, smelling the sweet, pure smell.

'There's a note attached. You'd better read it. From one of your admirers, if I know *you*, my girl. Well, we hadn't heard from you for so long, so I said to Daddy, I'm jolly well going to get the early train and surprise her. I thought something must be wrong . . . Aren't you going to see who they're from?'

I unfolded the piece of paper that nestled amongst the delicate pale pinks, yellows, lilacs and whites. It read: 'I'm so sorry. Best wishes, Paul.'

'Anyway, you really should keep in touch, dear. We do worry about you, because you never know what happens, these days. Well, aren't you going to ask me in? I could just do with a cup of tea . . . Oh dear, what's wrong? Oh Caroline, why are you crying?'

Acknowledgements

The Glimpses © Penny Vincenzi 1990
Olive Oil © Alice Walker 1985
Subject to Diary © Fay Weldon 1990
The Leap © Louise Erdrich 1990
Crumbs of Wisdom © Penelope Lively 1990
The Room © Tim Parks 1990
Princess Harafa's Revelation © Georgina Tisdall 1990
En Route to Algiers © Douglas Kennedy 1990
Teenage Wasteland © Anne Tyler 1984
The Bolshybally © Lisa St Aubin de Teran 1990
Baby Love © Julie Burchill 1990
Loosing the Shoe © Mavis Cheek 1990
116th Street Jenny © Judith Rossner 1990
Mike's © Sarah Harrison 1990
The Moses Basket © Felicity Wood 1990
Dislocation © Patrick Gale 1990
The Butterfly © Rachel Billington 1990
Glasnost © Shirley Lowe and Angela Ince 1990
Over the Road © Bel Mooney 1990